Praise for Cecy Robson

"Eternal is a heartfelt and beautiful love story of two wounded hearts who find each other when and where they least expect it." –*USA Today, HEA*

"This is, hands down, one of my favorite books of 2016 thus far… *Inseverable*, the first book in the upcoming Carolina Beach series, is FUNNY, like really funny. Heartfelt and sweet and goofy and just plain amazing." *–Top Pick, The Romance Reviews*

"Just when I think I can't love Cecy Robson more, she comes along with a book like *Eternal*, a sweet and sexy love story that's verily bursting with good feels." *–Panda and Boodle*

"Robson builds a sweet and lightly dramatic romance that deals with love, hope, and forgiveness. Well plotted with an array of personable and defined characters. Smooth flowing conversational dialogue engulfs you and draws you right into the middle of their lives." *–Smexy Books*

"Absolutely stunning! This book was a wonderful love story. So expertly written and so beautifully done." *– Kimmie Sue's Book Review*

"Unforgettable! Callahan and Trinity will tug at your heart strings and keep you turning the pages. Inseverable is a great love story that will leave you smiling and in tears." *–USA Today bestselling author, Jamie K. Schmidt*

"Oh swoon, I quickly fell in love with this adorable couple and have discovered a new favorite author to stalk. This was my first experience reading the delightful work of Cecy Robson and am as giddy as a schoolgirl to report that I have stumbled upon treasure – and have since marked the loot with a big X on my Goodreads map." *–Books and Bindings*

"2016 Editor's Choice Winner…The emotion is so well grounded and layered, the characters rich and believable, the conflict complex with just the right amount of hopelessness. *Inseverable* is a beautiful romance and a story worth dedicating a weekend to." *–Grave Tells Romance*

"*Eternal* by Cecy Robson is a fast paced sizzling hot story of insta-attraction. Even with all the sexiness there was equal parts of sweetness as well." *–Lampshade Reader*

"This is just the start of a new series by Ms. Robson, and already a favorite. I can't wait for more." *– 5 stars, Give Me Books*

"[*Eternal* was] a straight forward, make you feel good, warm your heart kind of romance. And I thoroughly enjoyed it. This is my first book by this author and I cannot wait to discover more of her books in the future." *– Once Upon a Book Blog*

"Call this Rom-Com on Steroids-This story has teeth and it leaves little love bites" *–Addicted to Happily Ever After*

"I would recommend *Eternal* by Cecy Robson, if you enjoy second chance romances or books by authors Melanie Harlow, Jen Frederick, Cora Brent and Scarlett Cole." *– Book Magic, Under a Spell with Every Page*

"Equal parts sexy and funny! Cecy Robson's new book had me swooning and laughing out loud! A perfect beach read!" *–USA Today Bestselling Author Annie Rains*

"I am a HUGE Cecy Robson fan. I have adored everything I have read by her, so I knew this would be fantastic…I wasn't disappointed. Landon and Luci are flirty and sexy and both have such good hearts. You can't help but root for their HEA." *–Two Girls With Books*

"Absolutely loved this story! ... A great start to a new series - I'm looking forward to getting books on the rest of Trinity's friends. I see great things for all of them!" –**Sizzling Pages Romance Reviews**

"I wanted to hug this book... All the **feels** Robson gave me as I devoured *Inseverable* provided that book high I am constantly craving." *–Caffeinated Book Reviewer*

"A sexy, sweet, heart-rending story. Cecy Robson pushed every single one of my reader buttons. Loved this book!" *–Kate Meader, Author of Playing with Fire*

"This was my first Cecy Robson read, and it will absolutely not be my last. From the minute I picked up this book, I knew I wouldn't be able to put it down. *Inseverable* is definitely going on my list of memorable books that I can't wait to reread." *–Reviews From the Heart*

"Already [Cecy] Robson was becoming one of my favorite authors but Inseverable sealed the deal. Inseverable shows Robson's different writing style and I couldn't get enough of this new setting and the new characters that were introduced." *–Lush Book Reviews*

By Cecy Robson

The Shattered Past Series

Once Perfect
Once Loved
Once Pure

The O'Brien Family Novels

Once Kissed
Let Me
Crave Me
Feel Me
Save Me

The Carolina Beach Novels

Inseverable
Eternal
Infinite

The Weird Girls Series

Gone Hunting (Coming soon)
A Curse Awakened: A Novella
The Weird Girls: A Novella
Sealed with a Curse
A Cursed Embrace
Of Flame and Promise
A Cursed Moon: A Novella
Cursed by Destiny
A Cursed Bloodline
A Curse Unbroken
Of Flame and Light
Of Flame and Fate
Of Flame and Fury (coming soon)

APPS

Find Cecy on the *Hooked – Chat Stories App* writing as
Rosalina San Tiago

Coming soon: *Crazy Maple's Chapters: Interactive Stories App*: The Shattered Past and Weird Girls series

INFINITE

A Carolina Beach Novel

Cecy Robson

DEDICATION

To all the Beccas and Hales of the world who found families to call their own .

ACKNOWLEDGMENTS

For years I've seen beautiful dedications filled with love, devotion, and admiration from children to their parents. There are aisles filled with cards in stores proclaiming as much and beautiful memes from the heart circulating social media. I'm happy for children who have the type of upbringing and parents to justify their hero worship and their gratitude. This novel is written to include those who don't. Those who have known pain instead of compassion and whose recollection of childhood is better left forgotten. Sometimes in life it's best to leave the past where it is and to move forward. *Infinite* is for those moving forward. You can find a better life. You can make your own family, be it with friends or partners who love you. You can be happy. It's what I most wish for you.

To Nic, my agent and family, who always supports me with an open heart and gentle honesty.

To Jamie, my husband and friend who taught me patience and what it is to truly love someone. Thank you for our babies, our home, and for your simply being you.

To our children, L, L, and M. My babies, my biggest honor has been being your mother. I thank God that He blessed me with you.

To Amanda, Beth, and Mary Kate. Our texts get me through day, lift my spirits, and yeah, make me guffaw. I think 'make you an avatar day' was my personal favorite. I'll always be there for you.

To my assistant and friend Kim who takes care of everything. Thank you for understanding me, and for always searching for ways to help me succeed.

To Kristin, my artist and friend, your patience is admirable, but your work and creativity is inspiring. Thank you for putting up with all my, "How about we do this," moments and my sad attempts at artwork.

To Valerie and Gaele for making my work shine. Your attention to detail never ceases to impress this woman who is so easily distracted. Oh, look, a squirrel.

Lastly, to my fans. Not because you deserve to be last. You've stood by me and obsessed over my characters and stories almost as much as I have. Almost. The emails you send me praising my work, discussing my characters, and asking for more keep me going. Thank you! I love our interactions on social media. Keep the fun conversations coming! You have my heart.

Chapter One

Becca

I look through the rear window of Hale's Tahoe as he pulls
away from the house. The window is tinted and I can't see
worth a damn. I wish I could. That's my heart back there. I
look up at Hale.

Well, at least half my heart . . .

The headlights from an approaching car illuminate the
planes of his strong features. This is a man I first met when he
was a boy. It was first grade and our teacher, Mrs. Newsom,
sat him behind me. I pretended not to notice him. But how
could anyone miss that blond hair and eyes so filled with
mischief they sparkled like diamonds cast along the sand?

Hale was new to our prep school, his family finally
making the money it took to pay for the absurdly expensive
tuition. He should've been shy and intimidated to join the
ranks of the so-called elite. But even then, Hale was fearless.

He tugged on my ponytail almost the moment he sat.
This boy didn't know me and had no right touching the hair
Nana June had painstakingly brushed to a silky shine. I
remember turning around just to glare at him, until I caught
his grin. At the time, I thought it mirrored a boy clearly up to
no good. I failed to see his innocence. My, oh, my. It was so

pure, he could've sprouted a halo. Except, as he grew into the young man sitting beside me, that grin grew with him, transforming into naughty enough to set a nun's panties aflame. Did I return that grin, way back then? Yes'm, I most certainly did.

The boy I first smiled at grew up long before either of us were ready, all the while hanging tight to the other half of my heart.

I'm not smiling now and neither is he. Tonight was all about a goodbye that's been coming for too many years, despite our attempts to wish it away.

We're no longer children. We're college grads, taking that massive leap into the workforce and leaving the carefree life that comes with youth far behind.

I give another glance back. Even with the street lights, I don't catch more than the looming shadows of the palmettos. "Do you think Trin is all right?" I ask.

"Nope," he replies.

Hale sighs when I reach into the pocket of my jacket and pull out my phone, cupping my hand and lowering it until it skims just above the gray leather seat. His touch is gentle, kind, and one of too many reasons he's stolen my heart.

The warmth of his skin and those eyes that see all make me feel everything I'm not supposed to. I don't know when I fell in love with Hale. Maybe I've always loved him.

It only seems right I should finally tell him.

"Don't, sugar," he tells me when my thumb slides over the screen of my phone. His voice is set with worry and sadness as palpable as rain beating down during the harshest summer storms. "Trin and Callahan have to work their shit out on their own."

The harsh sting of tears spreads across my pale green eyes. It's not the first time I've cried tonight. The first was mercifully in Hale's arms, during an acoustic version of *No Retreat, No Surrender*. Our tight group of friends sang it as we sat around the fire pit at Callahan's place. I'd picked the song. It summed up our group and misadventures perfectly. I was right, and because of it, we all seemed to fall apart.

We're starting our new lives. Me, in Charlotte working PR for Carolina's football team, and Hale in New York, working on Wall Street. The song we sang was our final farewell to our reckless youth. We all knew it. It's the reason only one of us made it to the last lyric.

"Don't cry, sweet thing," he murmurs, his thick Southern accent as soothing as the taste of warm honey. "You know I can't take it when you cry."

He slips his arm around me, just as he did in front of the fire pit when the last string of the guitar was plucked and silence descended upon us like the weight of a thousand deaths.

The window is cracked, allowing the last bits of summer and the scent of salt and sea to drift in and join our memories. The smell of the ocean is among the finest in the world, second only to Hale's masculine fusion of musk intertwined with the lush foliage pushing through the clay-sand composition that makes up Kiawah. Hale's scent is the closest thing to heaven on earth. I know it now. Maybe I always have.

My head falls against his shoulder. I clutch him like I did around the fire pit, afraid to let go. "Where are we going?" I ask, my barely there words not quite enough to mask my Southern twang.

"To Sean's." He pauses when I adjust my body so it rests against the collection of muscle stretching across his wide chest. "He's your ride home, remember?"

"I don't want Sean to take me home," I say. My gaze fixes on the navigation screen of his SUV, each syllable I manage huskier than I intend. "I want you to take me home."

Those muscles holding me tense, loosening slowly until his grip on the steering wheel relaxes and the fingers of his opposite hand trail lazily down my arm. "I don't think your daddy will like that," he bites out, somehow keeping his voice soft despite the tang of bitterness drifting so close to the surface.

"I don't care," I reply. I don't flinch, though I should. I may be a grown woman of twenty-two, but Daddy still gives me plenty to flinch about. The harsh criticism he has for Hale and his family more than prove his remarks are as heavy handed as his strikes.

I glance up. "Will you take me home? Please?"

"It'd be my honor," he replies.

My father has never scared Hale, even long before Hale passed Daddy in height. It's a rare feat seeing how scary my father can be. I'm not brave like Hale is. Not when it comes to Daddy. But Hale's lack of fear scares me plenty enough for both of us.

I cuddle closer to Hale, the smooth blacktop road that leads to the other side of the island a gentle hum along the thread of the powerful tires. It's like a lullaby in a way. Not that I'm not ready to sleep. My hand slides across Hale's rock-hard abs to grip his hip. Tonight, I want a goodbye that means more than a hug between lifelong friends.

Hale stiffens. It's brief, long enough to make me question whether he wants me, but not so long that my insecurities surface and force me to withdraw.

Throughout my young life, I've turned heads and garnered more attention than I've wanted or deserved. I'm not as confident as I come across. I've been hurt and weakened by those who should love me most, and while those scars have toughened my hide, they've never quite healed.

I think Hale senses the fear my memories stir. It's just like him. He presses a kiss to the top of my head, giving me the green light to stay in place and wonder a little more where our time alone may lead.

I haven't prayed much since Nana June died. I do now. When it comes to Hale, I want more than a superficial farewell stuffed with an obliged promise to keep in touch. I want him. Every time we've been alone this summer, the air between us has thickened to tar. Too many words were left unsaid, as well as too many sexy thoughts better shared beneath cool sheets.

"You sure about this, Becks?" Hale asks, his voice like rust flaking off an old steel pipe.

I'm so mesmerized by the rhythmic thuds of Hale's heart against my ear, I almost don't hear him, nor do I initially realize how fast I'm breathing. He shouldn't know how badly I want him inside me, not when I've spent a lifetime telling him we can never be more than friends.

"Very sure."

I don't know how he hears me. I barely hear myself.

"All right then," he answers.

I sit up as he rounds the bend that leads to the colossal house my granddaddy built. Granddaddy had a lot of money, but it doesn't come close to the fortune my father accumulated.

"Not here," I say, clasping his shoulder when he draws closer to the house. "Pull into the service road."

He cocks a brow, easing off the gas so the SUV slows to a coast. "I take it your Daddy's home?"

"He won't be home until later, but just in case . . ." My gaze travels to the small road that separates the main property from where my father's thoroughbreds are kept. It leads to an overgrown path that thins out at the beach. The thick vegetation should be enough to shadow us and keep us hidden. At least, that's my hope.

Hale rolls to a stop in the middle of the road and sets his SUV in park. "I thought you wanted me with you."

"I do," I reply. "I just don't want any interruptions. Not tonight."

The muscles along his square jaw tighten and relax as he mulls through each word. He thinks I'm ashamed of him. His family will never have as much money as mine. What he doesn't understand is that the shame I feel is for my family and all the harm they've caused.

"Becks, if we go on that beach, what's going to happen?"

My nervousness lingers but stands no chance against my growing desire. "Anything you want," I reply.

He drops his chin, slowly shaking his head from side to side. I don't expect his touch to remain tender. Yet there it is, skimming down to hold my hand. "I don't think you know what you're saying."

Tears escape, moistening my cheeks and causing Hale's light blue eyes to darken to topaz. He's sad, just like me. God, I'm going to miss him.

"I mean every word," I promise. I thread my fingers through his. "Will you let me prove it?"

There's nothing left of that boy who played with my hair all those years ago or the one all the ladies fought to lay their blankets beside when he'd take his post on the lifeguard stand. All that waits is a man full of need and a trickle of restraint barely keeping him in place.

He releases my hand to skim his knuckles over my jaw. With all the desire I see and feel, I expect a harsh kiss, tasting of sin and fury. That's not what comes.

Lips too soft for a man who mere weeks ago knocked out a drunk for touching me, feather over mine, teasing me until I allow him further in. I don't quite manage to return his taste before he eases away.

For a moment, we simply stare at each other. It's our first kiss and one I'll never forget.

"That was sweet," I tell him.

"Becks, sweet is the last thing I want to be with you." He steals another glance at the path. "You sure?"

I nod, my voice quiet. "I'm sure."

He turns his SUV off the road and onto the path, the wheels crunching through the forest debris until we're swallowed by darkness. He cuts the engine, his shoulders rising and falling fast.

"Wait until I come for you," he says when I reach for the handle.

It seems to take forever for him to reach my side, his steady features latching onto mine as if he barely knows me. From one long second to the next, he flings my door open and helps me out. I'm tall, almost as tall as the men in my family, but not as tall as Hale. I don't quite have my feet planted when his hands slide along my hips, banding my waist at almost the exact moment his mouth brands my lips with white hot possession.

Men have eyed me since puberty and sought to touch me before I was ready. I never became used to the aggression and outran most of it. I'm not running now.

He pulls back, the force of the separation making me gasp. His gaze searches my eyes, trying to unlock the secrets I was always too afraid to share.

The mangrove branches stretch out, the moonlight cutting through to illuminate Hale in silver light. "Do you have any fucking idea how long I've wanted to kiss you?"

"No," I stammer. "Are you—" I glance around when I hear a chirp, certain my racing heart has woken the nesting birds. "Are you going to do it again?"

"Hell, yeah," he says, shutting the door to his Tahoe.

We laugh, the remaining tension evaporating in the cool breeze breaking through the trees. The shin-length weeds tickle my bare legs as we head forward, allowing the increasing lull of the ocean to guide us.

"I suppose I should watch out for snakes and such," Hale mutters, holding me closer. "But I swear, I can't keep my eyes off you."

I lean into him, shielding my face to hide my embarrassment. I don't usually come across as quiet or timid. Both will get me hurt and I'm done feeling pain. "There's no need for pretty talk," I say, smiling softly. "You have me right where you want me."

"Not yet, darlin'," he assures me.

I nibble on my bottom lip. His terms of endearment send my insides fluttering in all the right ways. Hale isn't playing me. He's trying each out as if deciding which one he likes best.

I take a breath, giving myself a moment to take him and our surroundings in. The mournful harmony of the ocean vocalizes signals summer's end, but I no longer share its misery. All I sense is Hale.

As the tree line arcs, he eases us to the sand. We land on our knees somewhere between the shadows of the trees and the sea we've swum in all our lives. It's symbolic, my feelings for him coming out of the dark to lie where the moon can cast its final judgement and where my reservations strip away, leaving me bare.

"Are you cold?" he asks, pulling me closer, his large hands skimming down my body and over my backside.

I pull my focus away from the small cresting waves ghosting over the sand. "Not with you here," I admit.

He pulls me to him, his mouth parting as it slides over mine. This is only our third kiss and everything should feel new. But with the way our bodies meld and the natural rhythm we fall into, it feels like we've had a thousand lifetimes to perfect our kiss.

At first, it's slow and cautious, reminiscent of our childhood and more innocence than I think I deserve. But as his tongue probes further, I'm reminded that young or not, Hale is all man. His hold and the growing press of his erection as he lays us on the sand allow me to leave all flickers of virtue behind.

I return his kiss like a desperate woman, fueling his need.

Hale frees me from my jacket, tugging my white T-shirt free of the waistband of my shorts and skimming his hand upward to play with my heavy breasts. He stops our kiss, his gaze locked on mine as he explores.

I pant, losing myself in his gaze while his fingers circle my tightening nipple.

I grunt when he pinches the taut center, my lashes fluttering with each of his greedy pulls. I suppose it's his way of asking for permission to do more. I don't deny him. I *can't*.

The pads of his fingers linger over my flat stomach, tickling my waist before freeing the top snap. He swallows hard. "Tell me to stop," he practically begs.

I don't recognize my voice. "I don't want you to."

His fingers clamp over the zipper, snagging it more than once before he's able to guide his hand beneath my panties. His moves are leisurely, teasing, giving me time to move away.

My pelvis tilts upward, meeting the calloused edges of his skin. His fingers slick over my center, his swirls making me quiver.

"*Jesus*," he rasps.

My back arches as he pushes further in until his palm presses against my tantalized flesh. He curls his fingers, stirring my sweet spot as he strokes in and out. The motions are careful, becoming rougher the more I moan.

Hale dips his head, trailing kisses down my neck until his hot mouth pulls my nipple through the lace.

"I'm going to come," I whimper, as if he doesn't already know. "Please, don't stop."

Grains of sand spray along my legs as I peak. My hands are frantic, desperate to touch Hale. I reach in through the front of Hale's board shorts, gripping his thick, rigid staff.

"What the *fuck* you doing here?"

We jerk at the sound of my cousin Kirk's voice. Hale hauls me to my feet, shielding my body with his. I scramble to fix my disheveled clothes, my mind whirling from the abrupt interruption. I manage to snap my shorts closed and pull my shirt down only to freeze when I realize Kirk isn't alone.

From the shadows, four forms, ranging from average to hulking builds, emerge. Brent, Davey, Sully, Parker—all my cousins are here, except Matthew, their self-appointed leader. But I know him well enough to know he's not far behind.

"Hale," I whisper. "You have to get out of here."

"I'm not leaving you," he grinds out.

"I asked what *the fuck* you doing here, boy," Kirk hisses.

Brent steps forward, his breath reeking of Wild Turkey. He spits on the ground. "Better question is, what the fuck are you doing with one of our own?"

"None of your damn business, *boy*," Hale fires back.

I try to shove my way between them. Hale doesn't allow me, lugging me back and keeping me behind him. "Becks, I need you stay where you are, okay?"

He knows what's coming and so do I. I snag my jacket from the sand, clambering to reach my phone.

"Whatcha you doing there, cuz?" Sully adds.

I don't have to look up to know they're closer, my fingers shaking as I text Mason and Sean.

We're in trouble.

"Shit," Brent says, dragging out the word. "You ain't got no one to call."

Get here now.

I barely manage to hit send when Hale's hands shoot out, shoving Brent off his feet when he reaches for me. "Get the hell away from her," Hale growls, his voice all primal rage.

"You've got some nerve telling us what to do on our land," Kirk says, sounding more amused than angry.

"This isn't your land," I counter, speaking through my teeth.

"No, it's your Daddy's," Sully agrees, showing me the first real taste of their collective anger. "You shouldn't be hanging with trash, Becca. Come on. Time to go."

Hale adjusts his position, guarding me when Sully moves forward. "*Don't touch her*," he says, his words stabbing the air like frozen daggers.

"We're not here to beat her ass, son," Sully says, laughing. "Oh, no, this is all about you."

The phone flies from my hand as Sully tackles Hale. Sully is a big guy and used to play ball. But so did Hale and Hale was always better than Sully.

Hale uses Sully's momentum against him, rolling them toward the water. Hale lands on top, his fist crashing into Sully's face.

The crunch of bone explodes over the sound of crashing waves. I scream when Davey dives on top of Hale and Parker and Kirk stomp forward. Brent lifts me by the waist, dragging me back when I lunge at them.

"Don't hurt him!" I shriek, kicking wildly. "Don't you fucking hurt him!"

Brent is twice my size. He drags me along the beach and toward the house. Through the tasseled strands of my long hair I watch them pound on Hale. "*No!*"

"Cut the shit, Becca," Matthew says, somewhere behind me. "You're already in it enough."

His voice is steady, silently watching the show. If he's here—if all my asshole cousins are home—so is my father. I can't let them take me back to the house. My father can't know I've been with Hale.

My heel crashes into Brent's shin. He hollers a curse, falling back and taking me with him. I rush to my feet when Davey and Parker hook Hale's arms, allowing Sully to get some payback for his busted nose. I'm almost to them when Matthew fastens his meaty fingers around my arm and heaves me backward. My fists punch against his chest and face, my panic mounting when I catch the first glimpse of my house.

I'm no match for Matthew. He whips me around, crossing my arms and driving me to my knees.

I cry out in frustration and pain when Brent shoves my head down, forcing my body to curl forward, immobilizing me. "Knock it off, Becca," Brent snarls. "We ain't here to hurt you."

In hurting Hale, they already have. I can't see anything, but I hear every grunt of pain and feel every fist connecting against flesh.

"Quiet, Becca," Matthew says when I start to cry. "You're only making it worse for yourself."

"You don't have to do this," I sob. "God, just leave him alone!"

Hale is hurt. I know he is. Just as I know it's my fault.

The sound of tires shrieking to a stop echo in the distance. I twist my head, ignoring the pain it causes my neck. "Sean, *Mason*!" I scream, begging to heaven and back it's them.

I choke back a cry when I hear our friends. "The fuck!" Sean yells.

Brent releases my head, racing forward as Sean's long, lanky body shoots toward the fray. But it's Mason, all stocky build and muscle who reaches Hale first, punching Davey hard enough to break his jaw.

I rip free from Matthew, racing toward my friends. They're outnumbered, but the element of surprise worked in their favor. Hale is already back to his feet, nailing Brent in the head as hard as Sean and Mason are swinging.

I'm almost to them when the blast of a rifle erupts, sending rows of nesting birds to flight. Aside from the ocean waves soaking the shore, everything quiets. Hale's T-shirt is torn open, his chest splattered from the blood oozing from his mouth. Sully is on the ground beside Brent, who is pressing his hand against the gash above his right eye. He's going to need stitches.

I could give a damn.

Davey blinks at the star-filled sky above from his position on his back. Otherwise, he doesn't move. Neither does Parker, his face contorted with pain as he lays on his side holding his ribs.

Everyone is breathing hard, except for Matthew and the man I feel looming behind me.

I start to turn when I catch Hale's bracing features. "Becca, come here."

It's the one thing I want to do most. But I can't.

In my gaze, I plead with him to understand that what I do next isn't to betray him. It's to protect him and our friends.

I turn slowly to where my father holds the rifle pressed at an angle against his chest. Everyone tells me I resemble him. I hate it. Especially now.

"Don't hurt them, Daddy," I beg.

My father passes the rifle to Matthew, as a child would a toy he's grown tired of. Like a good wannabe son, Matthew takes it without question, assuming the armed soldier's pose Daddy had.

"Seems to me, Becca June, these boys have been roughed up enough," Daddy says.

He doesn't mean that. He's only trying to save face. Hale, Mason, and Sean are as tough as any true southerner. It may have been three against five, but no way would my cousins have won that fight.

In the bright moonlight, I see it all. Mason's cheek is swelling like Hale's, and Sean's lip is busted up. Mason gives me a wink, his dark skin gleaming in the moonlight, all the while his deep frown remaining in place. He's trying to tell me I did the right thing by calling them. I feel horrible about doing so, except when it comes down to it, me and Trin, and Callahan, too, would have done the same for them.

In the south, you don't call the police where family and friends and grudges are concerned. You handle your own.

My cousins were wrong to show up and gang up on Hale like they did. Cowards, as far as I'm concerned. Daddy, he's wrong, too, for this and lot more. I don't tell him. Right now, I'll do anything so long as he leaves Hale and our friends alone.

"What happened?" Daddy asks.

He raises his hand, silencing me instantly when I try to speak. "I found the Wilder boy on top of Becca," Kirk answers.

Daddy cocks a brow high enough to disappear into the crown of his wheat-colored hair. "He was raping her?" he asks.

"*No*," I yell over Kirk's response.

"You know damn well I'd never hurt her," Hale counters, ire blanketing him like fire.

"I wasn't talking to you," Daddy replies, his repulsion at Hale and Mason's presence as tangible as my mounting fear.

I push down my need to cower. It won't help me or Hale. But fear always enlivens memories better left alone.

"What happened?" Daddy asks Kirk.

"I don't know, sir. Like I said, I only saw him on top of her."

Kirk knows Hale wasn't forcing me to do anything. But he fears Daddy, just like his brothers and I do. Kirk won't say anything to defend me or to anger my father. Like a typical follower, he's merely along for the ride.

"Y'all trespassing on my property," Daddy reminds them, ignoring the swelling and bleeding faces.

"Just let them go," I say, wishing my voice didn't shake as much as it does. "*Please*. They won't come back here no more. I swear it."

"*No*," Hale says.

Hale's voice robs Daddy's spotlight. Sean and Mason recover first, flanking Hale's side.

"What did you say?" Daddy asks, his tone rising.

Hale ignores him. No one else exists now, not the way his steely features bore into mine. He holds out his hand. "Becca," he says. "Come with me. I won't leave you behind with them."

My breath releases in a stammer and for a long while all I see is Hale's outstretched palm and the olive branch he offers.

"Please, baby," Hale says, ignoring my cousins as they struggle to their feet. "You don't need to be here."

He's wrong.

It's only because I'm here that my father hasn't lashed out at him. My father walks forward, squaring his shoulders. I know that stance.

My racing pulse surges painfully as I hurry forward and intercept him.

I look my father dead in the eyes. "Go, Hale. Leave. Sean, Mason, you, too."

My back is to them. It doesn't matter. I know they're not leaving, because I wouldn't leave them, either.

A sharp pang squeezes my heart. "Please," I say, my composure dwindling as I continue to stare my father down. "I need you to leave right now."

Sounds of feet shuffling through the sand draw near and like the rising tide, the sense of danger returns. "Only if you leave with us," Hale's deep voice thrums. "I'll take care of you. I swear to Christ I will."

My composure crumbles and I clasp my hand over my mouth. My vision blurs with tears, but not so badly that I don't catch my father's smug smile. "Hale, if you feel anything for me, you'll leave without me. *Please*," I beg.

"Let's go," Mason mutters.

"Like hell," Sean says.

He's still itching for a fight. But Sean's family has money like mine. He's not in the same danger as Hale and Mason.

"We're going," Mason says, his promise stopping Daddy and everyone else from closing in.

"Becca," Hale says. "Becks, come on—*Get the fuck off me*," he adds, shoving someone away.

"I don't want you here," I say, my voice likely reflecting the dull hate overtaking me. "You don't belong here."

I mean what I say. Hale . . . he doesn't belong with this shit. I only wish it didn't sound so cruel.

I don't know how long I stand there, trying in vain to stare my father down. It's long enough for a truck to start and then another, their dense tires kicking back debris as they peel away and back onto the road.

With my boys gone, I'm on my own. I should be used to it. After a lifetime of being treated like I'll never be good enough, loneliness is more friend than foe. Except I want to be good enough. My word, I need to be.

My first mistake is standing this close to my father. My second is speaking.

"He didn't do anything I didn't want—"

My father cracks me across the face. The force is so hard it vibrates through my skull and instantly shatters my nose. My hands and knees slide through the sand as I fall. He hasn't hit me in years. I suppose he thought I was long overdue.

"If you wanted that shit from the likes of Hale Wilder, you're nothing more than a whore," Daddy says. "Just like your mother."

He means to hurt me with his words, just as he has every time I didn't measure up to his standards. I was eight the first time he called me a whore, all for playing with my mother's makeup kit. I didn't deserve it then. I don't deserve it now.

I spit out the taste of metal coating my tongue and swallow even more. It was a powerful strike. If I'm lucky, I won't need surgery to repair it. Not that my father cares. The damage is just one piece of the punishment.

For the next few weeks, every time I look in the mirror, I'll be reminded how I disappointed him and let the family down.

"Get in the house," Daddy snarls.

"No."

"What'd you say?" Daddy asks me, kicking sand up as he stomps forward.

"She's hurt, Uncle Lloyd," Matthew says. His bare feet stop near me, his immense size barely enough to keep Daddy away.

"Becca, get up," Kirk mutters.

I do, but not because Kirk tells me to. This is what's called survival and stubborn refusal to bow down.

I'm wobbly on my feet, my face throbbing and my balance askew. Somehow, I keep my feet, but not by much.

"Get in the house," Daddy says, his voice so eerily still it borders on psychotic.

I yank my arm away when Matthew reaches for me. "I'm not going anywhere with you." My voice trembles with unsurpassed rage. "I don't want anything to do with you—"

Another strike, this one causing me to spin before my body crashes onto the beach. Stars explode in my vision. I'm hurt. Jesus Christ. I'm really hurt.

Daddy's voice comes in and out as if speaking under water. Through the hard pounding in my ears, I catch enough. "After everything I've done for you, this is how you treat me?" he growls. "Becca June, you're no daughter of mine!"

I force my mouth to move. "Good."

I don't realize how loud I speak until Daddy's Burberry loafers step in my line of vision. "What did you say to me?"

This is the part where he expects me to beg for his forgiveness, to say something to placate him enough so he returns to the house after one last parting insult. I rise slowly, my legs rubbery from how hard I'm shaking and the adrenaline pumping through me in merciless waves.

A small twisted sneer cuts across his face.

He's happy I'm injured. Didn't he show me who's boss?

He thinks I'm afraid.

He's never been more wrong.

"I said, 'good', you fucking redneck piece of shit."

I don't know who is more stunned. This man in front of me, who dares to call himself my daddy, or my cousins. They gasp, an air of shock and fear pelting the air. They think

Daddy is going to kill me. They're probably right. But I'll be damned if I go down without a fight.

Daddy takes a step toward me. I step away. As much as I hate him, and truly and desperately want him to die, I won't simply attack.

His gaze drags down my body, something he sees in me keeping him in place and deepening his sadistic features. "You're dead to me," he says. "You hear me? Your car. Your clothes. Everything, but what what's on your slut back, belongs to me. Get out of here. I don't ever want to see your face again."

He spits at my feet and walks slowly away. One by one, my cousins leave, but not before casting me a worried glance. I don't know what they're so worried about. They still have Daddy. They've never needed me. I was just one more person to split the inheritance with.

The last of my family to reach my house is Matthew, his solid form giving him away. He pauses, looking in my direction. He may be having second thoughts, even though, like the others, he probably blames me.

Ultimately, he opens the security gate and strolls inside. I can't fault him. Leader or not, he belongs to my father as much as the rest of them, including my mother.

The only person my father never could control was Nana June. It's one of the reasons I loved her as much as I did.

I stumble forward. I didn't notice anyone pick up my jacket or phone, but they're gone. I stagger toward the road and in the direction Hale vanished. I know that he left and that I made him. But it's only when I come to terms that he's gone that I finally break down. It's not a pretty cry. It's one of those awful, ugly cries that reflect the loss of a life and the one true love.

I dab my face with the edge of my dirty T-shirt. When it only brings a fresh jab of pain I give up and start the long road alone.

It would be several years before I saw Hale again. It didn't hurt any less when I finally did.

Hale was my friend, confidant, the young man I could laugh with and cry to. The one man in my life I could always count on.

He was never supposed to break my heart.
And I was *never* supposed to break his . . .

Chapter Two

Hale

Ten years later.

"You know what your problem is?" Priscilla barks into the phone.

For someone who swaggers like a peacock, fanning her feathers to make sure everyone takes notice, this bird has a lot of bite.

"I'm emotionally unavailable?" I offer. "I don't hang around long enough to cuddle and I could do without buying you more jewelry?"

"You asshole!" she screeches.

And when I say screech, I mean, *screech*.

I turn down the volume on my earpiece. Wall Street titans need their hearing and, being their king, I'm no exception.

"Pris, you knew what you were getting into the first moment you came up to me at the Governor's Ball. I told you then. I'm telling you now. I don't do commitment. I won't wake up in bed beside you with puppy eyes, begging you not to leave me, and I'll never give you more than I think you deserve."

"You don't think I deserve a ring?"

My driver glances at me through the rearview mirror. The privacy window doesn't stand a chance against Pris' shrill tone. In fact, I'm going to have to ask Al to double-check it for cracks. I flip through the report the new hire put together. It's basic and juvenile, the research so sloppy and outdated, I'm surprised he didn't top it off with a Hello Kitty sticker and some glitter. This guy went to Stanford?

"Are you listening?" Pris demands.

I give up on the report after noting he missed a major investment opportunity despite listing all those "facts."

"Hale Wilder!"

She's using my full name. Pris is real mad now.

"Pris, you really thought marriage was where we were headed?" I ask, sounding more laid back than maybe I should. "Correct me if I'm wrong, but wasn't that your half-naked body getting awfully close to that professional golfer? What's his name? The one who cheated on his first wife, the second wife, and the third?"

"I can't believe you!" she yells, sounding genuinely aghast, bless her heart.

"It sure looked like you," I say. "It was in the headline of page six just the other week, if I'm not mistaken."

"Of course it was me," she shrieks (again).

"Good, I'm glad we established that." I hold out a hand when the Town Car rolls to a stop.

"Traffic," Al mouths. "Going around, Mr. Wilder."

A loud gulp followed by several hiccups replace the screeching.

I pause in the middle of straightening my tie. "Are you crying?" I ask.

"What do expect, Hale? I fucked a golfer in really ugly pants."

"I didn't need a visual," I mutter.

"I was trying to get your attention!"

Great. Back to the yelling.

"It was one last desperate attempt to see if you care," she tells me. "Do you think I'd ever want someone like him over you?"

I pinch the bride of my nose. How is it only eight in the morning?

"I did it for you, Hale. For us. I'm practically clawing off my face just to see if you'll notice a scratch."

Before, I was annoyed. Now, I'm damn well pissed. "Do you hear yourself? You think I want this for me? For anyone? Hell, Pris, you shouldn't even want this for yourself."

"Why am I not good enough for you?" she demands.

"Pris. I told you. I don't have it in me."

I'm not yelling. Just being honest. Me and Pris, we've done our share of using throughout the years. She needed arm candy for an event, I was there. She wanted to go hard and feel desirable, I'd open the door to my penthouse and rock her world between the sheets. But I never promised her more. I've *never* promised any woman more.

Well, almost never.

"I told you this from the moment we met," I remind her. "If you wanted Prince Charming, you needed to look elsewhere."

"I know what you said. But . . . dammit, Hale, I've given you two years! Two years of my company and enough blowjobs to make my jaw collapse. Two fucking years!"

She's screaming, hollering. I wonder briefly where exactly she is. I'd say she's alone. The thing about Pris is, she doesn't care who hears what when she's pissed. She thrives on attention, puts everything she has into it and always gives it her all. If she feels like yelling in the middle of Grand Central Station—if that's what's going to make her feel better—she's going to do it, hellbent on getting and doing whatever she wants, even if it means delaying the Metro out of town.

The thought of her screaming in her office—the one her father drops seven grand a month for her to do absolutely nothing in—in front of twenty staff members who do everything else, riles me.

Part of me doesn't think she has any business yelling. The other part of me, who recognizes the princess and pain-in-the-ass she is, also recognizes she's a woman. One I've clearly hurt. Regardless of what people think of me and what I've had to do to make the money I've made, I've never intentionally hurt anyone. I'm not a bad guy. Just a man who's had way too much bad.

"You may have spent two years with me, but in that time you've spent it with plenty of others," I remind her. "I'm not perfect, Pris. But what you gave me isn't marriage material. It's not genuine. It's nothing at all when you sit down and break it apart."

"You're not going to marry me, are you?"

"No, ma'am, I'm not."

"Fuck you," she says, abruptly disconnecting.

My head drops against the headrest just as Al pulls up to my building. I wish for two things right now: a strong cup of coffee and that I could care even a little about what just happened.

"Good morning, Mr. Wilder," the security guard says, rushing to open the door for me.

"Mornin', Jim," I say.

The chorus of greetings meets me as my shoes tap against black marble tile as I make my way to the elevators. I don't smile. I nod curtly. That smile I used to flash left me long ago.

I take a glance at my phone where it buzzes.

Where are you?

I almost grin. Almost. I don't have to glance at the name or contact information to know it's Neesa, my Nubian goddess of an assistant.

"On my way up," I voice-text into my phone. "My coffee better be waiting for me, woman."

It's too early in the day to be an asshole, Hale, Neesa writes back.

The grin bypasses me straight into a chuckle. Still, the moment the elevator doors part, that grin I mustered fades. I step into an open floor plan laid out with enough white and gold marble to blind a man.

A redhead with legs as long as mine appears, handing me a steaming cup right away.

"Good morning, Mr. Wilder," Red says.

"Mornin'." I take a sip of my coffee, moving fast. Just a splash of cream, exactly how I like it. "Are the reports on my desk?"

"Yes, sir," she says. "Everything you need and more."

I nod as I pass the rows of cubicles. The staff jolt to their feet, anxious to greet me and articulate their good mornings. My intern, Clark, rushes to my side. He snags the briefcase from my hand when I lift it. Like a horse at his first derby, he takes off in the direction of my corner office.

Humph. Neesa trained him well.

I take another sip of my coffee as my phone buzzes with another text.

Two FUCKING YEARS, is all it says.

Damn. Pris is raging.

Was it two years? I suppose it was. Considering months went by when I'd fall asleep working at my desk and Pris would fall asleep in another man's bed, it doesn't seem like that long. If I had to guess all the times we were actually together, I don't think whatever we had lasted more than three solid months.

I shrug . . . and that's about it.

I'm halfway through my coffee and only a third of the way through more crap reports when there's a knock on my door.

The redhead steps in, shutting the door carefully behind her.

She leans against the heavy wood. "More coffee, Mr. Wilder?"

"Nope. I'm good." I frown when I see Neesa's name at the top of the next report. Well, I'll be damned.

"Are you?" Red asks. "How good?"

She flashes me a smile most women offer only when they're naked. Maybe that's what she meant about having more than I'd need waiting in my office.

Here's the thing about me. Insensitive bastard or not, I don't fuck my employees.

"I already I told you. I don't need more coffee," I tilt my head toward the door. "You can go now. Next time, *ask* for permission before you step in here or leave through the elevator and don't bother coming back."

Her face turns almost the exact same shade as her hair. Red has probably never been rejected in her whole life. Well, welcome to the real world, hon.

I'm rude. I'll admit it. Momma taught me better manners. But I don't really care. The door cracks open and in steps my queen and goddess among mortals.

Neesa takes one look at Red and scowls, her brown eyes flashing with irritation. She throws open the door. "Coffee and reports," Neesa tells Red flatly. "I told you not to expect anything more from him. Pull anything like this again, you'll be searching for employment in Alaska, do you understand?"

I flip through Neesa's report. She doesn't need me. Neesa doesn't need anyone and my conversation with Red is long over.

The door slams tight. "You dumped Priscilla De La Terra?" Neesa demands.

I pick up a pen, crossing out a line item that reads more like bullshit than actual fact. "You did this?" I ask, motioning to the report.

Neesa squares her shoulders and tugs the jacket of her yellow suit. "I've learned a thing or two working here," she replies. "And good morning to you, too, sir."

"That's, 'your highness,' to you." I flip a page. "It's good. Much better than the total shit I read earlier."

"You didn't answer my question." she presses. "Did you or did you not break up with Pricilla?"

"Tiffany, why would I bother answering a question you already know the answer to? My time is precious, sugar cakes." I lift the stack of reports I read through and toss them in the garbage where they belong. "Tell the Wall Street wannabees that if they don't receive feedback, they need to redo their work if they intend to stay on with me. Oh, and kindly inform them that they didn't get a proper enough education regardless of how much their mommies and daddies paid."

"Tiffany? Sugar cakes? Really, Hale?"

Neesa is the only one in my firm allowed to call me by my first name, although she tends to use "asshole" more frequently than the name Momma bequeathed me. I'll give her this, asshole is often a better fit.

"Hale?"

I look up, twirling the pen in my hand. I know Neesa. I know when her birthday is and that her favorite color is sunflower yellow. Just like I know I'd be nowhere without her. Calling her any name I want, just because I can, is sadly my only opportunity for a good chuckle given my workload and so-called life. Besides, it's plenty fun. "My apologies, Marianne. I know you're sensitive when it comes to your name."

"Asshole."

There it is.

Neesa leans at the edge of my desk, yet another thing she is allowed to do that no one else is. I know she's only attended secretarial school or whatever the hell it's called these days, but Neesa is razor sharp. If I died, right here where I sit, she could run this entire firm single-handedly. One day, she may even kill me for it. And if I keep up my pestering, that day may come sooner rather than later.

I flip through the next report. Better than the first few, but not as good as Neesa's. "Where the hell are they getting their information from?"

"I'm not answering any more questions until you tell me why you ended your relationship with Priscilla."

I take a sip from my coffee and voice command my laptop to fire up and open my email and stock market apps. "Ladasha, is now a good time to remind you you've hated Priscilla since the first time she called here, yelling at you and demanding you put her through to me?"

Neesa shoves her hands onto her hips. "I'm not defending her nor am I telling you that she's not a terrible human being. I'm respectfully asking, why did you break up with her?"

The word respect was in there somewhere. I heard it. But her tone is anything but. The way she's speaking and how she's coming across? She's ready to lift the ten-thousand dollar mahogany desk she's looming over and crack my body in half with it.

The incident surrounding Priscilla has gone from a barely there memory to some highly entertaining interaction with Neesa. I flash her the "smirk," that lopsided smile she hates more than anything else. "Pris called you, didn't she?"

"And texted and sent me an email, and Gosh Almighty and cheese and crackers, will you wipe that stupid grin off your face!" She rolls her eyes and checks her phone, ramming the screen three inches from my face so I can read it.

I don't bother, too entertained by Neesa's fussing. "You know, you could poke my eye out with that thing."

Neesa ignores me. She does that a lot. Call it a strategy to hold tight to her sanity. "Do you have *any* idea what it takes to run this office and to put up with your crapola on a daily basis?" She doesn't wait for me to answer. "No. You don't."

"I don't?" I ask innocently, which only fires her up more.

She leans forward, using all five-feet-seven inches of her to her advantage. "Absolutely not. I don't need to deal with the likes of Priscilla all day long, sending me messages like this." She waves the phone at me. "You know what she said?" Again. She doesn't wait. "She says you have a small member."

"You mean my brother, Carson?" I pretend to give it some thought. "He is a little shorter than me, but I wouldn't exactly call him small—"

"She's saying you have a small—" She glances at the door, as if suspecting someone might be listening, and drops her voice to a whisper. "—*penis*."

I sigh. "Now Neesa, we all know that's not true."

If she wasn't ready to beat me with the desk before, she is now. "For the last time. Why did you break up with her?"

I scrunch my brows. "Why do you care?"

Neesa has this ability, a gift, if you will, to singlehandedly shrink men's balls inward and cause them to scurry behind their kidneys. All it takes is one glare. The same glare she's pegging me with now. I've grown accustomed to the glare and it's not a regular day if I don't see it at least once.

I still have my balls, mind you, and after all these years with Neesa, they barely even twitch anymore. Except, the glare I know and love so well doesn't last. Not this time. Her small features soften, matching the delicate ringlets of soft black hair she gives so much care to keep professional. "It's not that I care about Priscilla. I don't like her. I never will." Her voice quiets in a way I've never quite heard. "It's that I don't like you alone."

In the world of cutthroat business, where men and women use the knife they stab their friends in the back with to slash their enemies' throats, all the while laughing at the blood pooling on the floor, Neesa's words shouldn't bother me as much as they do.

I reason it's because no matter how much I make her mad, Neesa wouldn't pull that knife on me. Nope. She's too busy wiping off the sweat and blood pouring from my body when I return from battling my competitors. Just because I'd never hurt anyone doesn't mean I won't stand and fight. Like I mentioned, it's a cutthroat business and the way it stands, I hold the biggest blade.

"Anything else?" I ask.

"Hale, don't push me away."

Neesa is the first person to praise me for doing right and the one shoving people aside to slap me upside the head when I'm being a prick. In other words, she's a real friend. One of the few I have left.

"Send her a golden retriever puppy." I reach for another red pen when the one I'm using stops working.

"A puppy?"

I glance up. "A *golden retriever* puppy," I stress. "With a pink bow."

"You know what?"

"Let me guess," I say. "You don't like bows?"

"Hale."

"Or puppies?"

"Hale."

"Pink?" I offer.

I think today is finally the day Neesa will kill me. If hate were sand I'd be looking at the Sahara Desert.

"Hale, from the first moment I interviewed for this position, I knew a day would come when I would have to sneak into your apartment and kill you in your sleep."

See? I was right.

"What do you mean?" I ask. "I thought you women liked that shit?" I huff. "I mean what kind of sick fuck doesn't like puppies?"

"Priscilla," she says. "She'd skin that puppy alive, cut off its tail, and storm in here to smack you across the face with it." She points. "After she dropped the decomposing body on my desk."

"Flowers?" I suggest.

Neesa pushes away from the desk. "You have a ten o'clock with the Strubinskis, an eleven o'clock with the Holloways, and a lunch meeting with your top three."

"Anything else?"

She whirls around. "Yes. You're an asshole."

I chuckle. The door barely finishes shutting when my cell phone rings and Sean's face lights up my screen. "What's up?"

He's chewing on something as he speaks, but that's just Sean. "Hey," he says, his South Carolina accent just as thick as mine. "I think I have an ingrown hair on my ass."

Normal people say good morning. That sort of shit is lost on Sean.

"You don't say," I mumble, scrolling through the stock report.

"I asked the woman I'm seeing if she'd take a look at it. She told me no. You think Mason will look at it this weekend?"

"I'm certain he won't," I say, making a note to call Mrs. Valez and tell her I just made her a millionaire. "And before you ask, I ain't looking at it, either."

"Well, hell. If your best friends won't look at your ass, who will?"

"Probably a doctor is my guess."

"Hmm," Sean says. "You may be on to something there."

"Mm," I agree. I'm ready to discuss the excursion to Vegas we have planned for this weekend, but Sean's not done yapping.

"You know how I'm not supposed to mention the 'B' word?"

My head falls into my hand and I rub. "Yeah?"

"Or the 'F' word?"

Sean means football, not fuck and the "B" word . . . well, there isn't a stronger word out there. That word is capable of skinning me faster than Pris would that puppy. *Becca* . . . well, I'll be damned. Why is Sean bringing her up now?

"Yeah?" I ask again.

"The 'B' word and the 'F' word are on TV."

"They shouldn't allow that on television," I mutter. "Not with so many children watching."

Sean pauses long enough to swallow whatever he's munching on. "Hale, just put it on."

Against my better judgment, I flick on the giant flat screen perched along the far wall. "Which channel?"

"All of them. You pick. Becca's made national news."

Of course she has. I switch on FS1. Yeah, there she is.

After all I've done and all I've suffered through these past ten years, seeing Becca should not have this effect on me. If my mind were as brilliant as everybody always told me it was, it should simply place Becca someplace between a childhood friend and one rough night. Just looking at her face should *not* shove those memories front and center or sharpen them to a dagger capable of puncturing my skull. But here I am, wondering how one woman can wield such a knock-out punch.

Sun-kissed blond hair streaked with platinum and assets capable of rendering a man powerless at the groin, Becca is *that* woman. The one every heterosexual man has fantasized about at least once in his life.

Her smile is as brilliant and heart-stopping as ever, threatening to knock me off my feet if I wasn't already sitting. And her voice? Lord, help me. The moment I hear her sweet southern twang I'm that young man again, the one who never dreamed our friendship would die as brutally as it did.

What has to be wall to wall male reporters duke it out to ask the next question, "Miss Shields, Miss Shields," one close to her calls out. "The Carolina Cougars are headed to the playoffs and hailed as heroes—not only in the South, but in the entire football league. Are you responsible for catapulting this once has-been, drug-addicted team into superstardom?"

Becca tosses her long hair over her shoulder, smiling like the angelic virgin she resembles, instead of the devil in high heels she is. "Of course, I am," she says, adding a wink, because she's not already sexy enough. "But I also think the hard work and unyielding spirit of this brilliant young team might have something to do with it."

That earns her plenty of laughs from the crowd, and the way she tosses her hair, again more fans than all the players combined. Each word that flows from those full pretty lips laces the air with enough powdered sugar to taste it from here.

"Miss Shields," another numb nuts beckons. "The Carolina Cougar cheerleaders are now the most recognizable faces in the entire league thanks to the success of the team."

Becca nods, feigning curiosity. Like me, she already knows where this conversation is headed and she's ready for it. "Is it true that there's a new swimsuit issue planned where the cheerleaders have the option of posing partially nude or in lingerie?"

"Yes, sir," she adds. "It's also true that proceeds will go to the victims of the recent massacre in Yemen." She tries to lead him away from the partial nudity and into a better PR place. "Every member of the squad was thrilled to be a part of the issue. These goodhearted ladies are not only committed to the professional aspects that accompany their duties as NFL cheerleads, but to aiding humankind beyond the world of sports."

Damn. She's good. Her response should be more than enough to placate the reporter and move the press conference along. Except this guy is more of dick than I initially thought. He speaks over the next reporter asking about the banquet Becks organized to raise money for the children's hospital. "Will you be featured in the swimsuit issue, Miss Shields? The centerfold perhaps?" he adds with a laugh.

I can't see this idiot, but recognize his question has at least some merit. Becca is all curves, tiny waist, and legs as long as Tennessee. She could be Playmate of the year and probably every year that follows. Gorgeous looks aside, Becca's always been more brains than bust, an attribute she takes tremendous pride in and has valued more than the money she's from. Anyone who's ever taken the time to listen to her could sense as much.

This reporter though? It's clear he ain't listening.

"Stefan," Becca says, her smile fading just enough to reveal her tough side. "I don't grace the covers of sports magazines or pose for calendar shoots. I don't even find it necessary to make the front page of the newspaper unless it's to represent this team I'm so proud of. My job is to make sure that anyone associated with the Carolina Cougars uses his or her presence to give back to a world that's been good to them and this future Super Bowl Champions team." Her smile widens, still sweet, but with an edge, so it's clear her final statement ends with an unspoken "you worthless piece of misogynistic shit," rather than a period.

I shut the TV off when she turns to answer the next question. Not because I don't want to keep watching, but because I do. Jesus Christ in heaven. When the *hell* am I going to get over this woman?

"Did you turn it off?" Sean asks.

There's enough sound coming from his end of the line that I can still hear Becca's voice. Unlike me, Sean is still watching. He and Becca remain close, but then again, they never got as close as Becca and me got on that beach.

"I have work to do, Sean," I say, trying to keep my voice casual. "Anything else you want to tell me?"

"Yeah." He takes a sip of his drink. "I think Becca broke off her engagement."

I straighten, every muscle along my spine turning to stone. For once, I'm glad Sean's not around. I don't want him to see me like this.

"To the owner's son, Paris," Sean adds. "Hmm. Or is it Lynda? Could be Brooklyn or maybe something fancy like Minnesota. Whatever his name is, he's out of the picture. Did you see? She's not wearing a ring no more."

I didn't bother looking, but if Sean's telling me, it's because he did look. Ever since learning she accepted that jackass's proposal, I've forced myself to stop wondering what could've been between us. Who the hell am I kidding? I've *never* stopped wondering about us. How her hair fanned over my shoulder and the feel of her when I climbed on top of her.

My chest tightens with anger. Memories of Becca always start out so good. No matter what, though, they always end the same, with me in a bad mood and in too much pain to be reasonable. "Why are you telling me this?" I ask. "You think I care what she does with her life?"

Sean is the type of guy you want on your side in a fight. He's strong and all limbs. He's not as lean as he used to be and definitely has more bulk than when we worked as lifeguards. But like a good ol' boy born and bred in the deep south, he can knock out a man with one good punch, step over him, and take on the next guy who follows. Is he the most PC and appropriate guy you'll ever meet? Nope. Not even close. But Sean has one of the biggest hearts I've ever had the privilege of knowing and he's more brother than pal.

"You should care," he says. "Becca's my friend." He takes a breath. "And regardless of what's happened between you, she's your friend, too, Hale."

"Later Sean," I say, disconnecting before he can say more shit than I need to hear.

Shit, nothing he says make sense. My "friend" he called her. God damn. That's not what it looked like all those years ago and all those that followed. Every time I saw Becca after that night on the beach, every time I thought that maybe we could somehow start over, I'd hear things. I'd see things, too.

I'll never understand why she didn't leave with me that night her family caught us fooling around. I all but fell to my knees, begging her to come with me and promising to take care of her. Her family was never good to her and she was never good enough for them. Her Daddy wanted a son. When he didn't get what he wanted, he treated her like garbage instead of embracing the special person Becca always was.

Still, she chose them and not me.

I return to my work, but I don't do more than type a few words to an email before my thoughts return to the next time I saw Becca after that. It was a New Year's party two years ago. Sean and Mason told me Becca wanted to see me, that she felt bad about missing dinner with our friends Trin and Callahan. Except, from the moment I arrived at her party, Becca seemed scared for me to approach.

A few women, friends of hers, I thought, found their way to me. I spoke to them while Becca spoke to some of the players who couldn't seem to get enough of her and would lick the floor at her feet if she asked nicely enough. When those women got too close, Becca lost it, storming toward me, spewing nonsense about them keeping their distance from "her man."

She meant me. It shocked the hell out of me, but more than anything it sent rage burning through me like a dam of hell fire.

I rub my eyes, replaying that night. Callahan got in trouble and we went after him. Becca looked scared. We'd fought and we were both upset, but without thinking I reached for her hand. It was my way of letting her know pissed or not, I'd stand with her. She held me tight, refusing to let me go. I thought we were going somewhere. Again, I was wrong. Denver (*that's* his name) called Becks and ordered her back to Charlotte.

Fast forward to this past New Year's. I mutter a curse and lean back into my seat.

Once more, Becca invited me to a New Year's party in Kiawah. Once more I showed up like the pining idiot I was. After sending me multiple texts insisting I come and that she missed me, how could I refuse? I had my doubts. Trust me. After the previous New Year's fiasco I wasn't keen on what might go down. Instead of listening to all those warning bells going off in my head, I decided to go, thinking it was time to give us another chance.

I didn't RSVP, hoping to surprise her with a bottle of champagne and a grin. I arrived as she hurried off to the beach by herself. I thought this was the perfect moment. The thing was, the surprise was on me.

Becca walked toward me all shy-like, the ocean wind whipping her long hair against the side of her face. For a second, we were twenty-two again, two kids on verge of falling in love.

She smiled and I swear I saw a flicker of grateful tears. She looked—I don't know—moments from racing across the sand and throwing her arms around me. But then she froze. My guess is she noticed my eyes widen to saucers when I saw that giant rock glistening on her ring finger. If that wasn't bad enough, she tried to hide it behind her. It was too late. I stomped back to my Aston Martin, ignoring her when she tore after me. She begged me to come back. I didn't. To hell with that. Instead, I took off, blocking her number as I burned rubber around the bend.

Becca was engaged. She didn't bother to warn me like a real friend would. Instead, she set me up like a fool. She sold her house in Kiawah soon after that. Probably so she and that loser can buy one on together.

"Mother fucker," I mumble, glaring at the screen as if it somehow wronged me.

I reach for Neesa's report, but I don't get far. Yelling and scrambling erupt behind the double doors leading to my office. Like a bomb detonating, the doors burst open. I'm already to my feet when men covered with FBI jackets swarm in like an army invading a small country, their guns out, hollering at me to freeze.

"What hell is this?" I ask.

Strong bodies lurch forward, pinning me to my desk. "Hale Wilder," a big man barks into my ear. "You're under arrest for fraud and stock market manipulation."

Chapter Three

Becca

"Miss Shields. Miss Shields!"

LeeAnn is a wonderful young lady, but if she wants to keep up with me she needs to learn to run in heels. Every steel magnolia I know, including my best friend, Trinity, who prefers sandals to stilettos any day of the week, can scale a maple tree in three-inch platforms.

"Yes, Leanne?"

She's huffing and puffing where I have yet to break a sweat. It's barely lunch time and I've already clocked more than two-thousand steps. Welcome to my world, y'all.

"Miss Shields, if I can just have a moment?"

I stop. Leanne's not looking good. The way she's hunched over, I'm not sure if she'll pee or puke.

"Becca!" New voice. New woman to please. I glance behind me. Callista, the manager for the cheer squad, races down the hall. She's in better shape, so it doesn't take her long to reach me. Fine by me. Leanne appears to need a moment.

I reach for my cell phone when it buzzes inside my giant hot pink purse. "Yes?" I say, when Callista reaches me, flipping through the eight texts I've already missed.

Callista sighs. "I wanted to talk with you before the conference. Since the girls were allowed to pose partially nude for this issue of the *Cougar Times*, they're upset that they can't pose in the nude for other magazines."

"They can if they want," I say as I reply to the head coach's text. "All they have to do is quit the team and they can pose for whomever they want and in whatever position they see fit."

"Some have been offered six figures," Callista presses, as if I didn't hear her the first time.

"Have they?" I ask, making it clear I don't care, all the while replying to another text.

"You're not going to change your mind about this, are you?" Callista asks.

I stop typing, more than miffed. This isn't the first time Callista and I have had to chat about her squad. "Here's the deal. I didn't want the partial nude shots. I didn't want the lingerie shots. I didn't even want the paint by numbers bathing suit shots, regardless of how you referred to them as art. I didn't want any of it, knowing the ladies who chose to pose this way did so to launch their modeling careers. They want to be models. Wonderful. It's their right. But, Callista, this has been a PR nightmare. Mothers Against Smut, the local churches, even the Girl Scouts lost their minds, which is why all proceeds are going to charity."

"Becca—"

"Callista, do you know what it's like to be woken at two in the morning by the former legal team of the Reverend Billy Graham? When you've only been asleep maybe twenty minutes? No. You don't. If those ladies want to keep showing their bits, partially or otherwise, fine. They just need to leave the team to do so, or be slapped with a breach of contract lawsuit."

Callista starts to interrupt again, but I'm not done. "One more thing. I know you've offered to manage these girls' careers, just as I know you're taking meetings with all the skin mags. If I find out you're doing it on our time, you can leave, too. There are plenty of other folks who would just love to have your job.”

Callista regards me as if slapped, but she doesn’t respond. I take off, Leanne close on my heels. I don’t have the authority to fire Callista, but the extremes I’ve gone through to repair this team’s reputation have bequeathed me the power to request her termination from the big boss.

“Miss Shields,” Leanne whimpers. “I still need to talk to you.”

I reply to another text. “Sorry, precious. You go right ahead now.”

“Denver, I mean, Mr. Singleton the Second, wants to know if you’re available for lunch?”

I try not to roll my eyes. It’s hard not to. If Leanne is referring to my pseudo-ex-fiancé by his first name that can only mean he’ll be taking a peek at her panties real soon. I huff. If he hasn’t already.

“That’s not happening,” I reply, lifting my chin when I push through the double doors leading out of the stadium. The brisk March breeze wafts the first trickle of blossoms into my nose. Ah, lovely. “Speaking of lunch, Mrs. Singleton’s auxiliary club would love a tour of the stadium following their luncheon with the governor’s wife. Be a dear and arrange that, will you, hon?”

“You’re saying no?” Leanne stumbles over her words. “I mean about lunch with Mr. Singleton?”

My driver holds open the door to my town car. I pause a few feet away, more because of the hopefulness in her tone than what she’s actually asking. “I always mean what I say, Leanne.” I drop my smile. “Especially now. For your own good, keep your distance from Denver.”

Her face burns a deep red. Just as I suspected. Denver’s already taken a peek. “I don’t know what you mean, ma’am.”

Oh. So, now it’s ma’am? “Yes, you do.” I push my hair away from my face when the wind intensifies. It’s still winter up north, but the very start of spring in Charlotte. “Regardless of what he’s promised in soft, sultry whispers, Denver Singleton is not a good man.”

I smile and slip into the car. "Take care of the ladies' auxiliary club and show them a good time, won't you?"

Leanne's dark hair shadows her face as she stares hard at the ground. "Yes, ma'am," she answers.

Twain, my driver, shuts the door. He doesn't say anything until he pulls away from the curb. "Careful what you say about the boss's son, Miss Becca," he warns.

I pull down the mirror and check my makeup, reaching for lip gloss when I realize how much the color has faded. "If you think I'm going to keep quiet, you're wrong."

"I'm not saying stay quiet. Learned a long time ago that's useless advice when it comes to you, Miss Becca. I'm only remindin' you that he's the boss's son. As much as Mr. Singleton likes you, he's not going to take kindly to what you say about his boy."

"The boss will take kindly to me keeping his brat son out of trouble. *Again*," I remind Twain. I cap my lip gloss. "Mr. Singleton doesn't want another bastard grandchild running around, whose mother he has to pay off to keep the kid hidden from the press. He's got enough of those. His words. Not mine."

I like Twain almost enough to call him a friend. He watches out for me. But if he was one of those rare jewels I could call a friend, I'd be able to trust him with more than I do. "The boss," he refers to, this man of prestige and wealth, pinned me against the wall the first day I came to work for him.

I'd been beaten by my daddy weeks before and was still reeling from the trauma. My face remained bruised and it was clear I'd been through a lot. I suppose that's why Mr. Singleton felt I was an easy target. And if it hadn't been for the generosity of Trin and her family, I probably would have been at Mr. Singleton's mercy. But the Summers didn't just provide me with money to get settled in Charlotte. They armed me with love and support my own family never felt I deserved.

"You don't know what I could give you," Mr. Singleton told me, his breath wreaking of old expensive scotch.

"And you don't know how close you are to losing your balls," I fired back, shoving him away and causing him to stumble. "How dare you put your hands on me?"

"A hellcat. I like it," he said, unbuttoning his jacket and marching forward.

"No, a smart woman," I clarified. I reached for my phone and played back our conversation. He froze, his eyes widening. "Here's the thing, Mr. Singleton. You hired me to make you look good and I will do that job to the best of my ability. I'll promise to take the lowly Cougars everyone has given up on and make them into the golden boys the NFL never saw coming. Under my leadership, they won't share the spotlight with the greats of football, they'll seize it."

He frowned, insulted and likely nervous. But he was listening. I pushed away from the wall and straightened my suit, my hand holding tight to my phone to remind him it was there. "Just so we're clear, if you ever put your hands on me or make assumptions that aren't there, the software attached to this recording will distribute our conversation to every major newspaper and online journalist in the Deep South and beyond."

Mr. Singleton knows little about technology and often grumbles about mobile applications. But he knows enough to believe my threat is possible. Thanks to brilliant engineers like Landon Summers, technology like this does exist.

To his credit, Mr. Singleton didn't try anything with me after that. Well, at least not physically. More times than not, Mr. Singleton hinted about the oh-so glamorous life I could have being one of his mistresses—even at events where his devoted wife of forty years stood graciously smiling mere feet away.

Every now and then, Mr. Singleton invites me out for a "business" meeting at one of the premier hotels in town. Every time, I've shot him down. Now, he mostly ogles my breasts and ass when he thinks I'm not looking. On a good day, I think he respects me. On a bad day, he thinks I'm a bitch. It doesn't matter. I'm the one he came to when Denver's drink and drug induced antics with a prostitute (at the very hotel his father had invited me to) made headline news.

"Did you love him, Becca?" Twain asks me from the front.

"Who?"

"The boss's son."

Twain should know better. He was there for all the smoke and mirrors from the word go and polished said mirrors when they threatened to crack. "I loved Denver as much as I was supposed to," I respond.

My, isn't that the truth?

I "loved" Denver long enough to spruce up his reputation. I spun his hot mess, cleaned up the multiple indiscretions as best I could, and reshaped him from screw-up to a hurt young man, living in his father's shadow and unable to live up to his heroic persona—no matter how hard he tried. I even had him crying real tears on Good Morning America.

I'm good at my job. So good, I'm willing to play the fake fiancé who stands diligently and lovingly by her man, pretending I don't sleep alone with my thoughts on nothing but work.

Well, almost nothing.

Twain drops the conversation almost as fast as he flicks on the turn signal. Maybe he's hurt that I don't come clean with him. Maybe he considers me a friend and would tell me as much if I'd only open up. I hope not. I only spill my soul to one person and she's not here. I wish she was. Trin's always my sunshine when the dark clouds roll in. And for someone like me, who speaks to close to thousands of people on a weekly basis, I'm lonelier than I should be.

I think I reply to three emails and two texts by the time Twain rolls to a stop in front of Fernando's, an exclusive club for professional athletes and their guests. Sometimes it includes their wives, but most of the time it includes whoever they're sleeping with that week.

I fluff my hair more out of habit. The way Lizzie, my makeup artist and stylist, hooked me up before the press conference, I don't have to touch this hair for days.

Twain opens my door. "How long you going to be?" he asks, waving off the attendant who rushes to greet me.

I shimmy to the edge of the seat and rise slowly, putting on a dazzling smile and speaking through my teeth. "You know me. Just long enough to appear social." I give a wave to a TMZ rep who calls to me. "Or maybe sooner."

Twain mutters something I don't quite hear. He doesn't strike me as someone afraid to tell me what he thinks, more like a man who chooses his battles. He wants to give me advice, shake a reprimanding finger at me, or perhaps tell me what I should do instead of what I am doing. Here's the thing about me. I've always attracted men for one of three reasons: to control me, to bed me, or to protect me, and during the worst of times, to do all three. At thirty-two, I'm not sure which I hate more.

I strut toward the club as if I have all the time in the world. Four of our newest cheerleaders light up when they see me. They're stunning women, one of the many requirements of joining the team that makes me roll my eyes. This time, however, their looks aren't helping. Like many of the fans and wannabee baby mamas waiting behind the velvet ropes, they're not being allowed in.

"Becca!"

"*Becca*!"

"Miss Shields!"

The cheerleaders call to me and so does everyone else. The majority of the crowd is unfamiliar to me. I imagine they know me from watching me on T.V. They stretch their hands, pressing their bodies against the velvet rope hard enough to tip the stand, all for a chance to mingle with the best of the best.

"Sorry," I offer to the row of blonds I pass. "Team members and guests only."

The women swipe at their teary eyes. My smile falters. I wonder which player has already gone back on his word to call, or his promise to leave his wife. I hope none of them are pregnant. I've worked hard to fill this team with good people, but power has a way of smashing souls and filling egos.

I motion to the cheerleaders as I reach the bouncer. "They're new on the team," I tell him. "Let them through, John."

John gives me a stiff nod and steps aside. The girls squeal. "Thanks, Becca," they offer.

It's loud and cold here on the streets, but not as loud as it is inside. For an exclusive club, there's no high-tech music or overly processed auto-tune. This is the south. If it isn't country booming over the speakers it's good old fashioned rock 'n roll.

"Miss Shields," the hostess says to me. "Nice to see you."

She takes my coat. "Thank you, Marcella," I say, grateful to get somewhat of a breather.

My butt isn't quite on the stool when more cheerleaders accost me. "Becca, that bitch, Madison, stained my uniform with ink and then put it back in my locker."

I nod to the bartender when he asks me if I want my usual. "Sue Ellen," I say. "I'm neither your momma nor your babysitter. You're a grown ass woman. Take it up with Madalyn or whatever her name is, or hell, even your coach."

"You're not going to help me?" she asks, seemingly affronted I'm not going in guns blazing.

I offer my thanks when the bartender sets an Old Fashioned in front of me. I take a sip. I love these things a little too much. On a good night, I'll have one, on a bad, I'll have three. Tonight is a good night. I'm going to enjoy every last sip. "I like you, Sue Ellen," I tell her. "So, let me give you the best advice I have. Don't reinforce the stereotype of an angry, petty woman in this field. You're not doing the rest of us any favors."

She practically stamps her feet. "But I didn't start it."

"I don't care. Finish it."

Did I just dismiss this sweet little June bug? Yes, I did and I smiled while doing it. I mean what I say. I'm the nicest person in the world, usually, but the pettiness that exists between women has led to more catfights than I can count.

Santiago slides onto the stool beside me. The bartender knows what he wants without asking. He places a Dos Equis beer in front of him, hurrying down the bar to tend to the next superstar.

"Becca," Tiago says.

I lean forward, giving him a really good view of my large breasts. Tiago doesn't stop to admire them. He never has. Have I mentioned I *really* like Tiago?

"What's her name?" I ask.

His dark brows furrow menacingly, tight enough to form a unibrow that looks surprisingly good on him. "What?"

I grin. I have him exactly where I want him. "I asked you what her name is."

He stares at me like I've lost my mind. "I have no idea what you're talking about," he replies, his face unreadable.

"Yes, you do. Want to know how?" I take a nice long sip of my drink, my eyes closing as the sweet taste of sugar and whiskey glides down my throat. Mm, heaven. I open my eyes slowly, staring at him seductively from beneath my thick veil of lashes.

Tiago doesn't even blink, watching me in that same broody way. I point at his face and then to my chest and he still keeps his attention on my face. "That's how I know," I say. "Unlike the rest of mankind, you've never stared at my tits."

He swivels back in the direction of the bar and returns to his beer. I laugh. "Tiago, you didn't even look when I pointed." I take another long taste of my drink, enjoying the slow burn traveling to my stomach. No one else can make an adult beverage this good.

"You're not gay," I say, ignoring the way Tiago is ignoring me. I know he's listening. "I would've seen you with a man by now."

"Becca, stay out of my business."

"Why?" I ask, giving my drink a swirl.

Tiago glares at me. "Is now a good time to remind you I'm only one of three players from the original team? I've never given you a reason to question my ethics or professionalism."

"I know, sugar pie," I agree. "Why do you think I like you so much or care enough to ask?"

Segon Murphy ambles up beside Tiago, bending his arm to rest against Tiago's shoulder. "Hey, Becca. Looking good tonight," he says. Unlike Tiago, Murphy does look at my tits. "When are we gonna go out?"

"We're not," I inform him. I pull the fancy plastic toothpick piercing the garnishes from my drink and pop the bourbon infused cherry in my mouth, relishing the sweet taste intermixed with strong liquor.

"Why not?" Murphy presses.

I swallow the cherry, barely blinking. "Because you're a whore."

Tiago chokes on his beer. He wasn't expecting that one and neither was Murphy. "You don't have to be a bitch," he says.

"And you don't have to be a whore," I counter. Murphy storms away in a huff. "See you at the Children's Hospital next week. Oh, and don't forget to write a nice speech."

"What the hell, Becca?" Tiago says, laughing.

I laugh with him. Subtle is something I've never been accused of being in social circles. Why start now?

My laughter fades as his does. I turn in the direction he's looking. No, not . . . uh-uh.

The quarterback, Zack Anson, strolls in, his confident smile cutting through the dimness. His team members scramble to attention, just short of bowing before him.

Tiago doesn't bow. He doesn't offer so much as a curtsy for his life-long best friend. Oh, no. He's too busy eyeing Marilyn. Zack's girlfriend.

I whip back toward Tiago, his chin briefly lowering before he takes a purposeful swig of his beer. "You're in love with Marilyn?" I ask.

His eyes widen briefly before his frown returns. "Tiago . . . don't go there," I warn. "He's your best friend—Jesus, so is she."

Tiago doesn't respond, returning dutifully to his beer. "Tiago?" I press. "Tell me you won't go there."

He shakes his head slowly. "You don't get it, Becca. I loved her long before he did."

And unlike Zack, I'm betting Tiago would have remained faithful.

I'm not certain whether to cry with or for him.

Vulnerability tends to come at the most inopportune times and when you least want it. Maybe it's the atmosphere or the conversation we were just having, or maybe it's the combination of innocence, beauty, and kindness Marilyn effortlessly carries. It could be all of it. Whatever does it, for the first time since I've known this imposing man (who's always been comfortable letting his friend Zack take the spotlight, all the while guarding his back on the field), that vulnerability spills out.

"Tiago," I say, searching for the right words and the compassion he needs. "Be careful. Even I can't spin that."

"There's nothing to spin. I'm no fool. I won't ever let anything happen. No matter how bad I may want it."

My eyes flicker towards Marilyn as she approaches, smiling. She's happy to see Tiago, and maybe a little relieved. But there's something else. A look she gives him that's foreign from the way she looks at Zack. Damn. Maybe she loves him, too.

I slam back the rest of my drink and slip off the stool, greeting Marilyn briefly as she makes her way to Tiago.

Marilyn isn't like the rest of the women who come here. She's *nice*. It's not to say the other women are heartless. They just have different priorities, like landing a Sugar Daddy and achieving WAG status. I don't fault them, exactly. I suppose I just recognize that the fall-outs and the headaches outweigh the prestige and celebrity status.

As I near Zach (and yes, he does eye my rack), I can't help but turn back to Tiago. There's no scowl in his expression. Not with Marilyn near him and not given how softly she appears to speak to him. This isn't a man looking to cheat with his best friend's girl. This is a man in love with someone he can't have.

"Hey, Becca," Zach says. His focus once more darts below my chin. "I wanted to discuss the visit to the Children's Hospital next week."

I don't hear his next few words, not when my attention latches on the flat-screen above his head.

It's a media shit-storm. Camera lights creating a strobe affect as *Hale Wilder* is led into a courthouse in handcuffs.

Zach says something about footballs and autographs, but it's all white noise, my full attention on the news anchor. "Hale Wilder, also known as the Anaconda of Wall Street by the way he puts the squeeze on the competition, was indicted on multiple charges of embezzlement and stock manipulation today . . ."

My body shudders, thinking back to that horrible night. No, sir, that's not why he's called the Anaconda.

"Becca? Are you listening?" Zach asks. "Hey. Are you all right?"

"Shit," I mutter. My eyes sting with tears that shouldn't be there. It's over between us. All my screw-ups made sure of that . . .

"Becca? Sweetie, what's wrong?" Marilyn asks.

Tiago is here, too, reaching for me as the doors to the courthouse slam shut behind the cluster of FBI agents escorting Hale. My heartstrings break apart and my stomach does another flip when I realize Sean is calling me.

"Becca?" Sean says, not bothering to greet me or wait for me to mumble a response. "Hale's in trouble. Fuckin' A, Becca. Are you there? Hale needs you . . ."

Chapter Four

Hale

You ever watch the People's Court? Judge Judy? That kind of thing? Okay, picture it in real life. Instead of a few rows stuffed with nosey people likely paid to be there, imagine multiple rows of nosey reporters waiting on Judge Stein here to beat my balls with the gavel.

Judge Stein could have her own show. Not because she's pretty or elegant, but because she has that, "Take no prisoners, I don't care if you die, attitude," required of all T.V. judges, near as I can figure.

"How do you plead?" she asks, her hawk-like stare targeting me.

"My client pleads not guilty," Mason answers for me.

I have to give it to Mason. He's a criminal trial attorney representing gangbangers from some of the shittiest communities in Philadelphia. He has no experience defending anyone charged with a white collar crime. But he's my friend, who passed the bar in both PA and NY. For now, that's good enough for me.

"Bail is set at five-hundred thousand," Judge Stein declares, more like a warning than a ruling. She narrows her eyes. "I'll allow the defendant to return to Kiawah, South Carolina, under the condition his bank and credit accounts are frozen and all assets, including properties, electronic devices, vehicles, and personal belongings, are barred from sale once bail is set."

Are you fucking kidding me? My glare on the judge turns on Mason. He gives me a firm shake of his head. In other words, don't argue, this is as good as it's going to get.

The Feds argue flight risk, etc., just as they did the first time Mason made a motion to return me to Kiawah. Where am I going to go? Judge Stein stripped me of every dime I have.

Thank God, the reporters are still waiting on me when Mason, Sean, and I walk out. I haven't had enough humiliation for one day.

Sean leads the way, the long arms of his lanky body swinging casually, even as he narrows his eyes at anyone who dares to get too close.

Mason takes a protective stance beside me, his deep, booming voice assuring the press of my innocence, affirming that justice will be served. What he should say is that I'm going to find the fuckers who did this and bash their damned faces in.

The door to the limo Sean secured slams shut behind him. And since Sean was in charge of securing the limo, there's a damn stripper pole right in the middle.

Sean lifts his arm, gliding his hand up and down it. "I feel sorry for dem strippers who have to perform in here," he says thoughtfully. "I mean, there's like, not much room to spin." He frowns, glancing up. "Not to mention, they must have to wear helmets or some crazy shit so as not to bang their heads too hard. Helmets can't be an easy thing to pull off as sexy, s'far as I'm concerned. What do y'all think?"

If you think Sean's epiphanies are flying out of his mouth because I've had a rough few days, he thinks I could use a laugh, or is trying to distract me, y'all are giving Sean too much credit. Sean is being Sean and he's damn good at it.

I look at Mason. Unlike Sean, he's not contemplating the dangers of pole dancing in limos. "You're fucked," he says quietly.

"That's the spirit," I mutter, rubbing my face and leaning back against the seat. I don't think a minute passes before I sit up again. Unlike Sean, whose added bulk has only gone to his stomach, the muscles lining Mason's shoulders, back and chest, make him look more Marvel hero than lawyer.

"I'm serious, Hale," Mason says. "I'm the last person you should have called to represent you." He flips through his phone. "Trin and Callahan opened up an account in her name for your legal defense fund. They dropped a hundred grand in it, her brother, Landon, dropped in another hundred grand, and their daddy is texting he's adding another two and to let them know when you need more."

I mutter a curse. "They didn't have to do that."

"Yes, they did," Mason says. "They're your friends. Friends who recognize you need the cash for a lawyer who can help you out of this mess."

I meet him square in the face. "I've got one. I trust you, Mace, and that's good enough for me."

"Maybe it wouldn't be so bad if the helmet was clear to match the heels those ladies like to wear," Sean adds, giving the pole another stroke. "That'll work better, won't it? Women like to match their outfits."

Mason ignores him, scrolling through his messages. "Trin's letting you stay at the house she and Callahan flipped last summer. It's by the water. She says you'll love the view."

Trin and her family hooked me up with funds and a place. Not Emer and Carson, my brothers. They've waited years to watch me fall on my face. I can't imagine which one of them is laughing the hardest or celebrating my downfall more. Then again, they probably don't care enough to do either.

"Trin's a good friend," I manage. I should ask Mason to reply with a thank you or call her to tell her as much. But with Trin always comes Becca and . . . God damn it. Becks is the last person I should be thinking about. It wasn't okay to think of her during the best of times. When I had money, a reputation, and women ready to claw eyes out to get to me. It's sure as hell not good to think of her now when I'm being framed for shit I'd never do. I may be an anaconda like Wall Street dubbed me—never backing down and crushing my opponent—but I'm also ethical. I'm not sure what upsets me more. These charges or what these charges have done to my reputation.

"Do you think they should charge more?" Sean asks. "To cover the cost of the helmets? They can't be cheap if they're clear. Otherwise, more strippers would wear 'em. The floor in here is hard. But a stage strikes me as harder and more dangerous."

Mason glances up, grimacing. "Sean, I don't think now is a good time."

"I know." Sean's expression grows sad and weary. "Just worried, y'all."

It's not his comments that make Sean a real friend. It's his heart. "Me, too," Mason agrees, nodding softly.

I glance away. It hurts knowing they hurt for me. "Where're we headed?" I ask.

"A hotel on the upper west side. Your PA is waiting for us and is in the process of securing a private plane to take us to Kiawah by the end of the week."

"Us?" I ask.

"We need a better plan than we have," Mason says. "That will take some time and I may need to file a few petitions while we're still here. We'll get you settled in Kiawah and then fly back here." Mason swipes at his short, buzzed hair, sweat glistening along the crown of his dark skin. "If you're hell bent on me representing you, I have a lot of research to do and attorneys to consult with. I'll need to get a team together, other counsel, private investigators, whatever it takes."

"Thank you. Get who you need," I say.

"I will," Mason promises. "I'll take care of it."

I believe him. Not that the hole burning its way through my gut lessens in severity. I'm innocent. I am. We'll find a way out of this mess. Someone was smart enough to frame me. With any luck, he or she will be stupid enough to get caught.

My issue is, people don't soon forget scandal. I learned a long time ago how much people value money and how they'll cut you to pieces if they learn that you messed with theirs.

Shit. Wasn't it just the other day I was in my office taking millions and making them billions? Wasn't I telling the finance world to bite me and enjoy the slow chew? Now, every client I have thinks I screwed them, even sweet Mrs. Valez, who went from cleaning houses to cleaning up at the bank.

The tension, the hate I'm feeling, it becomes too much, especially for Sean.

He holds out his arms. "Let's hug it out, bitches."

Two more hugs and more than his share of much needed back pats later, we reach the hotel. I haven't seen Sean this upset since his parents split up and we spent an hour washing his puke out of Trin's hair. We were in high school and half running, half-staggering from a busted keg party. We can laugh about it now. But that's about all we can laugh about.

Just like back at the courthouse, the reporters are right there. Oh, and look, so is what has to be a throng of paparazzi. Pris is New York's celebrity socialite. As much as we're no good for each other, it pissed me off that one of those leeches snapped a picture of her sobbing as she left her apartment and smacked it on the front cover beside an old picture of us.

I called her and told her I was sorry about putting her through this. She told me, "Fuck off. I hope you rot in prison."

Good to know she's taking our breakup well.

Neesa sprints across the lobby as we shove our way through the press. "Hale. Jiminy Cricket, I don't know how they found out you're here—"

Neesa grinds to an awkward stumble, her hip and knee twisting in a way that seems unnatural. I snag her arm, steadying her.

Her eyes are wild, her eyelids peeling back behind her head. I turn around, expecting more FBI and another set of cuffs. I do a double-take when I realize Neesa, my go-to, my consummate professional, my never sweat in the face of danger, my super assistant minus the cape, is gaping at Mason and tripping over a word that sounds like erpaw. That's right. *Erpaw.*

I cock a brow. "Mason, this is Neesa. Neesa, this is Mason. I thought y'all had met."

Mason's nod is barely perceptible, unlike Neesa's stammer. "He-lo-lo. No, we've only spoken on the phone."

Mason gives my sweet little princess the once-over. Great. He likes what he sees, too. Mason steps forward, lifting Neesa's hand and kissing it gently. I'm still holding her. In case you're wondering, it feels as awkward as it sounds.

"Why haven't we met?" Mason asks, his deep voice as solid as the marble tile at my feet. "After all these years of talking, how is it possible?"

Women love Mason. They always have. This here display is a good example of why.

Neesa giggles. *Giggles* like a little girl, then nods like she's having a seizure. I'll give her this, it's a better response than the "erpaw", or whatever the hell first came out of her mouth.

Sean clears his throat. I don't think he so much cares about what's happening between Mason and Neesa. Sean is like a Hobbit and he's probably starving, having missed his third lunch to stand by me in court.

"Oh," Neesa says, suddenly remembering that she's not alone and that yes, I'm still holding her.

"Yup, I'm still here," I remind her. She shoots me a dirty look and addresses Sean. "Nice to see you, again, Sean."

"Hey, Neesa," Sean says. "While we're on the subject, do you have an opinion on strippers and safety gear?"

Neesa doesn't know Sean well. But she's interacted enough with him to not be too surprised by his comments. She smiles politely. "I haven't given it much thought," she says, looking back at Mason and blushing.

Christ, help me. I love Mason. I do. Most likely he and Sean will be Godparents to my kids if I ever accidently knock someone up. Except, the last thing I need right now is my attorney making babies with my PA. That shit don't mix in a time of crisis.

"This way," Neesa says, blushing *again.*

Mason watches Neesa walk off as if she's trying to keep a tennis ball clutched between her knees. He smiles, approvingly. Evidently, I'm not the only one who considers Neesa a queen among peasant folks like me.

I exchange glances with Mason, following closely behind Neesa as she heads toward the elevator. "You all right there, Lavina?" I ask.

She stiffens at the name. "Fine," she squeaks, attempting to pry her legs apart. "We're in the penthouse. It has plenty of room for you and Ma—I'm mean, your friends."

I think she meant Mason, "your hot, sexy, I wish you weren't here so I can get naked with him, friend." I want to ask her about it, but I'm not happy with how hard she's struggling to hold herself upright.

"Did you hurt your knee?" I ask. Damn, when she saw Mason, it's as if she hit an invisible wall. For all I'm joking, I think she might be hurt.

Neesa's leg does this jerky thing that can't possibly be human. "New shoes," she says.

"You wear those all the time," I counter.

That's about when the shy schoolgirl Neesa has warped into vanishes and Sasha Fierce returns with a vengeance. She hits the button to the penthouse, even though she already pressed it, speaking through her teeth. "They're *new,*" she insists.

I snatch her arm when she loses her footing while Mason presses a hand to her back. I'm not exactly shocked it's Mason Neesa looks at. I am, however, dumbfounded by the way she reacts.

I've never seen a woman truly swoon. I used to think it was a gross exaggeration of how women fall all over men. That shit can't be real. Well, I've been wrong before and it appears I'm wrong again. Neesa is *swooning* over Mason. Now? Today? Could they have maybe picked a less disastrous time in my life?

Sean shoves his way between us when the doors swing open. "I've got this," he says, lifting Neesa into his arms like Tarzan would with Jane. I almost expect him to do the Tarzan yell or maybe do the Chewbacca howl. Sean's all sorts of talented.

His talent and strength sadly go unappreciated by the lovely Jane. Neesa kicks her legs like a little kid learning to swim. It's all she manages before she covers her face with her hand.

Mason makes strangling noises in his attempt to not full out guffaw. Sean doesn't notice, which shouldn't surprise anyone. He returns to his stripper safety wear tirade. "Clear helmets," he insists. "Like dem heels."

I lift my arms, trying to save Neesa. "Here. Give her to me."

"I got her," Mason says, his offer to save the damsel in distress, draining the color from said damsel's skin.

"She's my assistant," I say, trying to spare her.

"She's his assistant," Sean agrees.

"For the love of chocolate and strawberries," Neesa whimpers. "Just put me down. I'm fine. Goodness gracious, I'm fine."

Maybe she is. I'm not. We step into the sunken living room of the penthouse. A tall, leggy blond rises from the couch like a bright sun in the horizon, disintegrating the darkness and making the clouds her paltry bitches.

Becca Shields steps forward, her killer stilettos crushing what's left of my heart.

"Hi, Hale," she says. "I'm at your service."

Chapter Five

Becca

I was prepared to see Hale. On my grandmother's grave, I swear I was.

Until I actually saw him.

His hair isn't as blond as it was when we were young and taking advantage of the sun and surf. The lack of boyish charm is also something new, likely hidden far beneath his pristine suit. Life away from Kiawah hardens and ages you faster than you're ready. So does life away from those who most love you.

Hale steps through, anger displacing his shock and what remains of the young man I fell in love with.

The sapphire blue skirt suit I'm wearing draws most eyes. Hale's focus remains fully on my face. I try to smile, but my smile doesn't come. All the tender thoughts I'm feeling at seeing him are kicked aside by Hale's sharp tone.

"What the fuck?" he says, his steely gaze meeting Mason's.

"Hale," Mason says. "Take it easy."

"Take it easy? Are kidding me?" Hale asks. "What the *hell* is *she* doing here?"

Hale storms forward, stopping inches from me. My breathing has increased for no apparent reason, matching his harsh intakes of breath.

The last time we stood this close, his touch sent sizzles of raw hunger penetrating through my chest. He's not touching me now. He might as well be, his ultra-masculine presence like liquid fire.

Mason appears, standing between us. I wasn't aware he'd moved, let alone sensed him cross the room. He warned me Hale wouldn't take my presence well. He'd insisted we meet downstairs. But downstairs, be it the bar for drinks or for dinner as he suggested, wouldn't work. It would be too easy for Hale to dismiss me and that's the last thing I want.

Mason folds his arms over his chest. It's a protective stance most bouncers take at a bar. But Mason isn't letting Hale know he'll fight him if he lays a hand on me. As furious as Hale is, he'd never raise a hand against a woman. Mason is just letting Hale know he supports me, as well as my presence. My, that pushes Hale over the edge.

The menace in his tone . . . Jesus, what's happened between us? "What are you doing here, Becca June?" Hale asks, his voice low, but no less vicious.

Wow. He had to call me that. I'm not certain it's because it's what my daddy used to call me, or because Hale is just that angry. Either way, I stand to my fullest height. It doesn't help much. Even in these heels and given my tall stature, I'm still shorter than he is. "I'm here to help you," I say calmly. "Saw the news. Looks like your image could use a little fluffing."

"Not from you," he assures me.

My lips press tight as if I'm unaffected, while I swallow back the hurt he causes. I didn't expect to be forgiven. I also didn't expect this much anger.

"I called and asked her to be here," Sean says.

My eyes widen when I realize he's still carrying Hale's assistant, Neesa. Sean shuffles forward, not bothering to put her down or even remember that he's still holding her. "Becca didn't hesitate and caught the first flight here that she could. She wants to help."

"I think she's helped enough," Hale replies.

"That's not fair," I say, my voice reflecting my hurt. I hate that it does. What happened to the woman who high-tailed it from the airport, so she could be here when Hale returned from court? The one hell-bent on not taking "no" for an answer?

"It's not fair?" Hale counters. "Surprised your fiancé would let you out of his sight? Did you have to ask for permission or did you have to lie about where you were going?"

"I don't need permission from any man," I fire back, my temper flaring. "I do what I want, when I want."

"Unless that man snaps his fingers or makes a fuss."

"Oh. I see," Aneesa says, her understanding causing our faces to flush.

Hale walks away, but not before hurling another hostile expression at me.

His anger practically sets the cool space of the open living room aflame. I'm certain he'll start swearing or demanding I leave. Instead he addresses Neesa. "Bedroom, this way?"

"Yes, Hale," Neesa replies. At her insistence, Sean sets her down.

If Neesa was hurt, she doesn't show it then, scrambling after Hale. I follow, too, albeit not as quickly. I need these next few steps to gather my resolve and to rein in the self-assurance that has all but left me.

I'm just barely crossing the threshold of the large suite when Hale tugs off his tie. He tosses it aside. His jacket follows.

They don't notice me, not that I'm exactly waving a flag.

"Clothes in there?" he asks, motioning to the immense walk-in closet with his chin as he removes his cufflinks.

"Yes. I went to Barneys, Saks, and ultimately, Nordstrom."

He pauses in the middle of unbuttoning his shirt. "Why so many stores?"

"Because, and I quote, 'I don't want any metro-sexual looking pieces of shit, Neesa,'" she counters. "It's New York, Hale. It's either high-class or five-dollar T-shirts off the street."

"All right," he mutters. "Thanks, sweet thing."

Sweet thing? I start to worry there's something between them when he tosses his collared shirt behind him and peels off his undershirt like a seasoned model. He gives no mind to what effect his long lean muscles and bare skin might have on Neesa. My guess is she's seen him in less before.

A pang of jealousy follows each step I take forward. I can't be jealous. No. I *shouldn't* be jealous. But that's exactly what I am. It seems I left my pride back in Charlotte with all that pesky confidence I once possessed. I should leave them alone and return to the living room. Yet, here I am, drawing closer to Hale.

I almost kick myself. *What the hell is wrong with you, Becca?*

Oh, darlin, my obnoxious lady parts reply. *Regardless of what he says and how hard you try to deny it, that hunk of man has always been yours.*

Sometimes, my lady bits just need to shut up.

I venture further in, head high, attitude out. Hale is down to just his pants. He sets his watch on the bureau beside the cufflinks while Neesa lays out his clothes. Neesa is moving so fast, I barely catch her disappear into the bathroom to start the shower.

Hale uses this moment to lean forward, placing his hands on either side of the dresser. His anger has all but vanished, leaving the weight of his problems to sag his shoulders. As psychotic as it sounds, I want to kiss the spot between his shoulder blades, that small spot that rests behind the heart I've always cherished. But the way I feel around him, I wouldn't want to stop with a kiss.

I'd wrap my arm around his waist, press my cheek against his warm, bare skin. I want to be there for him. In all the ways I should have been so long ago. The way we were meant to be on that beach. On that night that was supposed mean everything, only to become one of the worst times in my life.

Could I comfort him now? With my words? With my body?

Hale lifts his head, the muscles stretching across his back stiffening when he sees me in mirror, just a few paces away. As easily as that, his momentary display of vulnerability abandons him.

I should give him a moment and plenty of space. Yet the best I can do is not to gawk. Hale does pissed-off, broody, hot guy well.

It's not my fault. I swear it's not. My womanly desires are fully awake and they don't seem ready to shut the hell up.

"Don't you think that's a little degrading?" I ask. "Asking your PA to draw you a bath?"

It's pathetic. I know. Right now, it's all I have.

"It's a shower," Hale says, likely wondering how I had the ovaries to come in here. "And it's something Neesa does all the time."

"Baby you?" I offer.

"No." There's no hint of humor in Hale's response. But there is something else. "She takes care of me, Becca. Like a real friend would."

Neesa exits the bathroom, her hurried steps slowing as she nears. Her expression softens, demonstrating a caring demeanor she didn't reveal until now. "Hale's offered to get us matching tattoos," she says, pursing her lips when Hale winks.

"How else does a big shot say Happy Birthday?" Hale asks, acting as if I'm not standing there.

"I don't know. A paid vacation. A shopping spree. Candy. Maybe flowers?" Neesa offers.

"Nah. Navy ships across our chests it is." He waggles his eyebrows. "Unless I can talk you into a World's Greatest Boss banner dangling over a life-sized image of me giving the thumbs up."

Neesa makes a face. "I'll take the navy ship." She places her hands on her hips, attempting to appear as if she's had it with Hale, despite the lingering concern in her tone. "Is there anything else?"

Hale analyzes her closely, noting the misery she attempts to hide behind her no-nonsense persona. He seems prepared to offer words of comfort and support, something to assure her that he and the company will be all right.

I don't know Neesa, and in many ways, I don't feel like I know Hale any more. But I can read others well enough to know what these two are thinking. Hale wants to assure her he won't fail and that he'll take care of her. He doesn't realize Neesa isn't worried about her future. She's worried about Hale.

"Food," Hale replies. "You know what I like." He whips off his belt, smirking in her direction. "That is, if you and Mason don't already have dinner plans."

As easy as the strike of a match, Neesa's genuine affection for him morphs to annoyance. You might call it one of Hale's superpowers.

"Sometimes, I really hate you," Neesa tells him.

"And?"

"And you're an asshole," Neesa finishes, storming out the door.

"Is that a no to food?" Hale calls after her.

He chokes back a laugh when she flips him off. I turn to him, playing with the necklace I'm wearing. It's the only thing I can do that makes me appear somewhat relaxed. It's something I really need now.

Since I haven't seen enough of his muscles today, he gives me yet another show. An eight-pack of abs stretch and protrude as he bends forward to tug off his shoes and socks and, because that's still not enough, his arms bulge from the effort.

He makes quick work of disrobing.

He looks good.

Really good.

Why does he have to look so good?

No offense, God, but couldn't You have made him bald? Maybe had tufts of hair growing out of his ears? What about love handles? I could use some love handles on this man right about now.

In one slick motion, Hale rips off his pants and flings them onto the bed. I jump as if stung. "What are you doing?"

Hale tilts his chin, as if realizing I'm standing here and that, yes, that is my jaw scraping along the floor.

The floor of his bedroom.

Watching him get naked.

Seriously. Why does he have to look this good?

He frowns, affronted. But as his features relax, his mood changes.

Slowly, oh-so slowly, he slides his palm down his chest, over the center of his pecks and further down to his belly, his fingers skimming the small hairs below his navel, and lower yet. His voice is gruff, his words as tangible as rough stone dragging across my skin. It's similar to how he first addressed me, except, instead of anger, there's something else. A very naughty something else.

"What's wrong?" he asks. "Doesn't this look familiar?"

I'm gifted with spinning lies into gold bricks heavy enough to stone him to death. You'd never know it then. "You mean like when we were lifeguards and you wore swim trunks?" I want to kick myself and send me back to preschool. *This* is the best I can come up with? "Sure. I suppose."

"No," he replies in that same gravelly voice, sin dripping like droplets of rain from his tongue. "You've seen me in less. A lot less."

And felt even more, he implies.

Muscle memory. I believe that's what it's called. When your body remembers what to do by acting and feeling, ingraining the motion with the moment and searing the experience into your thoughts. I only intimately touched Hale once. It doesn't matter. It was long enough to brand it into my thoughts and get me through those lonely nights. His hardness, his long rigid length, and the silky skin filled my hands. I remember. I only wish I could forget.

My skin prickles heat. I'm blushing. I know I am. But I'm not alone. Hale watches me closely, his jaw tightening.

Hale's face is a deep shade of red. But he isn't embarrassed. No. He's something more.

"What are you doing here, Becca?" he asks. "What do you want?"

You, I almost say. *I want you back. I want us back. I don't want you to keep hating me.*

My thoughts war with each other, scrambling the words that race through my head. Hale, Mason, Sean, Trin, and I. We were so close. Inseparable. Until my friendship with Hale became something more and ended up hurting us all.

"I want to help you," I manage.

"I think your fiancé might have a problem with that." He peels off his underwear and marches away.

He's trying to hurt and embarrass me and he manages both just fine. I wrench away in the direction of the living room. I don't get far, barely making it to the door leading out of the suite. Without any trace of remorse, I glance over my shoulder, watching his rock-hard cheeks clench and unclench as he walks toward the bathroom.

What am I going to do? I can't leave now. That ass is practically begging me to take a swat.

"I'm not engaged."

Hale freezes.

"It's over," I say, tripping over the words to the point that I almost spill the truth.

I want to admit that Denver and I were never real. That it was all part of my job. It's what I think I need to do so Hale will trust me. But the anger and resentment Hale unleashed like a storm remains. As much as I want to trust him with the truth, now is not the time to come clean.

He glances over his shoulder, frowning. I expect him to accuse me of lying or demand that I give him some privacy. Instead, he walks toward the sound of the running water, not bothering to shut the clear glass doors leading into an ultra-modern bathroom.

I follow, drawn to him, barely noticing my steps until mere feet separate us.

The bathroom isn't like those you find in a regular hotel, even in some of the five-star hotels New York is famous for. This is an extreme penthouse in a building that caters to the wealthy and the famous. The ceiling is clear glass, permitting the sunshine through and the lingering clouds to float over a masterpiece resembling an Asian-inspired garden.

Wood printed tile surround a sunken Jacuzzi and makes up half the open room, fooling the eye to believe I'm in an outdoor terrace surrounded by stacked stone walls. I step onto the round pavers pressed into a gravel path leading to the open shower.

Instead of glass walls like the exterior, exotic plants surround the shower, barely concealing Hale's wet body and the steam rising from his skin. This is a fantasy. *My* fantasy of what my night with Hale should have been, instead of what it became.

Reason abandons me. The pull of Hale tempting me to strip and join him.

I can feel the warmth of his body as I wrap my arms around him. I can taste the water slicking my lips as I kiss and nibble his throat. I can sense the gentle stream of the rain shower drenching my hair and skin as my hands wander.

Would he let me touch him? Like he did so long ago? I'm not sure. But I owe Hale better than that.

I'm sorry I hurt you, I want to say.

I'm sorry that I wasn't stronger.

Things went too far.

I should have stopped them.

I should have stopped him.

I should have let you love me . . .

The apology that has gone too long without saying grows more burdensome, years of guilt making it heavier and impossible to say. "I'm sorry," doesn't feel like enough. I need to show him and to prove how sorry I am.

I lean against the pillar and cross my arms. The steam will wreak havoc on my hair. I let it. I have something more important to do.

"I want to help you," I say. "Will you let me?"

When he doesn't answer, I look up, watching as he soaps his hard body in slow, lazy circles. He doesn't miss a bulge. He doesn't miss much of anything.

Hale's no longer that young guy who made me laugh. He no longer carries that playfulness in his gaze that would always make me smile. He's all man and muscle and, my, *so angry*.

His voice cuts through the steam in a vicious swipe. "No."

"What?" I demand, my temper rising.

A stream of water flies in an arc with how fast he whips his head in my direction. "I don't trust you. Damn it, Becks. I *can't* trust you."

Hurt dissolves my anger, softening my voice. "Why? We used to tell each other everything."

"Not everything," he says. He flicks off the jets, the gesture as stiff as his tone. To his right there's a towel and a robe. He doesn't bother with the robe. Why would he? Clearly, he doesn't care that I'm here or what I see.

I turn around, giving him my back as he starts to dry off. For all that he's naked, I'm the one who feels exposed.

In the quiet that lingers, I hear every rough pass he makes with the towel as if he were on top of me.

On top of me. Excellent choice of words, Becca.

I fuss with my hands. It's a gesture my mother often made when she was nervous and worried about how my father would react. I hated it. It made her look weak and him more dominant. Mostly, I hate that I'm doing it in front of Hale.

Hale's feet slap against the tile, his steps closing in. In the reflection of the glass wall separating the bathroom from the bedroom, I see the robe where it dangles from the bamboo rail. It's not on the hook. He'd taken it down, but then had second thoughts . . . .

Without warning, the heat from his body strokes against my back in a boorish caress, rough, its only care to feed its desires and need.

My heart rate speeds up as the warmth increases to a raging fire.

"You're wringing your hands," Hale murmurs, his breath tickling the ridge of my ear. "Do I intimidate you?"

I squeeze my eyes closed, just barely managing not to curse aloud. I'd told him about my mother's nervous habit. He had to remember now.

Slowly, I open my eyes, gathering the nerve I'd evidently kicked aside. "This is what I mean, Hale. You know me. Just like I know you and how to help you."

The way he snaps his towel has me jumping out of my skin. The fabric shuffles and I think he's wrapping it around his waist. It's what I'm hoping. Seeing Hale naked again will be the knock-out punch I don't need.

"People change, Becks, and it's not always for the better."

He eases away from me and walks away. From the front of the penthouse I hear Neesa giggle and the faint sound of Mason's chuckle. Somebody closed the door to the suite only partly. My money is on Mason. He knows we needed to talk. He also knows he may need to step in if things grow heated between us.

With a deep breath, I follow Hale into the bedroom. He's donned a pair of black briefs. I should be thankful. I would be if he didn't look like he should be on a giant billboard in the middle of Times Square with a giant bottle of vodka shoved between his thighs.

In a way, the briefs are more alluring than seeing him naked. My inner sex kitten would love to snap the waistband with her teeth.

"Hale, about New Year's . . ."

Jesus. I don't mean to start where I do. I'm not even certain I know where I'm headed. But I can't stop. Not now. "The last few months haven't been good," I finish, not bothering to explain that the last few years haven't been great, either. Not when it comes to us.

He tugs on his jeans, the waist falling just below his hips to give me a grand view of the "V" at his waist. Incidentally, it's just as tempting as the rest of him.

He snaps his jeans closed. "What about the New Year's before that? You sorry about what happened then, too?"

My hands slap at my sides. I'm frustrated with him. But I don't fault him. Not when all that frustration stems from my mistakes. "I'm sorry about everything, Hale. I never wanted to hurt you."

He meets my eyes. For a moment, I catch a glimpse of the young man I used to lay my blanket beside, whose head of hair would illuminate like a halo in the sun and whose irises would twinkle when we couldn't stop laughing.

Hale places his hands on his hips. The jeans he's wearing are one of those that appear old and well-worn. His favorite kind. Aneesa knows him well.

I'm not certain what he's thinking, but he doesn't bother speaking until he pulls on a black long-sleeved T-shirt. "It's not just about New Year's or what happened that night at your father's place."

I stop breathing. I didn't want to bring up that night, not yet anyway, even though my apology was a part of it.

"You haven't been there for me, Becks. Not in long time," he accuses.

"I know I—"

Hale cuts me off with a look. "Did you know my daddy died soon after I got here?" He walks forward, his stride easy, unlike the memory pummeling his features. There's pain among those hard planes, despite the softness his skin promises. Pain he's reminding me I wasn't there to witness.

He pauses in front of me, this time keeping at least two feet between us. "Did you know my Momma followed a few months after that?"

"Yes," I reply. He doesn't mention she drank herself to death. He doesn't have to. Everyone from the area soon knew.

"Mason told me," I explain, once more fussing with my hands. But then I stop, simply stop. He's not the only one who's been hurt. When I meet his gaze, I don't blink. I allow my torment to reflect in what I say and how I say it. "He also told me you didn't want me there and that you didn't want me to know."

"Doesn't matter what I said," Hale says. "I knew he'd tell you."

He squares his jaw, like any man expecting a fight would do. But I don't take that verbal swing he expects.

I tilt my head, my brow knitting tight. "Were you hoping I'd show?" I ask. I shake my head, knowing his answer when he doesn't reply. "Things were so screwed up between us, Hale. I was humiliated about what happened."

He laughs without humor. "Yeah, well, your daddy never did think I was good enough."

"I wasn't upset by what happened between us," I snap, my sharp tone surprising us both. "*You* were never the problem, Hale. He was."

"And yet you still chose him," he fires back, every syllable clipped.

"No," I say.

The word is too simple to carry the weight I feel behind it.

My mind flashes back to that night.

My cousins on top of Hale.

The crunch of fists colliding against bone.

The grunts.

The cries of pain.

And my father's large hand striking me down.

God, if I hadn't gone to Trin, if her parents hadn't helped support me, I would have lost my position with the Carolina Cougars and been living in squalor.

And still I would have done it.

"I chose me," I say, my voice quivering as I remember how hard Daddy hit me. How much he wanted to hurt me. How much that sadistic bastard enjoyed watching me bleed.

With Hale so close to me and all those memories striking me as hard as my father had, it becomes too much. I start to leave, but instead of walking out of the penthouse and once more out of his life, I head in the direction of the window.

A million-dollar view. That's what the architecture magazines would call the landscape of cement and metal I see. Where Hale and I are from, there's lots of money, but in the outskirts of Kiawah, we see poverty that's existed for generations. That will continue long after I'm dead and buried. Throughout my life, my friends and I have done our best to lift up such communities. Yet, despite our best efforts, the majority won't ever leave the area. Some by choice, but most because it's not an option.

They dream of having better, sure, many likely willing to kill to spend one night looking out to a city that promises the success Hale found. I don't have such dreams. I've never liked New York. It's too loud. Dirty. Angry. But for them and all the blessings I have, I take it all in, because I can.

Beyond the landscape of tall buildings, the sun has begun to set, casting rays of red and amber to paint the sky. It's beautiful, temporarily drawing the eye away from the chaos below. There's a reason New York is known as the City of Lost Souls. Compared to where I'm from, the wealthy here are a different class of people. So are the poor. And so is anyone lured deep into its throes. Some make it. The majority don't, barely scraping enough to survive.

I know why Hale is here, and why he stayed for so long. What happened between us and with his folks made it easy for him to bury himself beneath the grit and grime, the bedlam, and maybe even its glory.

I want the Hale I know back. But to have him and the way we once were, I have to give him a bit of my soul and my pain in return.

"My father beat me up that night. Right after you left."

Hale's head jerks up. This time, I'm the one who laughs. It's not funny. The damage was so extensive, it took two surgeries before I could properly breathe through my nose again. A little bump remains near the center, despite the surgeon's best efforts to smooth it. Every time I slide my finger down the length, I feel it. I used to hate it. Now, I see it as a well-earned war wound and a stern reminder of all the misery I left behind.

"He *beat you up*?" Hale says.

"That he did," I reply almost robotically. "He broke my nose and gave me a concussion—"

Hale is suddenly there, cupping my face with his large hands. I don't expect this response or for his touch to be so gentle. My heart stalls, resuming its pace in painful thuds as I melt away in his gaze.

Carefully, Hale tilts my face, examining it closely. It's been years. I don't know what he expects to find. Yet, I feel every touch and every delicate stroke.

The door is thrown open and Sean is there. "Food's here," he says. He cocks his head, barely acknowledging the lack of space and intimacy between us. "Y'all want to eat? Neesa ordered a lot."

"Give us a moment. Will you, Sean?"

Sean shrugs and leaves. It's not until the door closes again that Hale lowers his hands.

I feel as if we were caught naked or doing something we shouldn't. I adjust the collar of my suit for all the good it does me. I'm not certain what happened just now. Whatever it was, it left me feeling vulnerable, yet craving more. I've been lonely for years.

I wasn't lonely just then.

"Hale . . ." I'm not sure what's racing through his thoughts. What I don't want is for him to dismiss our conversation and pretend it didn't happened.

He crosses his arms. "Why didn't you tell me he was hitting you again?"

I take a breath. Okay. Here we go.

As a child, Hale never failed to notice my bruises. The one time he and Trin convinced me to tell a teacher, nothing came of it, unless you count my mother slapping me across the face for embarrassing the family. It was the only time

Momma ever hit me, but it hurt more than my father's blows ever had.

As for the incident, it was disposed of like most indiscretions committed by wealthy families. The way I see it, my father's hands should be permanently tainted green with the amount of money he's used to pay people off.

Money has the power to silence anyone, including a well-meaning teacher. Miss Medera was her name. She placed unicorn stickers on our papers when we did well and made us popcorn when rain kept us inside at recess. I never saw her after she was "encouraged" to find a new place of employment. It was probably a good thing for her. For me, it was another example of my father's twisted and manipulative character, and one more reason to hate him.

My focus drifts to the hollow of Hale's throat, realizing he's still waiting for me to explain. "Daddy hadn't hit me in years," I admit. "But he made up for it that night."

"You should have told me, Becks," Hale says, his voice rising. "You should've called me. We would have come back for you and kept you safe."

My eyes burn with impending tears. Yeah. They would have.

"My phone was gone," I explain. I don't realize how tight I'm hugging myself until I try to shrug off the memory. "You had left and . . ."

Don't, I tell myself. *Don't you dare cry now.*

I return my focus to the soaring skyscrapers trying to out-wow each other. It's easier than facing Hale and every bit of emotion that day continues to stir. "I walked back to Callahan's place. He was gone, but Trin was there. She and her folks took me to the hospital. They helped me get settled in Charlotte and gave me money until I could stand on my own."

"I repaid every cent," I add, feeling the need to explain. "I wouldn't have taken their money if I had a choice."

"It should've been me," he says, cutting me off.

I don't think he means to sound accusatory, especially given his soft tone. Like me, he carries his share of guilt and shame from that night. Both feelings . . . damn. I learned a long time ago they can do strange and awful things to a person.

"Why didn't you come to me, Becca?" he asks. "Instead of Trin and her family, why didn't you go looking for me?"

"Hale," I say, feeling that familiar clench to my heart when it comes to him. "If I'd asked you for help, I would be exchanging one man for another."

"*Don't*," he says, the word as sharp as his features. "Don't you dare compare me to your father."

"I'm not," I say, my voice quaking with what I wish was only anger. "I would never do that. But you and I weren't—I mean, it was the first time you kissed me. The first time you touched me." I push my hair away from my face, feeling the gamut of that awful memory overwhelm me. "We weren't anything yet."

"We were *friends*, Becca," he reminds me. "The real kind, who always helped each other out."

"We weren't friends that night," I say almost silently. "That night we were more."

Hale straightens, squaring his shoulders. "I would have taken care of you," he rumbles. "I would have cleaned you up, taken you to the hospital, fixed everything, and made it right."

I swipe away the tear I can't manage to hold back. "I know," I say.

"Then why didn't you call me when you reached Trin?"

"I couldn't do that to you," I stress. "You were starting your new life and I was supposed to start mine. So, I let you go. It was hard and terrible being without you. More than once I wanted to call you and make sure you were okay and to tell you what happened. Jesus, Hale, you have no idea how many times I picked up the phone to call you."

"You're right. I don't. 'Cause you never did," he says. "All you had to do was tell me and I would have dropped everything to be with you. Becca, I would have done *anything* for you."

I don't know how to respond. His initial aggression had startled me, as well as his anger. But what he says and the honesty behind it, hurts more. Hale *would* have taken care of me. I don't doubt it for one second. But I also couldn't allow it.

"I had to prove I could make it on my own, that I'd never have to depend on another man again." It's hard to look at him. Somehow, I manage. "No matter how much I wanted to."

Hale swallows hard, forcing his gaze from mine to glare at the sea of imposing structures. "You had to show up, now."

"I did," I say. He scowls when he catches my soft smile. "Like I told you, we were close once. We were there for each other." I place my hand gently on his shoulder. "Let me be here for you now."

His gaze drops to where my hand lies. "You want to be friends again?"

"More than anything," I promise. "I want to help you out of this mess the best way I know how. Will you let me?"

Chapter Six

Hale

The limo we're in zips across the asphalt. I can't see the ocean from here, but I can smell it, even over the overwhelming aroma of freshly polished leather. There's no pole. Not this time. Partly because Becca's "people" arranged our ride from the airport and partly because Mason didn't want to spend the ride talking about Sean's latest and greatest stripper protection devices.

Becca yaps away on her phone, Mason on his. They're both forming their own sets of plans. One publicity. The other strategy.

Twenty professionals. That's who makes up my defense team. They range from former white-collar investigators to accountants to lawyers. It took a long week of sleepless nights for Mason to form this high-powered team, and another two to go through all the evidence against me, postponing our plans to come down to Kiawah by almost a month.

Apparently, the Feds were tipped off by an unidentified informant. I guessed as much, but I was still pissed. Mason didn't care and neither did the team. "We're getting you off," he promised. "You're innocent and we'll make sure the truth comes out."

I wasn't as certain. Not at first. Until James, the former white-collar detective, provided his first shred of evidence on our side. "Something doesn't sit well with me and my staff," he said. "You're accused of seven counts of insider trading."

"Yeah," I agreed. "Tell me something I don't know.

He smiled. "Where's the money? Me and my boys have gone through all your holdings. You're not married. You have no kids or close family. You have no other names or accounts linked outside your business. Nor did the prosecution provide any aliases. Aside from your apartment and your office, you own no other properties. Where is the thirty-five million you supposedly made off the trading? Me and my men can't find shit."

No. They couldn't, because there isn't any.

Which is why Mason and the legal team are going to go butt heads with the prosecution next week. Their hope is for the prosecutor to drop at least half the insider trading accusations, but also to flex their collective muscle. "Flimsy." That's how my top attorney, Vern Simmons, described the evidence against me. "This resembles a political move by the head of the federal agency more than an actual case against you, Hale."

Maybe. But my reputation is still demolished to shit. Even if every last damn charge is dropped, my firm—the one I built from the ground up—doesn't stand a chance without some major image repair, which is why Becca remains at my side.

I adjust my sunglasses, allowing them to shield my eyes so I can take my time taking in Becca. Have I flirted with her? Maybe. Just not as much as I'd like to. The whole thing sounds crazy, given that less than a month ago I could barely watch her on TV. Now, I can't keep my eyes off her.

These past few weeks have been mostly business. Like Mason, she's accompanied me to every meeting with my team, asking questions and offering support, all the while flying back and forth to Charlotte. I don't know how she does it. I'm just glad she does.

Lord, help me. When I first saw her at the penthouse, it was like someone swung a sledgehammer into my chest and swung it hard. I was pissed, shocked. Did I mention pissed? I mean whose side were Sean and Mason on, anyway?

"How do you spell synchromie?" Sean asks. Unlike the rest of us, mulling over next steps, working on damage control, and reassuring our staff, Sean is mulling over a crossword puzzle.

"Synchro what?" I ask, somewhat annoyed that I have to look away from Becca.

Sean slaps down his paper like I'm the stupid one. "Syn-chro-*mie*."

Mason casts a frown in Sean's direction, all the while ironing out the details of my next court date. I have to give it to Mason, even Sean and his Sean-isms aren't enough to break Mason's stride.

"Sean," I tell him. "That's not a real word."

"Sure, it is," he insists. "It's the process of buffing chrome or some shit."

"That's polishing," I say, not bothering to guess where he got that other so-called word.

Sean glances down at his crossword puzzle, his eyebrows as tight as the way he presses his lips. "Oh. That makes more sense."

Sean erases one word and pencils in another. He's in good spirits. Relaxed. Mason is anything but. He flips out when another call comes through the line. "No, *no*," he says. "This isn't getting pushed back another month, much less two. I don't care what the opposing team wants. Either they have a case or they don't. We're not dragging out this shit longer than necessary."

"Is denominate another word for exorcism?" Sean asks.

Becca covers her phone with a hand. "No, baby. It means to label or christen, that sort of thing."

"Fuck," Sean says. "Could've fooled me."

Becca gives him a "there, there," pat on the shoulder. She touches Sean like we all do, more like a little brother than capable brawler. The way I touched her yesterday, though, well, there was nothing friendly about that. We were saying goodnight following a long day of meetings. I stroked her chin and debated whether or not to kiss her. Instead, I stepped away, wondering if she'd follow. She didn't, growing flustered in a way that made me smile.

I straighten at the first sight of the ancient oaks that line the road leading to our old stomping grounds. I haven't been back here since New Year's. Becca broke my heart so badly, I was sure that I'd never come back. I'd experienced enough over these last ten years to make me hate Kiawah. It's a terrible thought. I once thought Kiawah was the place I would grow old and gray. Except, that was before the dream world I belonged to was ripped away.

What happened with my folks and my brothers left me in a very perilous position and dangling over a cliff of uncertainty. I wasn't sure this was a place I'd ever call home again. I wanted to, but when I saw the ring on Becca's finger, I went right over that cliff, sure I'd never want to make the climb back up.

Now look at me. Not only am I climbing, I'm letting Becca climb with me and allowing her bright demeanor to warm me every few feet.

She covers her phone. "Almost there," she whispers.

I nod. She's been doing that a lot, reassuring me, almost like I need reminding she hasn't yet left. Even if she didn't speak, how can I forget? Her sweet perfume fills my nose every time I inhale, and her spirit does me in every time I catch her smile.

It takes all I can to keep my eyes on the trees and Spanish moss dangling from their thick, twisting limbs. Tourists never come down this time of year. They don't realize how beautiful Kiawah remains even when the winds steal summer away and the cold of winter smacks us across the face. There's no place like Kiawah. Hell, I guess I should say, there's no place like home.

I lean back, adjusting my glasses and taking another long appreciative look at Becca. As much as I wasn't sure Kiawah would ever feel like home again, with Sean and Mason here, *and* Becca, it's more home than New York ever was.

I didn't expect a friendly reunion with Becca. At first, it damn well wasn't. The humiliation surrounding my current predicament and my resentment of her made her arrival strained at best. But when she told me what her Daddy did—*after* I left—the anger I held against her turned on him.

That son of a bitch. Of course he'd wait to beat on her until after we left. He may have held the upper hand with that shotgun, but he would have had to kill me before I'd let him raise a finger against her.

We haven't talked about that night since, but I meant what I said. I would have helped her. I would have saved her. I'm not too stupid to recognize her need to save herself, and I more than respect her decision to stay, now. Would I have respected it then? Probably not. Especially if I'd seen how bad he'd hurt her. I huff. Knowing me, I would have made sure Becca was safe before returning to her daddy's place and knocking on his door.

Yeah, there's all the shit from New Year's and beyond. Yeah, there's still plenty of hurt that remains between us. Life isn't so simple that I can toss all the bad between us aside, but I wish it was. I wish it could be that easy.

I take in Becca a little longer.

Nope. Life isn't easy. I suppose love isn't, either.

"Here we are," Becca sings.

Mason keeps his ear on his phone as the limo snakes its way through a long driveway with more curves than those strippers Sean is now hell-bent on keeping safe. I perk up. I know this place. In high school, we used to come here for parties. A ranch house had burned down years before we were born, leaving only the foundation, the perfect place for teens to dance and set their kegs.

The windy road and overgrowth gave us plenty of coverage from the road back then. Now, instead of weeds and wild ferns growing onto and through the cracked pavement, nothing but meticulously kept landscaping line the exterior of the freshly paved driveway.

I lift my glasses for a better look. Trin and Callahan didn't flip a house. They built a new one.

Bone white brick surrounds two stories of classic elegance. Sharp angles cut into the gray roof, creating arches over the doorways, the three-car garage, and picture windows. A modern twist to an otherwise traditional home. It's not a big house compared to the opulence found throughout Kiawah. It's not even as big as the house I grew up in, maybe just shy of four-thousand square feet. But it doesn't need to be huge or flashy to be beautiful. Just like my girl, Trin, it just needs a few touches of sweetness.

We step out, Mason grinning when he sees it. "Leave it to Trin to be all nostalgic and fix this place up."

Becca gathers the lapels of her bright blue coat when the wind picks up. "Would you ever have thought all those years ago that something this grand would stand in the same place we'd drink our faces off?"

"I think I puked right there," Sean says, pointing to a palmetto on the opposite side of the driveway. He turns around, searching as if he dropped his keys. "Or was it there? Hard to tell, it was a rough night."

Becca nudges me and motions with her chin to the tall tree at the center of the front garden. "I remember climbing that thing."

I laugh, surprised, considering all that's gone down. "I remember all of us working to get Sean down when his foot got caught between the branches."

"That was right nice of y'all," he says, helping the driver with the luggage. "And Trin was a real good sport about me puking in her hair."

"No, she wasn't," we all mutter, remembering her screeches when it happened and when we had to hose her down in Sean's back yard.

I reach for the last suitcase before the driver can, tipping him with a few folded bills. Anyone else would take more care in spending someone else's money. But I'm paying all of it back if it kills me. Besides, the driver seems like a good man and a hard worker. Why should he suffer just 'cause I have?

Becca unlocks the front door and steps in to hit the security code. "Trin will be by later and so will her folks."

"Is her momma bringing pie?" Sean asks.

"Yes, Sean," Becca assures him.

"Pumpkin or apple?"

"She didn't say," Becca says, pushing a strand of her hair away.

"What about dinner? Did she say anything about pot roast?"

"Yes, Sean. She's bringing pot roast."

"With dem little potatoes?" He holds out his long leg to keep the heavy door open, allowing me through with the large suitcase. "She knows I like dem little potatoes, right?"

"She does," Becca adds sweetly. "Miss Silvie is also bringing that scalloped corn you can't get enough of. While I don't know what kind of pie she's making, she promised to bring one just for you."

"See?" Sean says. "It's like I always tell Mr. Owen. If he dies, I'm taking his woman."

Mason holds out his hand. "I'm going to stop you right there," he tells him.

"What?" Sean asks, all confused like. "If I were Owen, I'd want to know my wife was well taken care of. As well as my kids. Besides, Trin and Landon would like a daddy like me."

"Sean, you're talking about sleeping with Trin's Momma," Mason points out.

"I guess," Sean replies as if Mason was asking him a question instead pointing out a fact. "But I was mostly talking about eating her food." He thinks about it. "But if I had to sleep with her, I think I could do it. Hey, do you think she's flexible and has all her working parts?"

Mason and I groan, pleading with him to stop.

Becca grins, speaking through her teeth. "Sean, precious, don't make us shoot you between the eyes." She releases the small carry-on she's pulling and motions around. She probably thinks Sean will forget all about marrying Miss Sylvie in another minute, just like the last time he ate her food, and the time before that. She's probably right. Still, no one needs to hear that shit.

"So?" Becca says. "What do y'all think?"

Aside from an office to our right when we first enter and what appears to be a guest suite to my left, the entire first floor is one open room. A tiled modern fireplace sits at the center, surrounded with circular and plush chairs. It's meant to give the space a cozy feel, and it does just that.

The kitchen carries that modern cozy feel as well. The backsplash is marble subway tile, matching the sleek quartz countertop and blending in with the dark wood cabinets and wide plank floors. A dining area runs parallel to the kitchen. The rest is a family room, the large floor-to-ceiling windows opening onto a stone terrace providing a breath-taking view of the ocean.

This isn't a house. It's a home, where family and friends gather to laugh and create memories. Exactly what I need.

"Trin's been watching reruns of *Fixer Upper* again," I guess. "Hasn't she?"

"Oh, you know she loves Chip and Jo," Becca gushes. She smiles softly. "Do you love it, Hale? Trin really wants you to love it."

I chuckle. "How can I not? It's a part of Trin."

I catch myself lifting an arm to put around Becca. If she wasn't fumbling through her purse to pull out her phone, she might have seen me. The hell? Wasn't I just saying things can't be this easy?

Mason tosses me a look. I try and pretend I don't know what that look means. "What are you doing?" he mouths, making it clear he knows where I was headed.

He's right. What am I doing? Look at me going full-speed ahead. Is that all it takes? Being back here with Becca to erase all the heartbreak between us?

Becca steps away from me, taking yet another call. "Becca Shields . . . What? . . . Oh, Amy, you are a Godsend," she says, the excitement practically causing her to jump in place. "You have the address where I'll be? . . . Wonderful. Thanks, baby."

She disconnects, beaming. "Operation Reputation is under way." She pats my arm. "We'll start first thing tomorrow morning," she adds proudly. She walks around, counting off on her fingers. "This is a good place for the photo shoot." She glances over her shoulder at me. "Are all your clothes designer?"

"Yeah," I say, still stuck on the photo shoot.

"We'll have to fix that," she says, like I'm somehow broken.

I hold up my palms. "Wait a second. Why are we doing a photo shoot to begin with? I want to stay out of the public eye, not remind everyone I'm here and under fire."

"Oh, don't worry about that. The article will be in Forbes—"

"Forbes?" I say. "Are you kidding me? The last time I was in Forbes was—"

"Just a few months ago, for their end of year issue spotlighting the biggest money-maker on Wall Street. Before that, it was last February. The same issue where you took over the center spread in the Alps, if I recall. You were celebrating, what? Oh, yes, the previous end-of-year-issue when you first made the cover all by your lonesome. Six months prior to that, for their November issue—"

"You've done the research. I get it. But you're forgetting, all those times celebrated me, my achievements, and the legacy I was building, *before* everything came crashing down."

Becca fluffs her hair as if I'm discussing sports, not my career-ending drama. "Oh, baby. The article won't run until December."

"December?" I ask. "But we're shooting it now?"

"That's right," she answers.

What am I missing here? "Becca, that makes absolutely no sense."

"Yes, it does," she replies casually, ignoring Sean's befuddled look. Never mind, he just remembered the word he needed for his crossword.

"Could you explain how?" I ask, glancing as he scribbles it down.

"From what I can decipher from the meetings and what your team has discovered, your legal problems should be behind you by December."

Mason nods, his fingers flying across his phone as he answers a text. "But dismantling your name won't be, Hale." He tips his head toward Becca. "This is where Becca's skills come in. No sense in saving your business if you have no business to return to."

"Picture this for a headline," Becca says, stretching her hands above her. "The Anaconda of Wall Street Slithers Back to Sink in His Teeth and Reclaim the Throne." She thinks about it. "Or something like that. I'm still playing around with the title."

I'd like to think Becca is as good as she claims. But she wasn't there when the Feds read me my rights and slapped on the cuffs. "You're nuts," I tell her.

"No, sugar," she says, her hands dropping away from her long mane of hair. "I'm just the best thing PR has ever seen." She strolls toward the large open windows. "I think we should do a beach scene." She squints, taking a good look at my face. "And as much as I'm not a fan of beards, I'd like you to grow out some scruff. Nothing neat. I'm going for relaxed. Think beach bum rather than this uptight businessman persona you have going on." She makes an irritated motion at my face. "This way, we'll extend your reach beyond your corporate circles and make you appear more sympathetic for the camera—"

"The fuck, Becca?"

Her fists slap against her hips. "Hale Wilder. You've developed a bad habit of interrupting me. If we're going to work together, that shit isn't going to fly? You hear me?"

I smirk. This is the first time I catch a glimpse of the real Becca, the one I fell head over boardshorts for. I stroll up to her casually, letting my gaze wander from the tiny black T-shirt dress she's wearing to the hot pink heels. I give her legs a nice, long glance. I don't try to hide it, allowing my appreciation for that sweet dress and the sexy woman wearing it to work in my favor. With every step I take, Becca's eyes grow wider. No, *wilder*, and those fists she rammed against her hips? Well, look at that, they slide down very sexy curves I'm looking rather forward to caressing.

"What's wrong?" I ask when only inches remain between us. "Do I intimidate you?"

She jerks her chin away. "No. I just think if we're going to have a working relationship, you need to respect my position."

"Position?" I drawl. "Darlin', I'll respect the hell out of whatever position you want."

Her slacking jaw is enough to crack me up and leave Mason and Sean to take a strong interest in the outside terrace. "Did you just—are you? Jesus, Hale. We're in a crisis here."

"And?"

"And you should calm your evidently out of control sex drive, that's what," Becca snaps.

Okay. Perhaps "snaps" isn't the best word here. Stammers. Yes, that works better. Oh, I like stammers.

"You sayin' I want you?" I ask. I scratch my head. "The way you keep staring at my ass, not to mention the way you watched me shower, I could swear it's the other way around."

Damn, she's cute when her face turns pink like that. In truth, I wasn't sure she was staring at anything at all. I am now. Just to be sure, I add a little more to my claims. "I saw you in the reflection of the glass."

I wink since that delicious remark wouldn't taste as good on my tongue without another sprinkle of naughty. It adds another coat of pink to that lovely face. For a second too long, I wonder what kind of fool her ex fiancé was to let her go. But as Becca's face resumes its sunnier glow, I'm reminded I'm on a roll.

"Do you like what you've been ogling?" I don't wait for her reply. Her pink cheeks are enough of an answer. "I wasn't sure if the tongue dangling to your toes was a good thing or a bad."

I cough into my shoulder, trying not to laugh out loud. I don't try too hard. My world as I know it was hit with a meteor the size of the sun and the ashes are currently floating into space. Y'all excuse me if I have a little fun.

Becca's eyes narrow and for a moment, just a teeny one, I think I've gone too far. She smiles. It's not that friendly smile I've seen her flash to her devoted fans. Come to think of it, I think sharks might have fewer teeth.

"You think *I* want *you*?" she asks, batting her long eyelashes. "Aren't you sweet? Don't think I didn't see you watching me last night. Remember last night, Hale? After dinner? When that warm, delicious chocolate fondue I was dipping my ripe strawberry into dripped down my lips, drawing a line all the way down?" She trails the corner of her cell phone between her breasts, to where the deep "V" of her collar ends and a peek of hot pink lace reveals itself.

Like a dumbass, I follow said phone, recalling said warm chocolate and wishing I had the chance to lick said incident clean.

I'm smarter than hell, but I'm all man and very human.

"My, oh, my, Hale," she purrs. "And the way you were eyeing me on the plane and in the limo, I was sure you'd take a bite right out of poor little ol' me." She snaps her teeth.

Yup. I be swimming in dark waters now.

Her Wonder Woman ring tone announces another call. The shark offers me a small pinky wave, tosses her long hair over her shoulder, and struts off. You might say this Southern Belle is capable of bringing any heterosexual man to his knees.

She pauses, just long enough to pretend she forgot her manners. "You'll excuse me, won't you, sugar?" she asks. "I have to take this if I'm going to save that sweet ass of yours."

I rub my chin. Okay, Becca. It's going to be like that? Darlin', it's on.

Chapter Seven

Becca

Trin and her family bring over dinner as promised, as well as all the media equipment my assistant delivered to their house. I need all of it. Their support and this high-tech equipment.

"I'm glad you know what you're doing," Trin says, staring at all the gadgets. "Alexa and I are always fighting. I can't help myself, really. I don't like machines that are smarter than me. I don't think it's natural."

She settles into the chair, shifting her hold on her baby. "Ever see the Terminator?"

"Only 'cause you made me," I remind her, adjusting the strap of one camera so it's easier to fit in the case.

"Someone had to," Trin says. "As far as I'm concerned, that's a lesson in the making."

"Meaning?" I ask.

"Meaning one day, you're asking Alexa for the weather, the next she's rigging the microwave to turn on you and ordering the furnace to set you on fire."

I laugh, knowing it's really what Trin is after. I don't know what I would have done without her in my life. Sure, we've shared some sad moments, but when we've laughed, we've felt that humor down to our toes.

I take a moment to stroke my Godchild and namesake's hair. Sylvia Becca, named after Trin's momma and me, is about the prettiest baby I've ever laid eyes on.

My ovaries give a little twitch. I wasn't sure about having children, ever. After the way I was raised, I couldn't be positive I'd make a good momma. But Little Silvie, the name she goes by, as well as Trin's first born, Cal, Jr., make me want a baby every time I see them, and some days, even when I don't. There's something special that happens when the friends you love more than life create a new life of their own. All the love you feel for your friends extends to their little ones. It's nothing you think about, nor is it forced. It just appears like the rising moon to thrive among the stars.

My thoughts of babies and holding my own make me a little sad. I return to the equipment laid out across the dining room table. There's not much to it, a tripod, a camera, a few small mics, and one of those mini recorders you can pin to your clothes. I don't think I'll need most of this high-end, high tech, bordering on spy, equipment. But I have it, just in case. Hale needs to show the side of him the world doesn't yet know. In case he can't manage that with the camera nearby, something subtle may come in handy.

"I saw Hale giving you the eyes," Trin says, adjusting Little Sylvie when she wakes so she can nurse her. My bestie is still as thin as ever. Seeing how much her baby eats, I think Trin gives every last calorie away.

I slice a piece of blackberry pie and place it and a fork in front of Trin.

"Thank you, Becks." She takes a bite. "Did you hear what I said?"

I double check the camera lens when I think I see a crack, doing my best not to happy dance all up in this bitch. "Hmm?"

"Don't hmm me," Trin says, wiping her chin when the crumbling crust explodes. "I'm serious. I think Hale still…you know."

"I don't know," I say. I try not to smile or think too hard about how good Hale looks in those jeans he changed into or that tight white sweater. I've seen D&G ads that were less erotic and naughty. "Trin, I officially declare this house a place of business. Not a brothel."

"Hey," I say when Trin smacks me in the rear.

"There," she says. "Now you can declare it a brothel."

"Cut that out," I say laughing. "You're a grown woman with kids. You shouldn't be touching anyone's ass unless it belongs to your hot husband. Even then, it should only be in bed, naked, with the windows and doors locked."

"I do that plenty," she drawls. "How do you think I got these two babies I have? I swear, Becks, with the amount of hormones raging through me, it's a wonder Callahan doesn't need a whip and wooden stool to keep me back."

"That could be fun," I add.

"Oh, and it is." She sighs. "You know how we used to love our men, sandy, muscular, and athletic?"

I check the memory card in the camera. "What do you mean 'used to'?"

She finishes off her last bite of pie, dabbing elegantly, even though our conversation resembles nothing close to sophisticated. "I'm only saying priorities and degrees of hotness change over time. Becks, I used to lose my senses whenever Callahan would emerge from the ocean following a long swim. Water drizzling down those muscular arms covered with Army tats, broad chest heaving in and out just so."

I pause, looking out on the terrace where her ass-kicking, former Special Forces husband, stands. "You saying he's out of shape? 'Cause if you are, I don't see it."

"Oh, no. I'm just saying it's been too cold to swim. That and that nothing gets me hotter than when he vacuums or helps me out around the house."

I'm certain I misheard. "Huh? Can we go back to the dripping wet, sexy men emerging from the ocean? I'm more familiar with that." It's true. When Hale and I were lifeguards, I got to see me plenty of that eye candy. *Rawr*.

Trin bats her hand. "I know you think I'm crazy. But when you've been up all night with a toddler with an earache and a baby permanently attached to your breast, and you head into the laundry room, praying you'll find at least one pair of clean underwear—only to find your man has everything washed and folded and your dishes all put away—just because he knows you're tired, I tell you, Becks. There's nothing that revs a woman's engine like that." She blinks up at me. "Ever have sex in a laundry room?"

"On top of folded clothes?" I guess.

"Are you nuts? I'm not about to mess up Callahan's good work. We placed the clothes in the basket first and then went at it like drunken elephants on parade. Candy and flowers are overrated, Becks. Give me clean floors and dinner started and Callahan can have me any way he wants."

"On the washing machine?" I ask.

Trin gives me the smile she does every time she thinks of her husband. "Spin cycle works best."

Her humor doesn't last despite how we both have a good laugh. "Hale isn't in a good place," she says. "It's not just the charges or how his good name has been dragged through the mud. He lost a part of his soul long before this."

My hands slow as I return the camera to its case. Trin's always been the one we all opened up to. The one with the biggest heart to share, and the warmest hugs to give. But even Trin, this perky, smiley, larger than life person, was no match for Hale's darkness.

"That's why I'm here, Trin."

"I know."

There's a lot my friend means behind those few words. Just as I know there's a lot she hasn't shared. As close as we are, she and Hale have shared a special bond. That bond is similar to the one that connects me with Mason and Sean. It prevents us from telling everyone, everything. I suppose it's best. Sometimes we all need our privacy, and some secrets need their silence. But there were times I could have used more news about Hale. As painful as it might have been, I needed to hear he was okay. Maybe because he wasn't, that news never came.

Trin pushes her long dark hair over her shoulder and adjusts her hold over the now content child. Like always, she's wearing her favorite ensemble, jeans, a T-shirt, and flip flops. "The Wall Street fiasco is plenty enough. But I think the damage to his reputation means more."

"Mason said more or less the same thing," I agree. "Every call that comes and the more information that's obtained, he's certain Hale will get off. But it's like you said, it's how bad his reputation has been slaughtered that's hurting him the most."

"He's always prided himself on being a good man."

I nod, thinking of all those times he defended those smaller and weaker. "I agree."

"But?" Trin asks, sensing my hesitation.

"I don't know, Trin. I think there's more there. No one wants their reputation questioned, especially when your livelihood depends on it. But I have the feeling it's brutalizing Hale even beyond what we see. Except, I'm not certain why."

"I hear you and feel the same. But there's more that troubles me. Being here, as much as I think it will help him to be around us and in the place he once loved, it's also going to bring up a lot of other problems."

She doesn't mention Hale's brothers. She doesn't have to. They're the unspoken part of his life we all know better than to ask about. "I know. I've thought about that, too."

Trin lowers her chin, appearing miserable, despite the smile she gives her baby. Yes. There's a lot she knows and plenty she's likely not permitted to share. "Becks, when word gets out Hale is here, his family may come sniffing around."

I carefully wind the cords to the small mic around my hand. "Maybe that will be a good thing."

"Maybe," she agrees. "But there's a lot of hurt there."

Trin is the friendliest person on the island and probably the entire world. Hale's brothers spent most of their lives ignoring her, despite her best efforts. It used to make Hale mad. It used to make *me* mad, seeing how hard she tried. I guess it was difficult for her to understand, since her brother, Landon, and his friends often hung out with us.

I wouldn't go so far as to say Hale's brothers were cruel. That's not fair. But they would snub us. If we showed up to a party, they'd leave. In school, they'd act as if we didn't exist. I didn't care then. I do now. Had I connected with them like I had with Trin's family, I could've reached out, softened the blow, and maybe better prepared them for his arrival.

"It's not just Hale's family I'm worried about," Trin says, turning to make sure we're still alone. "Becca, if your father finds out you're helping him . . . I don't want you to get hurt again."

I knew she wasn't done. Just as I knew she'd mention my family. "Daddy can't hurt me," I tell her. I take a breath, letting it out like I don't care, even though I'm pissed off that I do. "He's dying."

"What?"

I wish I could have said he can't hurt me, because I'm on my own or because he knows better or because he's a changed man. But my daddy doesn't change. The world changes for him or else.

I place my hand on Trin's shoulder when she tries to stand. I don't want to disturb her precious child and I've already upset her enough. "Daddy didn't beat cancer like he bragged about in the papers last year. And he's not traveling the world to celebrate like he told anyone who'd listen. He's home and he doesn't have much time."

"Your cousins just got back from Europe," Trin says. Her voice is quiet. Yet, the doubt I stirred remains. "They travelled with him. It was a family trip."

"No, on all counts," I admit. "He sent them and Momma, too. They were assigned to take photos and post them on his behalf like he was with them." I zip the nylon bag that protects one of my smaller recording devices. "The show I put on for the PR world, where do you think I learned such skills?" I press my palms against the dining room table, wishing it wasn't so hard to breathe and that for once, the ache my family causes me would lessen. "I learned everything from the best con artist I know."

"Oh, Becks," Trin says. "I'm sorry."

Trin is the best person I know. But she's not sorry my daddy is dying. She's sorry about what it will do to me.

Anyone else would remind me that he's still my father, and that I should make peace with him before it's too late. A member of the clergy might even encourage me to apologize for being a bad daughter, for not calling, for not obeying like all good children should. Not Trin. As kind as she is, she recognizes poison when she sees it, and she won't make me take a swallow.

"How did you find out?" she asks.

"My cousin, Matthew, called me. He explained the plan, how they followed it, and how they're all back now that there's not much time left. The doctors gave him six months with aggressive chemo. Without it, even less." I glance at my equipment, but I can't remember what's left to do. "Momma let me know when he was first sick."

Trin rocks her baby when she starts to fuss, but I know Trin well enough to know she's the one who needs soothing. Trin doesn't like me hurting. And as much as there were moments in my life I think I could have struck my father, and many more times that I've loathed him, it still hurts. My God, it still hurts to lose him.

"I'm surprised your momma would confide in you about his illness," she tells me gently. "I would have expected him to forbid her from communicating with you."

"Oh, he forbade her all right. But Momma wouldn't be Momma without writing the letters that she did blaming me for giving him cancer."

The color drains from Trin's face. "She accused you of giving your father cancer?"

"Not exactly." I glance up in the direction of the terrace, where Sean tosses another block of wood into the fire pit. Callahan and Hale fuss over Cal, Jr., teaching him to make s'mores. I don't see them as well as I should. Momma's words have always had that effect on me. "She told me I caused the stress that caused the cancer. I shouldn't have opened that letter. Or the other three that followed. They were among the worst things I've ever read."

I sigh, a tear escaping my eye. I sort of hear the chair being pushed back, but it's the embrace and all the love behind it that brings me back to the moment and causes more of my tears to fall.

"That wasn't okay," she tells me. "None of it is. Your father's illness, your mother's twisted words. Those are their issues. Their truth. But it's not real and you need to know that."

"I know I didn't do this," I say. "I know they're wrong and sick people. But what they say and do still affects me."

"I know, Becks," she says. "I wanted so much more for you. More kindness. More love. More patience."

"I wanted all that for me, too," I agree.

I want to wipe my eyes before anyone else sees me crying. But, for the moment, I simply sink into Trin's embrace and take in the reprieve it offers.

"I stupidly thought Momma might need help, or that she was the one who was sick, or that maybe she was finally ready to leave him."

"You're not stupid, Becks. You just have a big heart and you wanted to believe all the good things about your momma."

"After all these years, I should have known better, Trin."

Trin's eyes glisten. Real friends will never let you cry alone. "There's no shame in wanting the momma you've always needed."

I kiss the top of her head. "There is, when it leads to this."

I wipe her tears, leaving mine for last. Now that I'm here in Kiawah, I know there are more to come.

Chapter Eight

Becca

We all have our fill of food and dessert before saying goodbye. Mason and Sean are on the first flight out in the morning. I put in my request for leave. It was denied by the big boss almost immediately. Mr. Singleton informed me I needed to be back tomorrow and that my fiancé would be expecting me.

The fiancé part almost made me laugh. Almost. I wrote another email, reminding him I haven't had a vacation in two straight years. I also told him I'm therefore overdue for a minimum of eight weeks, per my contract. I almost called him and his son an asshole, but I refrained. I am a southern lady, after all. We ended with a compromise, one neither of us is thrilled with. I'm driving back to Charlotte tomorrow to tie up some loose ends, but I'm not staying to play the role of the devoted woman.

Mr. Singleton was less than pleased. His problem, not mine. I glance across at Hale. Mr. Singleton can fire me if he wants. I'm not going to sacrifice Hale in exchange for making Daddy Singleton and his disaster of a son happy. Hale is my priority, not them.

Hale looks from side to side. He even stands and lifts the cushion of his seat before plopping back down. "Humph."

"What's wrong?" I ask.

"Oh, nothing. I just can't figure out why it's so quiet around here."

I return his wry grin, knowing what he means. Most people can't get a word in when Trin or I are around. Put us together in the same room and good luck doing more than the occasional nod. She and Callahan were the first to leave, needing to get their babies to bed, and for the moment, I don't feel much like talking.

Discussing my folks with anyone, no matter how brief, always leaves me with a sense of dread. I wish it weren't so, but we don't always get what we want. Case in point, that beautiful man sitting across from me.

I stare at Hale through the flames of the fire pit. As much as I want to help his reputation, I don't want our time together to end too soon. I'll work to fix his problems. I'll make things right again. But this time, I don't plan to say goodbye so easily.

I rub my hands together. Every problem has a solution. It's been my mantra ever since I started with the Cougars. No matter how bad the situation or how stuck my players and staff were, I got them out of it. On the legal side, Mason will do the same for Hale. As much as Mason worried he wasn't the best attorney for the job, he was the best person to put a defense team together.

Tonight, Trin's family dropped another few mil toward Hale's legal fees. "Your team needs to fix this and fix this fast. You need more, you say the word."

"Thank you, sir," Hale told him.

Mason got word that the prosecution may be dropping more charges than he originally thought. It's becoming clearer that the feds rushed this case because Hale's name was attached to it, rather than it was a good case to stand on. I hope so. It's already been several weeks too many.

A thick fleece blanket drops over my shoulders, forcing me to look up. "You looked cold," Hale says.

I hadn't noticed him move, but he'd noticed the start of my shivering. "Thank you."

The ocean waves beating against the shore have lessened in their demand for attention. I guess the storm that was supposed to hit landfall is veering further away and out to sea. The wind, it seems, hasn't heard the news yet. It lifts my hair, bringing a large share of leaves scooting across the patio to make a big fuss. I arrange the blanket around my back. With this blanket around me and the sweats Hale lent me, I could sleep out here. Never mind. What I should say is with Hale this close, I feel safe and warm even through the harshest of storms.

Hale added a light jacket over his sweater. He has a blanket, too, but it's folded over the chair and it doesn't look as thick as mine. I suppose he's warmer by the fire, but the cold has never bothered him like the rest of us.

"What are you thinking about?" he asks me.

I run my fingers over the soft fleece. I recognize it from the pictures Trin sent me when she was deciding how to decorate. But that's not the only memory stirred by this blanket and the fire between us. "Remember when we used to sleep out as kids? All we'd need is a few blankets, some sweet tea in a canteen, and snacks."

"Potato chips," Hale says. "It was usually potato chips, extra salty, and marshmallows we'd roast over a fire."

I laugh. "Sean always ate the most."

"He still does. Miss Silvie promised to make me more pot roast, since Sean didn't leave but one of those little potatoes."

"She's always been great about feeding us," I agree.

"And Owen was always great about checking on us when we'd sleep out. I remember him showing up in the early hours, making sure we were all safe. He'd pull Trin's blanket up just below her chin. He had this gentle way about him. He never woke her. Came in like a shadow, left the same way."

"Your daddy would check on us, too," I say. "I remember seeing his big work boots step into my line of vision. They always smelled like oil and sawdust from all the construction work he'd do and oversee."

"Sorry," Hale says.

"What are you talking about? I loved that smell. It reminded me so much of him and how hard he worked."

Hale pokes at the flames, the aggression he uses alerting me something is up long before he speaks. "Daddy didn't start coming around until much later. When he thought I finally proved my potential and worth." He pauses, the edge of the stick glowing amber. "Owen didn't need us to prove anything. He just wanted us safe, and for his little girl to enjoy her time with her friends."

My hand is twisted in an odd angle. I meant only to adjust the blanket a certain way, not to remain in this position. But Hale's words froze me in place. I force myself to move it and shake it out, the tension I sense surging instead of lessening. "What's that supposed to mean?"

It's a strange question, but he knows what I mean.

Hale squares his jaw, his expression so harsh in the shadows of the flames, he's almost unrecognizable.

I don't back down. This is a battle I need to fight. "Hale, what did you mean when you said that about your daddy?"

When he doesn't respond, I adjust my position and lean forward. "Look, if I'm going to help you, I need to know things you may not be comfortable sharing."

"You mean private things? Things I don't want others to know?"

It's not really a question. "Yes."

What I've learned throughout my years of working closely with people is that the more you keep your trap shut, the more people will tell you what you want to hear. It's not so much a need to spill their darkest secrets. It comes with that desire to be heard.

I wait, watching Hale as he gives the ocean we love so much its due, all the while allowing the memories that stirred his bitter words to take life.

It takes a while for him to speak. When he does, I know he's ready and wants to be heard. "Do you remember how my daddy never missed any of my brothers' games, but how he always found a reason to miss mine?"

I'm not certain where he's going with this and my frown reflects as much. "He had to work. It's how he made his construction company the success it became."

My words trail at the slow shake of Hale's head. "No. That was the excuse my mother always fed me, and the one I'd eagerly swallow."

"What? I remember seeing him cheering you on all the times Trin and I went to watch you."

"I don't think you're remembering it right," he says, his voice so hollow, the breeze practically swallows it whole. "My father didn't catch my first football game until middle school when the coaches were noticing my talent and my teachers were noticing my soaring grades."

"But he went to your brothers' games no matter what," I say, repeating his words, since there's obviously more there and plenty more that I missed. His brothers were good athletes and made decent grades, from what I remember. But they weren't gifted or as smart as Hale. They also certainly weren't as popular.

"That's right," he agrees.

"Why?"

Hale's hesitation is brief. "Because, unlike me, they were blood. They were his real sons."

My knitted brow slowly lifts as shock hits me like a freight train.

"That's right," he says, opening his arms wide. "You're looking at one hell of a bastard. The real kind."

Hale reaches for a beer from the cooler near his side, popping off the cap before handing it to me. "You might need this," he says.

I take three hard pulls. Considering the bomb he just dropped on my lap, I might need a whole case.

"You were adopted," I say. "There's no shame in that."

It's a stupid thing to say. I knew it was before those lame thoughts flew out of my mouth. Clearly, he wasn't adopted. Oh, no. I take another few quick gulps, my head spinning when I realize I almost drank the whole thing.

Hale lowers the beer he took for himself, barely taking more than a sip. "Now, darlin'," he says. "We both know that's not where this conversation is headed."

In the far distance, lightning lights up the sky, signaling the start of the predicted storm and the wallop of a story Hale has to tell.

"Daddy had a heart attack a few weeks after I moved to the city," he begins, his focus returning to the flames. "I came right home. He was my daddy, right? At least, that's what I believed back then." He swallows a taste of beer. "We were in the hospital. He knew things were bad. He knew this was his time. Even though all the docs were telling him that with the right diet and meds he should pull through."

The flames reflecting and dancing across Hale's face would unveil darkness and bitterness on anyone else. On Hale, they reveal the soul of a damaged man.

"I think he wanted to clear his conscience before he died. Admit his sins and such. 'You're not mine,' he said. 'You're not my real boy.' I thought he was delirious or that maybe the pain meds he was on were having a negative effect." He huffs. "That's what I told myself, anyway. But I knew it then. I knew it in the way he spoke and in the way he looked at me. Hell, maybe I've always known."

I grip the longneck tightly, trying to keep quiet so he won't stop.

"He told me . . ." He drags his hand down his face. "He told me he was embarrassed about everything I had to do to win his love. How I had to work that much harder, while my brothers barely tried. About all those times he regretted walking past me when he could feel how much I wanted a hug."

Hale takes a hard gulp. "'You were always a good son, Hale,' he said. 'You always had a fire that couldn't be put out, and a heart as big as the ocean. I should have seen it long before I did. I owed you better than that as your daddy.'"

"He was telling you he was sorry," I say when Hale's thoughts take him away. "He was trying to make peace with how he mistreated you."

"Daddy never mistreated me, Becks," Hale says. "He ignored me. It's probably why I fought so hard to be the best in sports, in school, in everything. They were things I could do to make him pay attention to me."

"And make you the favorite."

"What in the hell are you talking about?" Hale asks. "No way was I the favorite. Not when I was the result of his wife's mistake."

He wants me to take back what I said. But I can't and he needs to hear why. "I'm sorry. Maybe I'm out of line. But from everything I saw when I was around your family, you were the hero. In your parents' eyes, you were the one who'd done right by them."

"I can't agree," he says. He tips back his beer. "Not after everything I had to do to make up for what my mother did."

He tosses his empty bottle in the garbage can. I down the rest of mine and pad over to him, blanket and all.

I take the second beer he offers and plop down in the cushy seat beside him. The cushion feels cold against my legs. I don't complain. This is nothing compared to what Hale is feeling.

"How did it happen?" I ask.

"Do you want Daddy's version or Momma's?" he asks me. He pats my knee. "You know what? I'll tell you Momma's. It's more interesting."

Interesting isn't the right word here. Not with the sadness that skims across Hale's aura like a rising tide.

"Daddy's business had started to take off. So much so, he was putting in sixteen-hour days and working seven days a week. He did that for two years straight, if you can believe it. Not so much as taking Christmas off, in order to please his clients and to make a name for himself."

"I always remember him as a hard worker," I say. I have nothing better to add. Although, for Hale's sake, I wish I did.

"You know what he did with the first of his fortune?" I shake my head. "He took his family on a trip to Europe. He'd never been. Always dreamed of going as a kid. But, instead of enjoying the trip, he'd stay behind in these fancy hotels to work and manage the business from afar. Momma couldn't take it. This was their time to be a family. He'd promised that all the sacrifice and dinners she'd spent without him was for them. But instead of just being lonely in Kiawah, she was lonely clear on the other side of the world."

My stomach turns inward. I know that loneliness well. I've just never known it as a wife and mother.

"She was young and attractive," he says. "You hear where I'm going with this, don't you? One night, while they were in Sweden, they hired a nanny to look after my brothers so they could go out on the town. But Daddy received a call about an employee acting up at a site. He couldn't have that. Not my father. Not when his reputation was on the line." Hale pinches the bridge of his nose. "Momma couldn't take it. For her, it was the last straw. She left my brothers with the nanny, my father to conduct his business, and went to the closest bar to a find a man who was willing to pay her attention." He motions to himself as he lifts his beer. "You can see it worked out well for her."

I blink several times. "This is what she told you?" I ask.

"More or less, a few days after the funeral." He rolls the bottle between his palms, not bothering with another sip. "You might have heard she was drunk at the funeral parlor. You might have even heard she was drunk at the service. I have to say, she was pretty lit when she spilled her secret. Some might have even referred to her as sloppy."

Hale's momma tended to drink more than the other mothers I knew. But I never saw her out of control even once.

"Her drinking wasn't bad until after Daddy died," Hale explains, reading my thoughts. "The guilt ate her alive. I think it took his death to make her realize how badly she'd hurt a good man." He pauses. "I also think she saw how badly she'd hurt me."

"Did you confront her?"

Hale rubs his eyes, appearing suddenly tired. "We talked about it. There was no screaming or yelling or accusing. It was just her talking and me sitting there wishing it was all a bad dream." He looks at me. "I don't think she wanted me to know. If it were up to her, they both would have taken that shit to the grave."

I look at the ground, my gaze practically singeing the stone pavers at my feet. I'm angry for Hale and disappointed, as well. Mostly, I'm heartbroken, just like he is. "What did your daddy say?"

Hale doesn't seem to be listening. I think the ghosts of his past speak louder than me, drowning out my voice and reducing it to a whisper. Eventually he answers, but it takes him time. "He blamed himself. I never expected a man as proud as my daddy to take the fall for his wife's mistakes. But that's what he did."

"He loved her," I say without thinking.

"I can't argue with that," he agrees, his tone heavy. "Even as he lay there telling me what she did, it was his love for her that made him break down. 'I was angry when I found out,' he said. 'And if she hadn't been pregnant with you, she may never have told me. But in trying to do right by my family, I neglected them. I neglected her.'"

"Shit," I say.

"That pretty much sums it up. Want to hear the best part?" He chuckles, as if knowing the punchline of a joke before he tells it, not that I find what he says funny. "My brothers figured it out long before they were told. I was blond, real blond back then. Hard to blend in, when you're a towhead in a room full of country folk with hair and beards as dark as midnight. My brothers never liked me. They used to gang up on me, remember? I know why now and why I chose my family in the form of friends like you."

I don't judge, nor reply. My family is just as screwed up as Hale's. It's the reason we were all as tight as we were with Trin, Mason, and Sean. We needed a family we could count on.

"Everything you just told me, every last word you said to me, we're putting on film."

"Excuse me?" he says.

"You heard me," I tell him.

"This isn't a joke or a publicity stunt," Hale says, his temper firing. "It's my life, Becca."

"And the side everyone who's already judged you needs to see," I press. "As much as you're known for your business savvy, you don't come across as warm, and no one out there has ever seen your heart."

"Why would they?" He jerks his chin. "Why would I show anyone what I've been through, especially when I've been part of the rat race, interacting with people who'd stab me in the back and rob me of everything I've worked for without thinking twice? One of them did this to me. Framed me or whatever the hell. Do you think that would have changed if they knew my heart? No, Becks. It would have been one more target they could aim for."

I can't say he doesn't have a point. But I won't shy away from what needs to be done. "You were the perfect man on Wall Street. Too perfect. So much so, your competitors and everyone else you managed to piss off couldn't wait for your downfall. Like you said, someone among them caused it, leaving everyone else to celebrate and wish you the worst. One less competitor, right?"

"Right," he agrees. "And one hell of a show. It's the reason the feds jumped on this case. The head of the agency is up for reappointment, and wanted something big to make him look good. Instead, he got a pitiful case, lacking any substantial evidence or good investigative work. The more my team finds, the more they're sure I'll get off with an apology."

He's smiling. I'm not. "A public apology won't be enough. Best case, it will be ignored by the press when the next big story hits, or shoved into the back pages of most papers beside the want-ads. Neither will win you back the public's trust, which is why we need to put your story out there. We need to humanize you for everyone who isn't so cutthroat. Those who trusted you with their earnings, and those who helped your firm become what it was."

"At the expense of my privacy?" he asks, growing testy. "Hell, no."

"It'll be tasteful."

For a second, I almost expect him to take that beer and smash it into the fire. But he doesn't. Hale wouldn't ever intimidate me that way.

"Is that all you have to say?" he asks. "That it'll be in good taste? What was I worried about? Hell, maybe all your hard work will even land you an Emmy."

"Maybe," I add thoughtfully.

"You're something else, you know that?"

He doesn't mean it as a compliment. Not with that tone.

I wipe my chin when I spill some of my beer, my thoughts racing ahead of my mouth. "I'm here to save your reputation. Right now, even your kindest and most genuine clientele think you're a crook, and they're convinced you screwed them. You've never shown them the side your friends have seen. You've never extended your hand in friendship."

"I didn't work as hard as I did to make friends. I was running a business, creating an empire."

"And you were damn good at it," I agree. "But you don't want to be perceived as an elitist, heartless, rich boy. We have enough of those. So, let me portray you as you are; a man who did his best to earn the love of his family. Who struggled to find his place in the world and succeeded against all odds."

"Damn it, Becca. Do you have any idea what it took for me to tell you what I did? Especially after all our time apart?"

"I think I do," I answer quietly. For all the horrible things we've endured, all the words meant to hurt and the actions that left impenetrable scars, here I am, still willing to bleed for him and make sure he recovers. We're friends at heart, Hale and me. Regardless of everything, that's who we are.

"I don't know what you hope to accomplish, aside from making me look like a pathetic whiner with Daddy issues and a drunk for a mother."

"Some people will call you a whiner," I reply, refusing to paint too rosy a picture. "They'll see you as everything you described and worse."

He nods. "Great. You are damn good at your job, Becks. Don't know what I'd do without you, girl."

"But the majority won't," I add. "They'll see you as a hero. As a man who could have easily succumbed to his pain, instead of embracing the American dream and kicking all the excuses to fail in the balls."

Hale just stares, pegging me with a sick amount of resentment I should be used to by now. But the emotions he feels aren't the result of anything I've done or said, but from what life has done to him. It makes it easier to take, but not much. For all I think this is the right direction, I'm asking a great deal and walking a fine line between exploitation and friendship.

"You've returned to the only place you've ever called home," I remind him. "Where you grew up and did your best to fit in. There's beauty in that and it's something many people will relate to."

"But how's it going to look when the world finds out that my brothers can't stand the sight of me? I can't come out of this looking good. Not with both of them against me."

"I don't know about that."

"How can you say that, Becca? My brothers won't even speak to me." He runs his finger along the stamp of the bottle. "The last I spoke with was Carson. He called me, drunker than hell, the night Forbes released their magazine with me on the cover, just to tell me how much he hated me. How much they both did." Hale works his jaw. "I'd taken my staff out to dinner at Tavern on the Green to celebrate, and every last one of them heard him screaming into the phone. Good times, let me tell you. Good times."

For a moment, I just gape. But this incident is another reminder of what needs to be done. "We can address that, too," I say, adjusting the blanket against my shoulders.

He cocks his brow. "On film?"

"Preferably." I pause, the next few words hard to say. "I'd also like to get their perspective if we can."

"You're off your rocker, woman."

"No," I reply. "Just strategic."

"Becks, at best, Carson will be too drunk to talk and Emer won't shoot us. No good will come out of reaching out to my brothers, and you know it."

I dump my empty bottle in the garbage. "No. I don't know it, Hale."

"You didn't see my mother at the end of her life. She was a broken woman who drank her calories. A fact my brothers sure as shit blame, and will never forgive me for."

"Why?" I ask.

"Because, unlike my daddy, I wasn't sure I could forgive her. After our talk, I left. Went back to New York to try to forget everything I'd learned. She'd call sometimes. I'd reach out and ask her if she needed anything. But it was all pretend. We knew there was no going back to the family I thought I had."

"How was she when you spoke with her?"

"Different." Hale glares at the fire. "Drunk. Always drunk. She tried to deny it. I begged her to get help. After a while we . . . I don't know. I gave up on trying to convince her and she gave up on life."

"Did you try to see her?" Hale winces. "I'm not trying to make you feel bad," I add, carefully. "I'm trying to understand what happened."

"She didn't want to see anyone. She locked herself up in the house. The only one she'd let in was some asshole she paid to deliver her booze. It'd been a few days since my brothers had heard from her. They broke into the house when she wouldn't answer the door and found her."

I expect tears. No. I *want* tears from Hale. They don't come.

I swear under my breath. I've learned the hard way that sometimes things are too sad for tears. I didn't see his momma near the end of her life, but I'd heard enough. Alcoholic liver disease is as ugly as it sounds.

Hale lowers his half-empty beer to the ground. Seconds pass. Minutes pile up. And the storm vanishes far away from us. I know we're done talking. At least for now.

I stand and fold the blanket, clearing my throat. "I might not see you for a couple days. There are things I need to do and people I have to reach out to."

"I thought you were done with all the prep work?" he asks.

I was. Until I realized how much more he needs from me and how much Mr. Singleton still expects. "I think we need a tad more," I say, keeping my tone professional.

I'm not blind to his pain and I'm not heartless. What I am is good at my job. "Hale, you're a victim of manipulation and greed. But you're not a victim of life and circumstance. I'll make sure you come across as the champion you are."

He frowns. "Why?" he asks.

I need to leave before I say too much. "Because you would help me if you could. Just like you offered to that night."

I walk through the house and out the door. Trin's house is less than a mile away. I need the air and I need the distance. Hale knows which night I mean. Like him, my memory is long and the pain I hold lingers unbearably close to the surface.

Chapter Nine

Hale

"What the fuck is that?"

A black and white creature, more mop than dog, blinks up at me from my doorstep. I can't see his eyes through all the fur covering them, but I'm pretty sure he's giving me the stink eye.

"Hey, Hale!" Becca waves and hops out of a white van. "Good mornin', darlin'."

Becca's hair looks the way it used to. Back when she didn't bother blowing it or whatever it is women do to make it movie-star perfect. It's messy in all the right ways, like when she used to let her sea-soaked strands dry in the bright summer sun.

There's a hint of waves and natural highlights most women drop hundreds in salons to achieve. I never told her it's how I like her hair best. Maybe I should. Hell, maybe I should start with a simple good morning, though not everything about it is good.

I barely slept. The shit I'm dealing with surrounding my court case gets less shitty each day. That's the good part. To me and my legal team's shock, all but one of the insider trading charges were dropped, and the ten counts of fraud charges were reduced to four. The bad news is the judge granted the feds another five months to strengthen their case.

"What case?" I asked Mason. "It's obvious they don't have anything to stand on."

Mason agreed. "Our problem is, it's turned political. The head of the agency wants to keep his job. When we prove he wasted time, resources, and money on a bullshit case, he's done, Hale. The judge knows it, but gave him the time anyway."

"Why?" I pressed.

"Because when we either prove your innocence in trial or get everything dropped, which is where we're headed, the judge can say he's given the feds enough time."

"What about the supposed informant who turned me in and led them to the so-called evidence?" I countered.

"They can't produce him."

"Can't or won't?" I asked. "Big difference there."

"We thought they had some kind of ace up their sleeve with this informant," Mason explained. "But even though he reached out to the feds several times, and sent them after you, they never pinned down who he was."

"What?"

"Tell me about it." Mason made a face. "These idiots never clarified who he was or how to find him. He provided plenty of tips and information about you, but then he disappeared. They couldn't even determine if "he" was a he. It's a good thing for us. No witness, no evidence, no case. Our dilemma remains that the Head Fed can't go down like this, so the agency is trying to find the informant and anything that justifies your arrest and the media circus this whole thing became."

"What about us? Can we find him?" We, meaning them.

"We're trying," Mason said. "But we have less to go on than the feds. This is their Hail Mary."

"Damn," I said.

"Yeah," Mason agreed. "But if they can't find him, they have to let this thing go sooner, rather than later."

In the meantime, I'm the one who looks bad, not the feds. I've spent the last few weeks making calls back and forth with Neesa—trying to keep the staff and what's left of my business going—paying their salaries in the hopes I can return. Except, as insane as it sounds, this whole experience is not what's keeping me up at night.

I told Becca what really happened with my folks. I'm still not sure why I did it. Maybe being around our friends and talking about the good times over supper triggered it all. Maybe it was Miss Sylvie's pot roast, warm and savory and full memories of better days. Maybe it was the ocean. The way the waves soaked the beach, bringing me back to a time where I was a Wilder, a real one, and everything made sense.

Or maybe it was just Becca.

Okay. I'm really starting to hate that word "maybe."

I'm not sure how I went from practically setting her pretty clothes on fire with just one dark look to spilling my soul like I would a slippery glass of milk. But Becca's always had a hold over me, long before I kissed her, and now, years later, when I want to do a hell of a lot more.

I lean against the doorframe, watching and waiting for her to explain why she's here with a dog who already assumes his place is with me. After a three-hour conference call with Neesa about what to do with the clients who have stuck by me, I'm ready to go for a long run and not stop until my worries are nothing more than a blur.

Too bad I can't. Too bad the woman who can suck my heart clean through a straw lingers mere yards away with some guy wearing enough pastels to shame a flower. Jesus, what a morning.

Becca and all her raving beauty surprisingly don't hold my complete attention. The sixteen-year-old looking dude, the one with the camera, pastels, and more eyeliner than should be humanly possible, brought friends. And when I say friends, I mean more than one mutt.

A fluffy white dog with (Lord, help me) barrettes on her ears like pigtails. wags her tail enthusiastically as Becca coos at it. Can't say I blame the dog. Becca could have that effect on the world if she cared enough about what the world thought of her.

"Momma will be right with you, baby," Becca says. "Oh, yes, she will." She turns to pastel guy, her voice all business as they fumble with some equipment in the rear of the van.

The black and white dog is still sitting beside me, watching, waiting, and apparently torn between looking for a good place to raise his leg, or going for my throat. I suppose that's the effect *I* have on the world.

I return the dog's expression and look back up toward Becca. "Becks, I asked you what the fuck this is?"

"A dog," Becca answers.

"I know it's a dog. But what is he doing on my doorstep eyeing me like he wants to chew my leg off and bury it?"

"Oh, you're just imagining things," she says, batting her hand dismissively.

"I am not. Look at him!" I say, pointing.

As if totally taking her side, the big mop of a dog whines at me.

"Hale Wilder, you're scaring him," Becca accuses.

I watch the dog hunker down at my feet, his head down. "I wasn't trying to scare you," I tell him. He whines, earning me another reprimanding glare from Becca. "Okay, pooch, now you're just making me look bad."

I bend, letting him sniff my hand. He wags his thick tail, hard enough to send the leaves the breeze stirred along the night to flutter away. But when I stroke his head, his tail really starts thumping. This dog is a hot mess and I can so relate.

"Tootles," Becca says. "Do you think Hale needs more cutesy?"

"Tootles?" I ask, giving the poor mutt a good scratch behind his ears. "Damn, Becca. The poor thing has it bad enough looking like a giant rug with a tongue. Did you have to call him Tootles?"

The photographer in pastels blinks back at me, horrified. He glances briefly at Becca. "Um. I'm Tootles. The dog's name is Twinkles."

I rise, ready to shut the door in everyone's face when Becca shoots forward. Her ball of fuzz in barrettes bounces up and down in her arms, appearing excited just to be alive. "I recognize that look," she says, all enthusiastic-like. "You don't think this is a good idea. I'll have you know, it's only because you haven't given it enough thought."

"Are we talking about Tootles or Twinkles?" I mutter.

"Maybe both, shug," she replies through her teeth. "He's a good boy."

"The dog?" I ask. He wags his tail when I look at him. "I suppose."

"A very good boy," the photographer says, like that will somehow change my mind about wherever Becca is headed. "He's already licked me twice and we just met."

"Well, he does seem right friendly, Twinkles."

"I'm Tootles. Benji Tootles. The dog is Twinkles," he reminds me.

This poor fucker. I don't know if his momma or daddy are alive. But if they are, and depending how the next few hours go, I may have to drive to their house and smack the shit out of his father for giving him such a stupid name.

"You used to get beat up on the playground, didn't you, son?" I ask.

Tootles' face turns roughly the color of his pink scarf. "Um. Yes. But I went to a school that didn't appreciate creativity or fashion."

As soon as he says it, I feel bad and offer him my hand. "I don't appreciate them as much as I should either, Tootles. But if you went to my school, I wouldn't let anyone fuck with you."

I mean as much. Me, Becks and our friends, we were pretty well known in school as the cool kids to be around. But we were never cruel. Not like some of the kids a man like Tootles must have seen in his time.

Tootles smiles at Becca as he releases my hand. "You're right. He's nice." He motions to me. "I wasn't certain when I first spotted you."

"Hale's bark was always worse than his bite," Becca assures him. She tosses her hair *and me* a look that informs me I need to behave. "Tootles was intimidated when you stepped out of the house and growled."

"I didn't *growl*," I say, all the while likely growling.

"What do you call asking me, 'What the fuck is that?,' instead of a decent good morning?" She skips past me. Twinkie, or whatever the dog is called, follows behind her, tail wagging and trying to keep up. What the hell? I thought me and him were starting to bond.

Becca puts the prissy dog down and rubs her hands. "It's chilly in here. But that may work to our favor, seeing we're going for a more wintery feel. Hale, did you get the linen pants and the light white shirt I sent over this morning?"

I stop in the middle of making coffee just to raise an eyebrow at her. "Those things were for me?" Shit. I haven't seen her in a few days, so I was hoping she was having clothes delivered here with the expectation of staying.

"They're designer," Becca says, as if that's going to make me jump on board the feminine-looking clothes ship.

"And linen breathes really well, in case you were worried," Tootles adds.

"Yeah. That's what I was worried about, Toot."

"It's Tootles," Becca tells me. "That's his professional name in the fashion industry. Kind of like Law Roach."

"Who?' I ask.

"Just put on the damn pants, Hale," Becca says, showing more teeth than either of the mutts. "We need to get this fabulous day started."

Translation: shut the hell up before I kill you in front of Tootles and the dogs.

I chuckle into my shoulder, trying to keep from full-out cackling. This little hellcat hasn't changed one bit. "Why the linen? I thought you preferred me in little to nothing at all?"

Tootles gasps, throwing up his arms and growing flustered. "You didn't tell me we were doing nudies. I think I'm going to need more light." He whips out his phone.

"Stefan? Did you leave yet? . . . What? . . . Go, back . . . that's right. We need more light!"

Becca doesn't bother correcting him, even though he appears close to losing his mind. She's too busy grinning at me with a smile capable of roasting testes on an icy tundra. "Hale, I have a vision."

"Does this vision involve dogs?" I ask, bending down to scratch the giant moppy head that rubs against me. "You plan to have me and Trusty on the cover?"

"Twinkles," Tootles interrupts. "Precious, I need you to connect. This dog needs to feel like he belongs."

Damn, he's stressed.

Becca ignores me, bending down to pick up the prissy dog running in circles at her feet. "Her name is Anarchy," she says.

"I would expect no less," I say.

She laughs softly, her gaze lingering on the wooden floors. The sweater she's wearing shouldn't be doing anything for her. It's light brown, almost gold, unlike the bright, bold colors she normally wears. But this one has a low neckline. Not too low, just enough to allow the eye to travel over the swell of her breasts. The color may not do anything for her skin, but it does bring attention to her pretty face and is more than enough to make me take notice. And those tight jeans she's in? Y'all, Becca has always looked good in jeans.

She pouts her lips, pressing the dog to her and speaking a sexy whisper that should be out-lawed in at least twenty states. "What's wrong, Hale?" she asks, cuddling the dog closer so its white fur rubs against her long, bare neck. "Don't you like dogs?"

"Sure." Sorry. What was the question? Damn, it's hot in here.

Tootles shakes out his hands. "Which bedroom gets the most light?"

I shrug. "They're all pretty bright. Feel free to look around."

And he does, taking off in a sprint up the stairs. "Yes, Stefan," he says into the phone. "We need nudies."

I'm barely aware of him rushing around upstairs and barely notice when he races down to check the other suite. Becca has my full attention, although she's too busy pretending not to notice. She's not wearing much makeup and the clothes she's in make her look younger, softer, not like the PR princess ready to fling her tiara at anything that messes with her.

Tootles returns, appearing less anxious and more determined. "I think his suite works best. There's more room to work. More light. We can get him naked and tuck the sheet around him at the waist. White works best and, bonus, there are already white sheets on the bed. I'm thinking, more romance, less color. Shades of gray or likely straight up black and bold whites."

He hurries to me. But I'm not all that focused on him. I'm still stuck on Becca and "naked." I don't know what this photo shoot is all about, but so far, I'm all in.

Tootles presses his hands on his hips, eyeing me up and down. "I'm thinking your hands tucked behind your head like so." He threads his fingers and demonstrates for me, thinking I'm not that bright and that the action may be too complex for me. Tootles doesn't have a lot of faith in me. I almost laugh, waiting, *just waiting,* to prove him wrong.

"I want you to look away from the camera," he instructs. "You're awake. Your focus is on the window. Toward the light and the future."

"Infinite," Becca says. "That's the title. Infinite possibilities. Infinite future."

"Love it," Tootles agrees.

Becca strokes the dog, sighing as if everything is falling exactly where it needs to. I don't pay much attention to her actions, but I should. Every mild gesture and expression draws me to her beauty, reminding me how stunning she is no matter how much time has passed.

"I know we haven't started yet, y'all," she says. "But if we're going in that direction, I think it should be the last shot for the Vogue spread."

"Vogue?" I ask. "What happened to Forbes? Newsweek? Time?"

"Don't you worry your pretty little head about that," Becca tells me, using that same sinfully delicious purr. "I have all the major outlets covered."

Tootles jumps in place, clapping. "Becca forbade me from telling you—"

"*Tootles*," she warns.

"But I'm going to, anyway. This woman, right here, has used up every favor she has. You're going to be everywhere, Hale. Every mag has an exclusive, releasing back to back. To give you an idea of all the awesomeness, you have Forbes in the winter issue followed by Vogue at the end of the year." More jumping, more clapping. Tootles is beside himself. "It's why I'm here. I *know* Vogue."

Becca smiles. "Tootles interned at Vogue and has worked for the greatest in the business for years before branching out on his own. You're looking at one of the hottest and most sought-after creative directors in the business."

"Oh, stop it," he says, turning to Becca. He eyes her up and down as if seeing her for the first time. "Hmm. Becca, I'm thinking you'll have to get naked, too."

And lose the purr in three . . . two . . . one . . .

"*What?*" she screeches, scaring the dogs.

I nod thoughtfully. "I like it," I agree. "Fuck the linen pants."

Tootles sucks his teeth. "I'm sorry, Hale. We'll still do linen for Forbes. Becca's right. You do need a little softening and nothing softens a man like linen and puppies."

"I'll bet," I agree. "Now, getting back to me and Becca naked in bed..."

"This isn't a good idea," she says, speaking over me. "I mean, this is a very bad idea."

"What's wrong, Becks?" I ask. "Tootles here is a professional. Don't you trust him?" I throw my hands up. "Don't tell me you're doubting a creative visionary with an unmatched reputation like Tootles?"

There was nothing better I could have said. Tootles places a very irate hand on his hip. "Is that what you're saying, Becca?" he demands. "That you don't trust me?"

"You know I do," she answers Tootles, all the while glaring at me. "I just don't know why *I* have to be in bed, naked with *him*."

Even the dogs look at me when she says it. Another man, a less confident and more self-conscious man might take offense. Me? I can't stop my grin. "You're worried you might not be able to keep your hands to yourself or something?" I ask. Her face reddens. "Damn. You are, aren't you? Hey, Tootles, mind if I get a few digital copies when you're done? When I'm old and senile, I want to remember this day when you and Becca saved my very naked ass."

Both ignore me. "Becca, precious, the shot? The one we agreed we loved? That's the money shot. You yourself said it should be the very last image Vogue readers see when they page through Hale's journey. He's pondering his infinite future, remember? Career, life, and yes, marriage and family, too. We don't need to show your face, but we do need to capture your vulnerability to reflect his. It will cement his strength, his hope, his return, understand?"

"Yeah. Why aren't you getting this, Becca?" I ask. "It all makes perfect sense to me."

Becca loves animals. *Loves* them. But I think she might beat me with that dog in her arms before the day is through.

"You'll lay across his chest," Tootles continues. He plays with her hair. "We'll cover your face. No one will know it's you. But they will know the man holding you close."

"*Real* close," I agree.

Becca lowers the dog. I half expect her to order it to bite my ankles. She doesn't, thank God. "I don't know about this, Tootles," she says. "It's not that I doubt your vision. It's just ..."

Tootles sighs all dramatic-like. I can't blame him and almost mirror the sentiment. "I understand. It's a lot to ask someone to capture and portray another's vulnerability."

She places her hand on her chest. "Thank you. That means a great deal."

"Wait, one damn minute," I protest. "This is the best idea I've heard in days. Don't I get a say?"

"Oh, we're still doing it," Tootles assures me. "Don't you worry about that. My creativity will not be silenced."

"Excuse me?" Becca asks. "You just told me you understand."

"I understand your concerns and fear about participating," he tells her. "But that's the shot we need. Hale needs. *The world needs.*"

"Are you using the dogs for this?" Becca asks, confused.

"Not for something as delicate as this," Tootles says.

"Then . . ." Becca asks. "Where exactly are you headed with this?"

Tootles chuckles. "You're not the only one with connections, my dear. Suzi Watertower just finished a week-long shoot with David Gandy. She's recovering in a luxury spa just a few miles from here. I'll call her."

He lifts his sparkly phone, scrolling through his contacts.

"Suzi Watertower?" Becca asks. "The super model?"

"That'll work," I add, ignoring the glower she pegs me with.

"I don't think you should disturb her," Becca interrupts. She sounds testy, despite her evidently deep concern for supermodel Suzi's well-being. "Poor thing is recovering. Like you said."

"Nonsense, dear," Tootles says. "Suzi loves me. Besides, once she gets a look at Hale, she'll be more than happy to take your place in bed with him—"

Like a ninja, Becca snatches the phone from Tootles' hand.

"I'll do it," Becca says, a little faster than even she expected. She clears her throat. "Let's not bother Suzi. She, um . . . *we* might need your connections for something else during the campaign. Let's not exhaust them this early."

It's then I know that God truly exists. Becca looks at me. "I'll get naked with Hale."

Chapter Ten

Becca

The crew Tootles brings on is small and among the best. Not just because of their skills, but because of their ability to be discreet. Their contract for this shoot, like most they're solicited for, includes their silence. They're kept from discussing any details about the shoots and are required to leave before the photography begins. Still, I'm not taking any chances. I made sure they signed NDAs ahead of time.

In addition to being a creative consultant, Tootles is a gifted photographer. He's taught me all I know about taking the perfect shot, and what I'll need to conduct the more intimate interviews with Hale. But for Vogue, Forbes—all the big names—I need better than me. I need Tootles.

Hale's laughter booms from the bedroom, overpowering Tootles' softer chuckle. Hale managed to charm Tootles with his kindness. I knew he would. Hale can recognize someone who's had it rough, especially those who soared to success regardless of it.

Right now, I'm not loving their budding friendship. It works against me, instead of for me. I'm in a robe and nothing else for the love of all. How do I get myself in these dilemmas?

The manicurist buffs my nails with expertise. I was wearing pink and was hoping for something similar. Tootles has other plans. "No," he says, hurrying in. "No color. French or nothing at all."

"Nothing at all," Hale echoes, leaning against the frame and crossing his arms. The dogs skip in behind him and spread out on the floor. After a few shots on the beach, a few more in front of the fireplace, he's won them over, too. Bastard.

The team worked on Hale long before they ever thought to touch me. He wasn't thrilled about receiving a new hairstyle and complained more than once. He's not complaining now, giving his hair another pass with his hand.

The stylist trimmed the sides and mussed the top, leaving the impression of a good night with very little sleep for all the right reasons. I never pictured Hale like this. Never mind, I have. I've always loved how he looks. Even at his most angry, I enjoy everything that makes him Hale.

All those mushy thoughts aside, I love his hair. It amps up his sex appeal and makes him look more hero than heartbreak. Whatever the team did to his scruff managed to add another helping of sexy and brightened his smile.

Like me, Hale is in a robe. My guess is, there's nothing beneath the cotton material. I try not to give it too much thought. Those thoughts eagerly appear when I'm around him and now even when I'm not, reminding me I'm no longer in control of my raging and lonely womanly parts.

Hale looks at Tootles, but that smug grin that casts a shimmer across his mesmerizing irises is all for me. "What do you think about a shot of Becca's short nails dragging down my back?"

"Oh," Tootles says over my very audible gasp. "That could be sexy."

"I think you're looking way too much into this vision," I say, my face heating.

Tootles disagrees, of course. "No. I like where he's going with this. Infinite, your title suggestion, not mine—"

"Which you love," I remind him.

"Agreed," he says. "It suggests all those long-term successes we want for Hale, including love."

"Love?" I stammer.

This time when I turn back to Hale, all evidence of mischief is gone. Only tension remains between us, accelerating with every stunned blink of my eyes.

"What's wrong, Becca?" he murmurs. "Don't you want me to find love?"

With a heavy breath, my attention falls to my lap. "Of course, I do," I say, wishing I didn't sound so sad.

Tootles' tone softens. It's not sympathy or understanding he feels for me. This is all about this shoot and how enraptured he's become with it. "Infinite," he says, repeating the word. "A long-term love affair with the one woman Hale will share his bed with, forever."

God, if you're listening, help me. I'm in trouble, serious trouble.

Tootles bends to look at me, appearing depressed. "Do you really think readers want Hale, their hero, in bed with a one-night stand when we're using a title like Infinite?"

"Yeah. Do you?" Hale asks.

Again, I blush. This time with anger. I may have to kill them and find a remote place to bury the bodies. "What does forever have to do with short nails scraping down Hale's bare back?" I ask.

"Passion," Tootles says like it's obvious.

"What he said," Hale agrees.

"Becca," Tootles says. "There's a horrible theory that when people marry their initial passion dies."

"Horrible theory," Hale reiterates.

"It doesn't have to be that way," Tootles says.

"Nope, not even close," Hale adds. "I say kill that awful theory."

"Agreed," Tootles says.

"Don't you let that passion die," Hale presses.

Tootles grins. "Not on my watch," he assures him. "Now, about the nails. Let's go a little shorter. We don't want them long. Just long enough to tease her husband."

"In bed," Hale agrees. "Hey," Hale interrupts when the stylist reaches for a straightener. "Don't touch her hair. I like it how it is."

The way he speaks, as well as how he eyes me, gives me tremendous pause. His irises shimmer, reflecting the heat streaming through my body.

"Excellent point. We don't want the images to appear overly posed," Tootles explains to the stylist, oblivious to the escalating tension spreading between me and Hale. "Same with the makeup. She shouldn't look like she has any on."

The make-up artist nods. "I'll just touch her up a little so the sheets don't wash her out."

"Lovely," Tootles confirms. "Hale and Becca will be the ultimate couple if it kills me."

My shoulders slump. It may very well kill me.

"Props," Tootles says, clapping to get everyone's attention. "I need a ring."

"A ring?" Hale and I say at once.

"Becca isn't a one-night stand," Tootles patiently reminds him. "There has to be a ring." He shoves his hands on his hips. "Am I the only one committed to this campaign?"

"No," Hale replies.

Nice. He can still talk. Good for him.

The dogs look expectantly up at Hale when he places his hands in the pockets of his robe. I used to own a lot of jewelry, mostly rings. But when I left my daddy and the life I'd experienced with him behind, the jewelry stayed with him. I've accumulated a few nice pieces throughout the years, mostly earrings and necklaces. I don't wear anything on my hands. I don't need any more memories of my time with my father or that stupid engagement ring I wore for show. That charade I had with Denver is over, regardless of what his daddy thinks, and so is a life that includes my father.

Fumbling of drawers ensues as Tootles looks through the accessories the team brought. "I need pretty. But not too sparkly," he says, his idea getting the best of him. "We want the focus to be on the commitment, not the jewels."

"I have something," Hale offers, the way he says it drawing everyone's attention.

Hale pays us no mind and disappears into the bedroom. I'm not certain what he's up to. The only ring he ever wore was his high school football ring. But that's not something I've seen in years and not something I imagine would fit with this shoot.

"Miss Shields," the make-up artist says. "I need to finish up."

"Yes, of course," I say, momentarily forgetting where I am and what's at stake.

The soft makeup brush passes along my skin. I stare at my reflection. The blush is mild and I'm not certain it will do much in front of the camera, but my lashes are dark and long, which will be more than enough.

"Excellent," Tootles says. "I think we're ready."

The team nods and begins gathering their equipment. They recognize it's time to go and forget everything they saw.

"Found it," Hale says from the doorway. "I just need a moment with Becca."

Tootles starts to explain that they're almost done, but like the rest of the team, he sees something different in Hale. No one moves, including me, our full attention on Hale and where he waits by the door.

The air changes in the room, growing somber to match Hale's mood.

Tootles moves toward him slowly, his attention dropping to the small black box cupped in Hale's hand. "Is that it?" Tootles asks. Hale gives a stiff nod. I can no longer see the box, but I hear the small creak it makes when it's opened.

"It's perfect." Tootles glances back at me, although I'm unsure why. "I . . ."

"A few minutes," Hale says. "That's all I need." He looks past the staff to where I'm sitting. I can't move. I want to, but Hale's mere force keeps me in place. My word, what's happening here?

"Of course," Tootles says, motioning to his team to hurry. "Let us know when you're ready."

I think I should rise from the portable makeup chair, meet Hale halfway, or at the very least assume a less submissive position. But although the shoot hasn't started, the one where I'm to reflect the vulnerability Hale can't outwardly demonstrate, I'm already unwillingly in character long before he kneels before me.

He holds out the square box. It's not one of those swathed in velvet. It's leather with a gold stamp framing the worn edges. He opens it to reveal a thin, platinum band with tiny diamonds embedded around the edge. It's not flashy. It's subtle. But I can sense its significance long before Hale speaks.

"It was my mother's," he says. "My father gave it to her the day I was born."

I meet his face, wishing I knew the right words to say. "Why?" is all I manage.

He frowns, looking at the ring. "I think it was his way of starting over and proving he was still committed to her."

"But not to you?" I ask before I give it much thought.

I start to apologize for my choice of words, but Hale speaks first. "No. He wasn't ready to accept me yet." He sighs. "Momma gave it to me the last time I saw her. She slipped it off her finger and handed it to me. I didn't understand why she wanted me to have it. I'd only just learned I wasn't his son."

"I think she wanted you to know that you were still a part of everything they shared," I say.

Hale averts his gaze. My fingers slide over his hand and I give it a squeeze. "There was a lot wrong between them," I add quietly. "A great deal of hurt and some things they never managed to forgive themselves for. But this ring was the first step toward healing and saving what they had." I shake my head. "They made mistakes, Hale. Big ones. Your father with how long it took him to accept you, and your mother for straying when she should have remained faithful."

I swallow hard. My next few comments are the hardest. Somehow, I manage without stumbling and without my voice breaking, although it very much wants to. "But if she hadn't strayed, if he hadn't created that wedge between them, if you hadn't worked as hard as you did, you wouldn't be you. You wouldn't have been born and I never would have known you. God, Hale," I say, gripping his hand tighter. "I'm so blessed to know you."

Hale trembles, not with fear, not with anger. It's raw emotion. The same thing I feel. "This ring was the first of many long steps toward healing and acceptance." I fight back the tear that threatens to fall. It falls anyway. "I think your momma wanted you to know that, no matter what, they did heal and that you were their son."

Hale bows his head. For a long moment, all I see is the top of his blond, mussy hair. I want to stroke it and clutch him to me. Instead, I give him the moment he needs.

"I don't know why I thought of it," he says. "And I'm still not sure why I brought it out. If you don't want to wear it, I'll understand."

"I would be honored to wear anything that's a part of you," I whisper.

He nods, his head appearing as heavy as our hearts. He pulls out the ring and places the box on the corner of the granite vanity counter. He's still on his knees. Without thinking, I offer him my hand, waiting for him to slip this bittersweet memory on my finger.

If he hesitates, it's brief. I watch him slide the ring that symbolizes his existence across my finger. I think I should say something. Before I can gather my thoughts, he wraps his hand around mine and draws me to him, lifting me to stand in one smooth motion.

Our gazes lock. "Come on," he says. "Time to play married lovers."

Chapter Eleven

Hale

When I crawled out of bed this morning on very little sleep, I was expecting the usual; calls with Mason and Neesa, and doing all I can to hang onto my staff. Things that needed to get done. The last thing I was expecting was to slip into bed naked with Becca.

Would I have wanted to? Hell, yeah. I have a pulse, damn it.

Except, for too many reasons to count, this isn't the way I thought we'd end up in bed. It's for a picture. I get it. And at first, I was having my share of fun with it. It was like something out of my wildest fantasies was suddenly coming true.

I loved teasing her and getting a rise. Loved seeing that blush I'm now officially addicted to. Except, all the fun and games wrapped up damn quick, didn't they? All it took was a big wrench from the past to screw it up and beat all the good humor to death.

I'm not sure what made me think of that ring. I'm also not sure what made me bring it with me. My assets, belongings, everything I owned was court ordered to stay in New York. But when Neesa slipped into my apartment before my court date and before the ruling, she found the ring and took it with her, exactly as I'd instructed.

Mason suspected that the seizure of my assets was coming, given all the original charges pending against me. But instead of watches, shit from my safe, and things of value that I actually need, that ring . . . that was the one thing I begged Neesa not to leave my place without.

When Momma first offered it to me, I refused. Part of me, that part I bury deep and keep locked away, knew she was saying goodbye. She didn't have much longer. She was done with life now that Daddy was gone.

So, what do I go ahead and do with that ring I *didn't* want? The one I couldn't leave New York without? I went and slipped it on Becca's finger. The woman who broke my heart.

I recognize the irony. Don't think that I don't. What I haven't fully wrapped my head around is why.

"Are you ready, Hale?" Tootles calls out.

He has his high-tech camera ready to go. I'd hate to tell him no. He's trying to help. They all are.

"Sure," I say, faking an easy-going persona I recognize has left me high and dry. From the moment I thought of that ring, everything that kept the jokes and the teasing coming abandoned me, leaving me stuck in the past, pretending to have a good grasp on life even though I don't. Nope. Not anymore.

I take off the robe and toss it behind me. From behind the closed bedroom door, the dogs whine. I'm hoping the little prissy one is trying to hump the moppy one like she did during the beach shots. That's just embarrassing for both of them. Mostly, though, I'm hoping to get through this shoot.

Becca waits in the opposite corner bouncing nervously in place. I'm not sure if she's looking my way. If she is, I hope she learned modesty isn't part of my vocabulary, especially when I'm around her. At first, I might have used my blatant nudity as an intimidation tactic, just a little one. I wanted her to high-tail it out of my life when I first saw her in New York. Now . . . shit. I'm not sure what I want.

I slip beneath the cool and crisp white sheets, their softness skimming along my bare skin. Trin had sent a cleaning crew to straighten up earlier in the morning. "They'll be there same day every week," she texted. I'm not sure if she knew about the shoot. Hmph. Who am I kidding? As Becca's bestie, Trin knows everything.

My hands make quick work of adjusting the sheet so it lays over my waist. Tootles fusses with the pillows, fluffing them. The heavy camera around this neck bats against his stomach as he directs me closer to the center of the bed. He dismissed the staff as fast as he could and got to work, fretting with the light and the layout, trying to create the best post-sex morning his little heart could envision.

There wasn't all that much to do near as I could figure. The home is staged to sell. Everything looks perfect, except for the bed that Tootles made appear very much played in. To add to the naughty night theme, he laid out a fresh pair of panties and a bra near where Becca's side of the bed will be, positioning them just so to appear as if they were tossed during the heat of passion.

I'm trying not to think about the see-through teal bra or its matching thong. Mostly, because I can picture Becca wearing them. Thongs, sweet lacy bras, these are things she would wear. To this day, I remember the feel of her bra against my teeth that night I pulled her taught nipple into my mouth.

Damn. Where am I again?

"Don't worry about what happens to your hair," Tootles says, pulling me back to reality. "Messy is better and leaves more to the imagination."

I drag my hand through it. "All right," I say, since, y'all know my hair is all I'm thinking about now.

"This is your moment, Hale," Tootles says, his excitement building. "Think of it as a story. Your story had all these twists and turns you weren't expecting, but now the drama is behind you. Now, there's only peace and the promise of a bright and peaceful future."

"Right," I say.

I don't know Tootles. He seems like a good guy and he strikes me as someone who guards a fair amount of secrets from being around the famous people he associates with. It's probably why he looked away and got busy when Becks and me stepped out of the bathroom.

Or hell, maybe he saw something between us we didn't want him to.

Tootles rushes to the tripod, adjusting the second camera he set up. This one has a remote that's hooked to his belt loop. According to him, he'll press it throughout the shoot to get several shots from different angles. It keeps the set intimate, he told us, and allows him to disappear.

I wasn't sure what he meant, but I understand now. I sink into the bed as instructed, thinking only of Becca and what the next hour will bring.

Tootles begins to fade away, his voice lowering so it's barely audible. He looks at me through the lens, adjusts the light just so, and peels back the sheet so it lays at an angle. The man who made a big fuss about the "nudies" is gone. The professional stager, photographer, and creative director has arrived and is very much front and center.

"Very good," Tootles says. "I'll direct you as we go, if needed. For the most part, forget that I'm here. Take my suggestions about altering your position and make them yours. It's the best way for them to look natural."

He shakes out his hand and, I suppose, the nervousness he's feeling. "One more thing. Don't look at the camera. You were good about it outside, but right now is especially important."

"Got it," I assure him, my voice lowering.

"Becca," he calls. "We're ready for you. Hale, tuck your hands behind your head. Tilt your chin in the direction of the window and toward the light. *No.* Too much. I need to see both your eyes. Good."

I sigh and do what he instructs, moving slowly as he suggested when we shot the outside pics.

Click. The first picture is taken.

Click. I move a fraction of an inch.

Click. I close my eyes.

Click. I open them slowly.

Click, click. This one from the tripod.

Click. One more. *Click.* And another.

The gentle sounds from the camera start to fade. Almost silently, Becca moves forward. I barely hear her steps. But I sense her. I always have.

The scent of her perfume, the mild flowery one she usually wears this time of year, drifts ahead of her, filling the room with her fragrance. I always knew when spring arrived in Kiawah. It wasn't the changing weather, or the blossoms poking their way through thick and battered vegetation. It was Becca, her increasing energy, her widening smile, and this perfume.

I close my eyes again, remembering the first time she wore it. It was high school, our sophomore year. There was a change in Becca when we started high school. She began caring more about what she wore and how she looked, fussing with her hair, giving us second glances when we told her she looked good, like she wasn't sure we meant it. It was also the time she tightened her circle of friends, as if she'd finally learned who to trust. But sophomore year . . . yeah, that's when this perfume made its presence known.

It fit Becca perfectly, light like how she moved and fresh like her spirit. I remember her walking toward me, laughing at something Trin was telling her, her long hair swaying and her skirt fluttering, her eyes bright, and the sweet scent she'd claimed as hers drifting closer as she neared.

I sink further into the pillow, relishing the scent and memories I have of her. There are too many to count and she's almost to me. Can she guess how many more memories I'd like to make of us?

"You know she's here," Tootles says. "Look up. See your lover."

I do, turning my head slowly. My eyelids are like a heavy curtain, unveiling the vision before me.

The intensity of the moment chisels the image of her into my soul. Becca's robe is gone. Another sheet, this one black is pressed tight against her breasts. She keeps her head lowered as instructed. Not in shame. Not in sadness. *Anticipation.* That and a shyness that I didn't quite expect.

Her heavy strands of tousled hair gather around her face, cloaking her features and concealing her eyes. I need to see those eyes. She can't hide what she's feeling within them, no matter how hard she tries.

Becca's back is exposed, revealing every curve and bit of her silky skin in the reflection of the mirror. Tootles doesn't seem to notice as he clicks away behind her. She's a prop. That's how he described her.

To me, she's something else. Hell, she always was.

"Don't move," Tootles says, when Becca quivers. "Look up at Hale, slowly. Use your body to tell him what you want him to do to you."

The light from the room hits her face just right, casting shadows from her hair around the perimeter and illuminating her features. Lowered lids, thick with eye makeup, meet me with full force, drilling me in place. I can't be sure what she's thinking. But I know what her body wants.

Blinding need builds within her, casting a shade of pink across her face and throat. She bites the bottom of her pouty lips, unsure, hungry with desire, and inexplicably frightened.

She has nothing to be afraid of. Becca has me. I'm all hers.

I just need to make her mine.

"Good. That's it," Tootles says. "It's okay, honey. Don't stress. No one will know it's you."

I want everyone to know, I almost say. *Want everyone to see she's with me.*

"Inch closer to Hale," Tootles instructs. "Slowly . . . slowly . . . good. So good!"

Tootles has no romantic interest in Becca. I know it as well as I know that ocean singing its gentle song beneath the sunny sky mere yards away. That doesn't mean I like another man seeing her. Touching her. No, not like I see her now, and definitely not when I want to be the only one whose hands glide across her exposed flesh.

He plays with her hair, bringing it down to further conceal her face and cloak her soft features.

Don't touch her, I want to say. *She's perfect.*

"Love this, Hale," Tootles says. "You're doing great and responding well. Rugged and strong, but willing to abandon it all to meet your lover's needs and fulfill her desires."

That sounds about right.

"Get riled," he instructs Becca. "Get hot. Go to him."

Becca lifts the sheet, allowing the bottom to pool in front of her. She crawls across the bed, struggling to keep her body hidden.

I don't want her to hide. I want to see her. No. I need to see her.

Click. Click.

Becca's doing all the work.

Click. Click.

But every emotion she reveals in me is captured in that camera.

"Reach for her," Tootles instructs. He's at the corner of the bed. The long lens of his camera captures the moment my hand grasps hers. He doesn't seem to notice the way we're watching each other, too busy telling me to turn her hand so he can see the ring.

I think I give him what wants. Although I no longer care.

God, it hurts to breathe.

Hurts not to touch her.

My muscles are shaking, burning from the warmth of her hand.

Her breathing increases and so does mine.

"*Hale*," she rasps.

She could be begging me to stop. Telling me this is all too much for her.

She could be pleading with me to take her. That she no longer wants to be without me.

She may even be telling me that she's not ready to feel what she does.

Or maybe that she's ready for more.

I don't ask.

I kiss her hard, my fingers tangling in her hair. She lets me, returning my affections, her tongue skimming across mine, begging for a deeper taste, and her short nails digging into my shoulders to keep me in place.

Jesus, sweet Jesus, don't let her stop.

I haul her on top of me, my fingers grazing down her bare back until they linger at the sheet and I wrap my arms around her.

Our lips audibly smack, seeking more of each other.

"And . . . release," Tootles says.

Becca whirls in Tootles direction. Like me, she seems to have forgotten he's here. She pulls up and away from me, her eyes wide, her breathing ragged, barely managing to keep the sheet pressed against her.

My hands drop to my sides. Other than that, I don't move.

Tootles busily flips through the images he captured. "That was hot. We'll have plenty of pics to choose from. Now, Becca, I want you across his chest."

"What?" she asks.

"Lay on his chest," he says. "It's morning. He's awake, thinking about the future and everything it promises. You're on top of him where you fell asleep after making love. You're content and at peace, knowing you're safe in his arms."

"Content?" Becca repeats. She nods quickly, appearing to regain her senses.

Good. I'm glad one of us has.

Tootles' vision. My reputation and career on the line. Sure. It's all coming back to me now.

Tootles arranges the sheet behind Becca. She hangs tight to the front, not willing to expose herself like she did for our kiss. I didn't see anything. But I felt it all. How good she fit against me and how damn good she tastes.

Once she's covered, Tootles drapes the white sheet I'm lying beneath over her. "All right," he says. "Settle into his body."

I gather her in my arms. At first, she tenses and so do I. But then slowly, very slowly, we relax into each other.

I'm not certain Becca knows that this is where she belongs, here with me. It doesn't matter. Her body recognizes as much, molding into mine as her breathing returns to normal.

"That's good, Hale. We'll start with this position and end with your arms tucked behind your head again."

"All right." It's what I say, but how on earth am I ever going to let Becca go?

"The sheet, the one beneath me is showing," Becca stammers.

"That's okay. The black sheet represents Hale's dark past, how he faced it, and how he's now able to leave it all behind. Now, close your eyes, Becca. No, too much. You're scrunching. Better. Better. Nice!"

Click.

Click. Click.

The sounds of the camera continue.

But all I know is Becca . . . How good she feels against me and how I *never* want to let her go.

Chapter Twelve

Becca

My hands are shaking so badly, it takes me a while to get dressed. I'm hoping it's adrenaline from the intensity of the shoot or what remains of my nervousness. I shake out my hands, pausing when I realize I'm still wearing the ring.

No, this quivering has nothing to do with adrenaline. It's everything I felt during that shoot. And everything Hale made that moment become.

He was so fearless, abandoning doubt and hesitation as easily as he did that robe. He stripped himself bare to me, different from when we were at the penthouse. There, he'd tossed his clothes as if I didn't matter. Today, he rid himself of what we were and embraced everything that's coming. Goodness, *everything*.

I saw the muscles that stretched along his spine and arms. But I didn't see much more, although I wanted to.

I should probably be ashamed of how badly I want to see him naked. It's the right thing to do. The *proper* thing. I drop my hand and sigh. I must be insane. Of course, I want to see him naked.

My only comfort is that if Nana June were still alive, she'd probably applaud me for showing what piddly restraint I managed. Except it wasn't exactly for my sake or Hale's. I just couldn't move.

Awestruck is the best way I can describe myself then. Hale's masculine persona robbed that room of time and space. It was only when Tootles instructed Hale to turn away that I could remove my robe and join him in bed.

Hale kissed me. To him, I wasn't merely a prop and this was no longer about saving his reputation. He kissed me like the lover I was supposed to become all those years ago. Each pass of his lips and gentle nibbles were a reckoning I never saw coming.

My fingers leave my lips, remembering how it felt to have Hale claim them with sweet aggression. He was making me his. God help me, I don't think I've ever felt more alive.

I'm barely able to snap my jeans closed. From the foyer, I hear Tootles' light tenor voice, assuring Hale he took a wide array of shots and that he'll select the best for the spread. If he doesn't like what he sees when he and I work on the layout, he may schedule another session.

"I have the cover for certain," Tootles says.

"Already?" Hale questions.

Tootles claps, excited. "Yes, I knew what it was the moment we snapped it. Should I tell you?"

"Why not?" Hale says.

He sounds distracted. Maybe worried. Neesa called shortly after we were done. He disappeared into the walk-in closet to dress and speak with her. Whatever it is, I'll help him through it. I'll do anything to help us grow closer.

I cuss when it takes me a moment to buckle my belt. Why can't I stop my hands from shaking?

"It's the one of you sitting on the beach in your suit. The black one," Tootles continues. Unlike me, he's very much in control. "The linen was okay, but not Vogue or Forbes. Do you want to know which one I'm talking about? Your feet were partially buried in the sand. Your tie was loose and the top two buttons of your shirt were open. You couldn't see what I saw, but I know you'll just love it."

Hale chuckles. "If you say so."

"I think the open bottle of champagne sticking out of the sand was a nice touch and your head bowed was fabulous. No matter what, I've got you. Becca and I will take care of you."

I shove my feet into one of my shoes, waiting for Hale to say something that will give me a better indication of his mood.

"But my favorite shots weren't of the beach. Oh, no, no, no," Tootles says. "Those shots with you and Becca were more D&G and Calvin Klein. Racy, *sexy*. I loved every minute of it."

I push my foot into the other shoe. I loved every minute of Hale and me, too. Even the scary one when I first approached him.

My phone rings where I tossed it on the bed. I've taken two calls since I ran in here but ignored the last few texts. Four were from my fake-ex Denver telling me to call him. One was from Mr. Singleton demanding to know where I am. It's only because I see Trin's bright smile flash across the screen that I answer.

"Hello?"

"Hey," she says brightly. "How's it going?"

"I got naked with Hale and made out with him on the bed while a photographer captured every pornographic and sinful second on camera."

A dramatic pause follows. I fall onto the bed, waiting for the response I expect.

"You showed Hale your titties?"

Yup. That was more or less the one.

"Not exactly," I reply.

"Were you naked or not?" she demands. "You said you were naked. Are you now taking it all back? You can't take something like that back without telling me to sit down or something."

"Fine. Sit down or something."

"Becca!"

I kick my feet, all the nervous energy I have left in my hands streaming downward. "Look. It wasn't something we'd planned. Maybe."

"Maybe? You said you were doing a photo shoot for a magazine. I was picturing Better Homes and Gardens not Maxim meets Big 'Uns."

"Um," I offer.

"Callahan," she calls. "Can you take the baby? . . . What? . . . Oh, I'm fine. Becca was just in bed naked with Hale . . . of course, I'm serious . . . yeah, I saw it coming, too . . . mmm-hmm, no surprise there . . . What? . . . No, I won't mind my own business. I've been waiting years for this . . . fine . . . *fine*. I'll leave her alone after she finishes giving me all the details. Something about midget wrestlers body slamming each other during all their nakedness. There was also some kind of circus fellow, twirling fire or something . . . what? . . . Callahan Sawyer, I do *not* sound crazy . . . those were her exact words . . . no, *no* . . . that's a lie. I've never exaggerated the truth in my whole life . . . I can prove it . . . some other guy took pictures and everything."

I drape an arm across my eyes. "Trin," I groan.

"One minute, Becks, just turning the baby over so you can tell me every last dirty and disgusting detail surrounding your sordid afternoon. But before we get started, were there pirates involved or any kinky stuff involving swings and chandeliers? That sort of thing is personal and I wouldn't want to invade your privacy like that." She pauses. "Unless you want me to."

"Run for your life, Becca," Callahan yells in the background. "Go someplace where they don't have phones or Trins."

"Well, that doesn't sound like a very fun place," Trin adds. "Go, ahead, Becca. I'm all ears."

"Hold on," I whisper, covering the speaker when I hear my name.

"Seriously," Tootles says. "You and Becca should consider modeling for fragrances, clothing, anything sexy. I'll shoot you myself."

"I'm not one for modeling," Hale answers, his voice quiet.

"I understand. It's not every man's dream. But, honestly, Becca missed her calling. She was a little stiff when we started, but that beauty. Oh, she slayed it, and the chemistry between you was something to behold."

"Becks?" Trin says.

"Shhh," I tell her. "They're talking about me."

"Who?"

"Hale and Tootles," I explain.

"Tootles?"

"The photographer."

"Oh. Well, what are they saying?" she presses.

"I'd tell you if you'd just let me eavesdrop like a real friend," I hiss.

"Becca never wanted to model," Hale tells Tootles. "She was really against it, even though I know she would have gone far."

"Why?" Tootles asks.

"She just wanted something different, is all," Hale says.

He keeps his voice easy, giving nothing away, even though he knows the truth.

"Well?" Trin says.

"Tootles was telling Hale I missed my calling as a model," I say, keeping my voice low. "Hale told him I wasn't interested."

"But that's not exactly true, is it?" Trin asks.

Like Hale, Trin knows what really made me run screaming from that business. "No," I agree. I start to laugh, recalling events I haven't thought about in years. "Remember when we used to practice posing?"

"After every America's Next Top Model episode and sometimes even during," Trin says, laughing. "You were always really good at keeping still and striking those poses that were so uncomfortable. They looked natural when you performed them."

I laugh. "And you were always good at the action shots, sugar."

"That's because I'd get bored standing still. I remember doing jumping jacks and squats in between my so-called modeling."

"Oh, stop," I say. Trin is the cutest thing ever. She always was. We both worked so hard that summer, trying to get our bodies just right so we could convince our mothers to take us to an agent.

"You were going to be the next big thing," Trin reminds me.

"No, we were," I remind *her*.

"Or so we thought," I add, quieting.

Our mothers were never close, despite the constant interaction between Trin and me. Miss Silvie was always tending to her children, her husband, or her garden, or raising money for people who desperately needed saving. Momma was always busy being seen at the right events with all the right people. She served on the board for several charities, but I recognized at a young age it was all about representing the family and looking good, not about helping others. That day, though, the one Trin and I spent preparing for, was my first real look at the life I was headed for.

We bought a white runner, the paper kind they used to cover the aisles during weddings. We had a runway show to put on and we couldn't have a show without a runway. Trin and I had so much fun setting up the Christmas lights on either side, decorating the rows with flowers and bows, and keeping the boys away. Her brother Landon was nice enough to help us set up a curtain and her father helped us with all the things we couldn't reach.

Our mommas weren't allowed to see anything until show time. Miss Silvie clapped, "ooh'd" and "ahh'd" in all the right places. She didn't make a fuss about us dirtying her sheets and she praised our creativity. She didn't even seem to notice all the times Trin fell and how she had to drag most of the ill-fitting clothes behind her.

Momma didn't notice Trin at all. She was so pleased with me. So happy. I've never seen her so proud. For the first time, I thought she was seeing me and my knack for becoming anything I put my mind to.

When our show wrapped and we finished tidying up, it was late. Momma rushed me to the car, fussing with my hair and excited to tell Daddy.

"We'll have to set up interviews in Charlotte. Maybe even New York, once we get a few head shots. Oh, Becca," she gushed. "You're going to be a model!"

I laughed, giddy. Until she said what she did.

"When word gets out you are a professional model, you'll have your pick of any young man at the club."

"What?" I asked.

She stopped listening. "You know that political function we're invited to every year in Washington? The one the wives of GOP congressmen and senators put together? They're normally so tired and overdone, but it's good for connections. One never knows when one might need a favor."

"Uh-huh," I said, already fearing where she was headed.

"Families are always invited," she stressed. "Sons, especially, who are interested in political careers." She glanced at me. "I never thought you were ready to interact among political giants. But you've proved me wrong, Becca June. Now, you have something to offer."

She meant she had someone worthwhile to offer them.

"This could be your chance to meet your future husband." She gasped. "One day, you could even become First Lady. Can you imagine? *My daughter*, the wife of the president of the United States."

My gaze drifted away from my mother and it took all my strength not to break down. Modeling wasn't my future. I knew it then. In those few minutes in the car with my mother, it became another talent to add to my resume, to make me attractive for a man and a future I didn't want.

"I don't want to be a model, Momma," I told her, immediately crushing her dreams and mine. "Trin and I were just playing. It was a project. Nothing more."

"Don't be ridiculous, Becca June," she said. "This is obviously something you're good at."

"It was just a stupid game," I said. "Something to do to pass the time."

Momma looked back and forth from me to the road. Her shoulders slumped dramatically. "Then why did you waste my time?"

"Your Momma didn't mean to be so cold," Trin says, hauling me away from another painful memory. "She just never knew any better. In her mind, she was being a good momma by trying to give you the best chance to meet a good man."

"But Nana June wasn't like that," I tell Trin. "She was more like your momma, caring more about her family than what anyone thought of her."

"I know," Trin says. "Our parents have the strongest influence on us. They're there from the start, molding us into what we'll become or helping us become something entirely different. The life your momma chose was the right and best one, as far as she was concerned. And because it was, she wanted that life for her child. It didn't matter that you deserved better. In her mind, she was doing right by you."

"I understand what you mean, but because of what happened that day and how I gave it all up, I held you back and I feel terrible about it." I'm not exaggerating. Trin dropped her pursuit of modeling once I told her what happened with Momma.

"No worries, Becca," Trin says. "It was all for fun and I only had fun when I was doing it with you. Besides, they usually prefer tall women, less freckles, and fewer squats down the runway."

I want to laugh, but my focus lifts toward the tiered ceiling and the alternating tones of blue and white. Kiawah was supposed to stir memories for Hale. But here I am, watching as they circle my mind. I don't have great memories of my family, but I always do of Trin.

"Thanks, Trin."

The front door opens and shuffling ensues as Hale and Tootles load up the van. It's only when it shuts that I tell Trin about the ring.

"He gave you his momma's ring?" she asks, her voice quiet and her thoughts drifting her away. "The one his daddy gave his momma the day he was born? Goodness, Becca."

"It wasn't like that," I say.

"It was like something," Trin points out. "You're getting closer. More so than either of you probably thought."

"I hope you're right. I can't stand the thought of losing him again."

"Becks . . . you sound so sad."

"I am. Mostly I'm scared. Hale's intense. That carefree boy we knew is long gone."

"Hale was always intense," Trin reminds me. "I mean, for the most part he was laid back and level-headed, unlike Sean, bless his heart. But when things were serious, be it on that football field or when push came to shove and one of us was hurting, that intensity always slammed its way through like a herd of wild horses."

"This time it was different." I try to explain. "You weren't there, Trin. You didn't see how he . . . *took me*."

"I didn't have to be there," Trin says. "Y'all got pictures. Don't you be thinking I won't be ordering a few eight by tens."

I laugh out loud.

"It might even be our Christmas card this year."

"Trin!"

"Nothing says Merry Christmas like a picture of your best friend's backside as she walks toward your other best friend, naked in bed. All I need to do is add, 'Hugs and kisses, the Sawyers,' and I'm all set."

I cover my face, laughing, the last of my stress erasing. Well, most of it, anyway.

Hale is almost done helping Tootles. I can't hide in here with Trin forever, but there's more I need to tell her.

"Do you know what happened with Hale's parents?" I don't outright discuss the affair. I just give her a nudge. Of course, she knows exactly what I mean. Trin keeps a lot of our secrets. This time, I wish she hadn't.

"He told me when I came home from the Peace Corps," she admits quietly. "He said he'd planned to write me and tell me about it. But he couldn't discuss something like that in a letter."

"You never told me," I say. "Trin, this was something I needed to hear long before now."

"Becca," she says gently. "It wasn't my story to tell."

"I know," I agree. "I'm not mad at you. I just wish I'd known. I could have been there for him. Instead I screwed things up and wasn't sure how to make it right."

"You weren't going to repair your relationship just because I told you something bad about his family, Becks. I love y'all. You know I do. But the people you are today are not the same people who left each other under those awful circumstances. And, if I'm being honest, I don't think either of you were ready for each other back then."

"We were going to make love," I say, remembering how much I wanted to. "I realize it sounds stupid to say it like that, but it wasn't going to be just sex. Not with Hale."

"I know. Y'all have loved each other forever. As friends first and maybe more now."

There was no "maybe" about it. But even to Trin I can't admit as much yet.

"It was a rough night," she says, thinking out loud. "Lots of goodbyes we weren't ready for. It played on our emotions and damaged us a little on the inside. For you to say you were going to make love, well, how could it have been anything else? Both of you needed healing and sought it through intimacy."

"I wasn't thinking about healing anything," I confess. "I just wanted him. I still do."

"I'm not saying you weren't physically ready to connect," Trin adds. "But I am saying there was an emotional component that was missing that would have tainted the experience. That night, we were all about growing up for good and moving on forever. None of us were sure we'd keep in touch. Even as well as we've remained friends, it hasn't been like we originally planned."

"We were all supposed to buy houses next to each other," I say, thinking back to the promise we'd made when we were little. "Our houses were going to be right next to each other. In the center. Hale, Mason, and Sean would be on either side of us."

"So they could watch over us," Trin finishes for me.

"Yes," I agree. "Or maybe so we could keep them out of trouble."

She laughs, the sad, quiet laugh that tender memories like these bring. "It's been hard having my babies grow up with everyone so far away. But, in a way, we've all benefited from the distance."

"How so?" I ask, knowing how much the friendship between the five of us changed when we moved away.

"Becks, as much as I hated that we all went our separate ways, everything I experienced prepared me to be a better wife and mother . . . just like all you and Hale went through together and apart prepared you for each other."

There's no gentle teasing to her voice. She's being honest and telling me what I need to hear.

"You think we're ready for each other now?"

"I hope so, Becks. You want to be there for him and prove your friendship, and make up for the years lost between you? I can't think of a better time than now. Hale needs you."

"I know," I agree quietly. "I wasn't sure we'd ever happen."

"Are you serious? Becca, I've seen how Hale looks at you. We all have. Those eyes he gives you are that of a man who never forgot you."

My eyes tear. "I hope so."

"I hope so, too," she says. "That emotional component that was missing so long ago? It's not missing any longer. I just hope you and Hale are finally ready for it."

Chapter Thirteen

Hale

"Y'all want some chicken?" Both dogs wag their tails at me as I stand by the fridge. They say dogs can't understand much past their names and a few simple commands, but I've never met a dog who didn't perk up at the word chicken.

I reach for the first of three rotisserie chickens Trin left in the fridge. I'm not certain how much that woman thinks I eat, but if the zombie apocalypse hits, I'm throwing the zombies a few of these fuckers.

I shred the chicken with my hands and pop it into two bowls. I look up when I hear Becca yelling from the bedroom. She's all worked up. I heard her on the phone earlier with Trin. I couldn't hear what she was saying, but I recognized that voice she always gets when she talks to her. It's a comfortable tone, safe, like when you know you're in a good place.

It's not the voice she's using now. Her phone rang as I was headed into the kitchen. I think it was roughly two point five seconds before the yelling began.

I wash my hands, wondering a little too hard about who has her so riled. I liked her talking to Trin. They must have discussed me and Becks at length. Women do that. It put me in a damn fine mood until the screaming began.

I dry off my hands when my phone rings. "You all right?" Sean asks.

I peer in the direction of the guest suite. "Yeah. Made out with Becca naked."

"It's about damn time," he says. "Later."

"Later, Sean."

Yeah. Becca and Trin probably analyzed every last detail of our kiss. What it meant. What it'll lead to. Me and Sean? I grin. We just got right to it, didn't we?

"You will not tell me what to do, ever," Becca shouts. "I don't belong to you, you little bitch!"

She throws open the door, startling when she sees me watching her. "Oh, hey," she says, fluffing her hair.

"Problem?" I ask.

She glares at her phone when it buzzes and shuts it off. She clears her throat, walking toward me with her head high and about the best "fuck life" strut I've ever seen. "Just taking care of a few things at work."

"Oh, all right," I say, not believing one damn word. "You hungry?"

She does a double-take when she sees the cheese plate I created. Brie, goat cheese, parmesan, big circle of Vermont white cheddar, and a multitude of little crackers. Don't be too impressed. Trin bought it. All I did was transfer it to a cutting board.

"I'm impressed," she says.

"You should be." I give her a wink. "I have mad skills, woman."

She covers her mouth, laughing, but doesn't quite conceal that blush.

"Let's go outside. It's a beautiful day." I frown when she hesitates. "What's wrong?"

"I'd like to go outside with you." She places her phone on the counter. "But I can't stay. There are a few issues I'm dealing with that require my immediate attention."

"All right," I walk toward the terrace, unsure if she'll follow. She does, which gives me hope, at least a little.

The lovesick puppies hurry behind her. Can't blame them. I'd do the same.

I take a seat in front of the fire pit, debating whether or not to start a fire. The wind is strong enough to lift Becca's hair off her shoulders, but the sun is winning the fight in terms of warmth.

"I can't stay long," Becca says when she sees me eye the stack of wood.

"So, you said." I pop a slice of cheddar and a cracker in my mouth, narrowing my eyes when the dogs get a little close to the food. "Don't even think about it," I tell them.

The moppy dog immediately lays down. The little one with the barrettes just sits. I'm guessing she's the brains behind Operation Let's Steal the Cheese, but it's just a guess.

"Where did you get these mutts, anyway?" I ask.

"The shelter," Becca says. She takes a seat beside me, appearing sad. "Miss Silvie started a program with them. She takes the calmer and more manageable dogs to the nursing home every Tuesday to interact with the elderly residents. It keeps up their spirits."

"The seniors or the dogs?" I ask.

"Likely both," she says, smiling. "These were the two she recommended for the shoot."

I toss a cracker in the air. The moppy one catches it, just barely out of reach of the little one. "Why?" I ask. "Out of what has to be a wide selection of dogs, what made her suggest this mismatched pair?"

"According to Miss Silvie, they've had it the hardest and need the most love."

Well, doesn't that say it all?

The little one pops onto Becca's lap when she makes a kissy sound. Damn lucky dog. I'd do the same if Becca puckered up. She laughs, cuddling the dog and stroking her head. "I wasn't ready for a dog, but I don't see how I'm going to let this little princess go."

"She likes you," I point out when she wags her tail. "Can't really blame her."

Becca blinks back at me, smiling, but not quite in the way that covers her sadness. "What kind of dog is it?" I ask, trying to distract her.

"Part Maltese, part poodle, and likely part Cavalier. The volunteers at the shelter aren't entirely sure. The big dog, they think, is a Golden Retriever and Saint Bernard mix. There's also standard poodle in there.

Moppy rests his head on my lap. "I can see the Golden in him for sure, and the Bernard because he's a big guy. But you lost me on the poodle. Where did they get that?"

"He doesn't shed," Becca says, leaning in to stroke his ears. "But he is due for a haircut, poor thing."

Moppy thumps his tail at Becca's soft tone. "What happened to them?" I ask.

"What didn't happen to them?" she says, making a face. "Both had mange and were starving when they were found near Bowman. They had to pull buck shot out of Twinkles' hide."

"Jesus," I say, scanning the length of the big furry bag of fluff. Whoever shot him couldn't have mistaken him for a wolf or coyote. But whoever did it is an asshole. "I can't fathom that shit."

"I know," Becca says. "People can be so cruel."

The dog looks up at me, his eyes twinkling. I suppose that's how he earned his name. He wags his tail harder when I smile at him. He knows I like him. "You said they were found together?"

"Yes," Becca says, her voice quieting. "They were always seen together, but the rescue doesn't seem to think they were from the same home. Twinkles was worse off, like he'd been exposed to the elements for a lot longer. Anarchy was slightly better nourished. The townsfolk said they'd see the big one feeding the little one." She shrugs. "They seemed to have found each other when they needed each other most."

I take a chance. "Kind of like us?" I ask.

Becca's smile is warmer. The kind I most love on her. "Yes, kind of like us."

"I'm keeping the dog," I say.

"What?" she asks.

"You heard me," I tell her. "He likes me. His name shall be Sam."

"Sam?"

"Why does that shock you? Sparkly eyes or not, no dog of mine is going to be named Twinkles."

She looks from me to Sam, unsure if I'm messing with her. "Hale, this is a lot of responsibility."

"I know. But I've wanted one for more years than I can count. Besides, he likes me just fine." I grin. "You think Miss Silvie will put in a good word for me?"

"She will, but . . ." Becca glances out to the ocean. "Are you sure, Hale? This is a good place to have a dog. But what's going to happen when you go back to New York?"

"I'll take him with me." I mean what I say. "I was playing with him on the beach during the shoot. Throwing a stick, that sort of thing. He likes to run. I do, too. My place is big enough. It should work out just fine."

I motion to the prissy dog. "What about that one?"

Becca cuddles her closer, growing protective. "What about her?"

"You think you'll keep her?"

She considers the question, glancing back at Sam. "I don't think we should separate them."

"What's that supposed to mean? Where are you going?"

"To Charlotte," she says. "I'll be gone a few days, settling some things that need settling."

"That's not what I meant," I say. "I was referring to you and me."

"Are you talking about our kiss?" she asks, her attention on the dog's head.

She's feeling shy. I'm not. "You mean the hot one we had in bed naked?" I turn around as if I can see the bedroom and hook a thumb. "That one in there, when we were feeling each other up."

She covers her face. "We didn't feel each other up."

"But we wanted to. Didn't we?"

The wind picks up, sweeping her hair to the side and away from her face. When it settles, I don't think her hair could lie across her shoulders like it does any better had I'd touched it myself. A gull caws overhead, peering across the dunes as if it sees something it likes. Another caw, and then another gull appears. It joins the first as they dive down into the sand.

It takes the wind sweeping in again before Becca answers me. "I wasn't expecting this," she says.

"You think I was?" I ask. "It's only been a month since you fluttered back into my life, waving your arms and pelting me with glitter."

"I didn't flutter," she says, grinning.

"Strut?"

She laughs. "Maybe. But there was definitely no glitter. That's a Trin thing to do."

"All right. Let me clarify. It's only been a month since you strutted into my life, swinging your hips just so and tempting me closer until I gave in to you and your nymph-like charm, and kissed you hard like you wanted and deserved." I smirk at her gaping mouth. "There. Was that better?"

"I didn't strut . . . much."

"Yeah, you did," I say. "You have ever since you learned to walk in dem heels."

"And I don't have nymph-like charm," she protests.

I throw my head back, laughing. "No, you don't. You come across as fine and sweet as sugar until you open your mouth and cuss viciously enough to send a drunken sailor staggering off and screaming."

"That's better," she says, seemingly satisfied.

My smirk fades, just a little. "Except when it came to me. In there," I say jerking my head in the direction of the house. "You've always had this hold on me, Becks. But I don't really think you've understood just how bad."

"I might understand," she says gently.

The way her gaze meets mine erases what remains of my smirk. This woman has me where she wants me, but she always has. After all these years, I still don't think she knows just how easily I gave her my heart.

"Hale . . . I have to tell you something." She adjusts her hold on her pup and reaches for a cracker. She tries to take a bite, but thinks better of it, offers it to the dog instead. "It's about Denver. Mr. Singleton's son."

I'll give Becca this, she's always delivered a good kick to the balls. "You're still with him." I huff, a bitter grin cutting into my skin. I rub my jaw. "You let me kiss you like that and you're with some other man?"

She smiles. *Smiles.* What the fuck?

"I was never with him. That's the part you don't understand." She looks down, appearing sad. It takes me a second to realize it's not so much sadness she feels, but rather shame. "I've had to do a lot for the Cougars. Most of it has been positive. But there are some things I've done I never would have entertained before."

"Like Denver?"

Hurt reflects in her irises, making me want to kick my own ass, regardless of how hurt I am in return. "Sorry. I should have guessed he was something special if you planned on marrying him."

"I never loved him, Hale," she says. "I never slept with him. I've barely stomached his kisses."

I frown, a mix of confusion and fury building in my gut. "Then why were you engaged to him?" She dips her chin, focusing more on the dog than I wish she would. "Becca, please look at me." It takes her a moment, but she does. "Why were you engaged to him?"

"He was in trouble, Hale. Lots of it. I can't go into too many details. I'm already violating my contract as is."

"Your contract?" I repeat, hardly believe what I'm hearing.

"It's an NDA, a non-disclosure agreement," she explains. "The Cougars were messed up when I first took over. They continued to screw up until I convinced the owner, Mr. Singleton, to make some serious changes."

She smiles down at the little pup when it starts to fall asleep on her lap. "The more I had to do to alter the team's reputation, the more I appeared in the public eye. The way the fans, commentators, and athletes took to me was a blessing. They liked me, and I became as much of a prominent member as their best players. It pleased Mr. Singleton in all the wrong ways. Denver was his only son, but lots of trouble. He did a lot of really bad things, soiling the new team's good name. Mr. Singleton thought Denver needed a good woman at his side. Someone the public adored and trusted."

"Someone like you?" I offer.

She sighs. "I didn't want to do it and flat out refused. I did some research and found an actress willing to pose with him and play fiancée for very large sum. Everyone was on board except Denver. He told his Daddy he wanted me and wouldn't pretend for anyone else."

"Nice." Sam drops a large paw on my knee. He feels my pain. This arrangement is about as fucked up as it sounds.

"Don't be mad, Hale. I'm not proud of what I did."

"I'm not mad. At you." I let out a breath. "Okay, maybe I am a little. I just don't see how you'd agree to something as sleazy as this."

"I saw it as part of my job and nothing else, but . . ." She adjusts her position, her hand never leaving her small companion. "You have to understand, Hale. My job became my life. I wasn't dating. There was no one in my life except for Trin, who's four hours away. So, instead of pouring myself into a glass and swallowing my misery, I poured myself into my work."

I hold out a hand, interrupting her. "Wait. I saw how all those players were panting after you. How close they stood and how much closer they wanted to be. You trying to tell me you never dated them?"

She raises her brow, a flicker of amusement dancing across her features. "I'm not telling you they didn't try. But I wasn't interested in more drama. I was trying to fix it."

"Then why Denver?"

"I told you. He was something to fix. Another part of my job that I needed to take care of." She shrugs. "We posed for kisses in front of the camera. We held hands and were seen at important events. But the moment we left the 'stage,' as I called it, I kept my distance from him."

"Did he keep his distance?" I ask. I'm not trying to be a dick. I'm just saying Becca is beautiful and damn near impossible to resist.

"No," she says. "He expected a lot more than a simple arrangement and had a hard time taking no for an answer." She makes a face. "That was him on the phone. For someone I never really belonged with, he certainly thinks I belonged to him."

If he was here, I'd break him in half. "I'm happy to talk to him and let him know that's not true."

"I'm sure you would, Hale, but this is not what either of us needs. We were supposed to be engaged a lot longer than we were, but then—" She curses under her breath. "This is more than I should be telling you."

"Tell me anyway."

Becca seems ready to burst with the truth. But I know her. She's wrestling between her loyalty to me and the team she's committed to defending. "Mr. Singleton wanted me to marry Denver. Denver did, too. They offered me a ridiculous sum of money to pose as his wife. It was then I came to terms with how desperate they both were. So, instead of continuing this pretense of love and respect, I gave the ring back."

"Where do you stand now?" I ask.

She rolls her eyes. "With a very pissy ex fake fiancé and a boss demanding I return to Charlotte and do right by him."

"You're leaving," I say. I'm not really asking. She made it clear from the moment she sat.

"I fix things." She smiles. "But I'm not leaving you, I swear it."

There are several things that infuriate me about this scenario. The main thing is the position I find myself in now. If I had what I had in New York, I'd tell Becca to quit and that I would take care of her. It's the same damn thing I promised all those years ago, but I learned the hard way all it would do is pry us apart.

The other things annoying the fuck out of me are those shitty excuses for human beings thinking they own her, or can buy her for a price. "You told me you never wanted to depend on another man again," I remind her. "What's the difference here?"

All at once she bristles. "I don't depend on them. They depend on me. The only thing I'm guilty of is being overcommitted to my job."

"This isn't work, Becca. Not when they're expecting more from you than the normal nine to five."

"I know." She looks out toward the ocean. The waves are starting to slow their rough caress against the sand. Better weather is ahead, but I'm not sure there'll be better times to match. Not with what the Singletons have planned with Becca.

"When I was in school getting my degree, it was all about making the clients happy, making them look good, and protecting them at all costs," she says. "The profs and career professionals who mold and shape you don't tell you about the white lies that have the potential to turn into storms, or what it takes to do a job well and still hang tight to what remains of your soul."

"It's not your soul I'm worried about," I say. "That and your heart were always your most attractive traits."

"Not my dual personalities?" she asks, motioning at her breasts as a bitter laugh escapes her pretty mouth.

"Now, don't you go putting the girls down," I say. "They've done the best they can to lead you right."

We laugh, this time meaning it. But the conversation is too heavy. It doesn't take much for that shame to return and make me see how much of her soul Becca's had to protect. "Would you leave your job if it came down to it?" I ask.

Her face softens in a way that breaks my heart. "I would do that and more if it meant helping you."

I move faster than I think is humanly possible, scaring the dog off her lap as I gather Becca in my arms. We fall back into my chair, kissing like it's our last moment while our hands drag over our bodies as if time is all we have.

Each taste, each tease, is sweet and possessive. I brand her as mine with each flick of my tongue while her lips press mine hard, leaving no doubt I belong to her alone.

I don't remember ever needing to kiss a woman like I do with Becca. I need every part of her, just not in the way that she thinks.

She clutches me, like she's scared of what's coming and that I alone can keep her safe. I hate her being afraid and reassure with my shielding embrace that no one will harm her with me by her side.

My rough fingers massage down her back. I want to feel more than the thick knitted sweater she's wearing. She gasps when I slide my knuckles down her lower back, teasing her bare skin. She likes what I'm doing, not fully comprehending how much hotter I can make her.

She groans softly as my teeth graze over her throat and behind her ear. We kiss. We touch. We make out like the teenagers we were so long ago. I want her and want to do so much more. But I won't allow things to turn to shit. Not this time.

I'm not sure how much time passes. But the change in position of the shadows against the terrace tell me it's been a nice, long while. All we did was kiss and here we are, ready to take it to the next level. How did everything between us turn out as bad as it did when we shared all this sweetness from the start?

I cup her face, my desire reflecting in her glazed eyes and the way her breathing releases in quick spurts. "Why didn't you tell me about Denver before I saw that ring on your finger?"

"I wanted to," she whispers. "But things were already, strained, between us. I was stuck with this contract. I wasn't expecting you that night and then . . . then you wouldn't speak to me."

"Did you tell Trin?"

She presses her lips, not wanting to admit what she does. "She kept a lot of our secrets. But I'm not so certain that's a good thing. If she were more of a blabbermouth, maybe it wouldn't have taken us so long to find our way back to each other."

"I don't know about that. You're a stubborn little thing."

She throws back her head, laughing.

My hands travel down to her waist and I give her hips a squeeze. "I want this, you hear me? I want us together."

"I do, too." She licks her lips, holding on to the taste of me a little longer. "I used to worry about it screwing up our friendship."

"Becks, we did that just fine without getting together."

She blinks back what I hope aren't the start of fresh tears. "It's been a shitty few years without you."

"It might be a shitty few more years with me," I tell her. I don't want to think like I do, but I owe it to both of us to be honest. "Becca, if for some reason the Feds throw in some bogus evidence just to save face—"

"Don't." She tries to pull away from me. I don't let her get far. "I don't want to hear you talk this way."

"Good. I don't like talking this way. But Becks, as much as I'm innocent, as much as I'll fight this, and as much as my team is swearing up and down that I'll get off, if I am found guilty, I'm looking at a few years, minimum."

Her head falls against my chest. I gather her close, trying to comfort her. She needs it more than me. "Nothing can happen to you, Hale. We have the best legal team money can buy. We have the pictures and the spread all planned out. Every magazine that matters is going to show the world that you returned to your throne. That in spite of all these bogus charges and sloppy work on the side of the Feds, you were innocent and all the lies are behind you."

"Twinkles did take some mighty fine shots."

"Tootles," she murmurs.

"I know," I say. "I just wanted to see you smile."

"I will when all this is over."

We hold each other for a long time. We finally see red and gold burn in the horizon, showing us our first hint of sunset. Our two pups sit near our feet, panting and waiting to see what's next.

I whistle, calling them to us, so me and Becks can give them some of our love.

Love? Damn. Is that what all this has been with her? I shake my fool head. Must be so, for us to hurt as bad as we did apart and to heal as easily as we're starting to.

"You sure you have to go?" I ask.

"For now," she says. "I have some fires to put out, a fake ex-fiancé to shut up, and a bullheaded boss to placate."

"They can't pay you enough for that shit," I mutter.

"It's something that has occurred to me more than once," she admits. "When we get back, I want to work on your 60 Minutes interview."

"What?"

"Or the one for Anderson Cooper. I haven't decided which one will air first yet."

"*What?*"

She nibbles on her lip, trying not to laugh. "Hale, I told you. You hired the best."

"We've never discussed payment." I waggle my eyebrows. "However can I make this up to you?"

"With kisses," she says. Her fingers trace over my lip. "And more when I get back."

"How much more?" I ask, flashing her a lopsided grin.

She teases the arch of my ear with her nose. "Enough to make me glad I'm on the pill."

"Nice," I say, taking a nip of her chin. "Just as a public service announcement, I'm clean as whistle and more than happy to prove as much."

She moans softly when I kiss her neck. "Same, but now isn't the time to show you."

"Huh?" I ask, my hands immediately stopping over the snap of her jeans.

"Hale, things are so screwed up in Charlotte. As much as I want to stay here, all night, I have to go." She glances down briefly. "And the last thing I want is to rush this."

I watch my hand as it splays across the soft denim of her jeans, not wanting to let her go, but not being too much of a selfish bastard to realize that, for now, she has to. "I don't want you to go. But I won't make you stay. When we make love, I want it to last. I want to take my time and make you feel good. I want to wake up with your bare skin pressed against me." I stroke back her hair. "I want you to scream my name in pleasure and beg me to give you more, just like I've always dreamed you would."

Her voice is thick with surprise and desire. "You don't just want to have sex? You want to make love to me?"

"What else would you call it?" I murmur.

I speak the Gospel truth. Becca was never a woman I could fuck. She was always Becca, my beautiful friend and the woman I've desired since I first realized what it means to want someone.

"I call it really hard to leave you now," she says, falling against my shoulder. "God, Hale, I really wish I could stay.

My body relaxes as hers does. I cradle her in my arms, not wanting to move. After a while, I start to drift, thinking she's already asleep. "Are you sure about the dogs?" she asks.

I chuckle. "Dogs?" I ask. "I'm only offering Samson the Mighty here a place to live."

She lifts her head. "Hale," she says, her smile content. "You can't keep these two apart. Not after what they went through."

My fingers thread through her hair and I pull her closer for another kiss, passing my lips over hers so tenderly I barely feel them skim over mine. "You're right," I say, my voice as soft as my gaze as it melts into hers. "Some souls were always meant to be together."

Chapter Fourteen

Hale

I woke up smiling today. My business is in ruins. I have the feds trying to make a case out of shit that ain't there. Oh, and Sean has some kind of rash on his ass he was more than happy to go into detail about. Again. I can't help my smile and it's all due to Becca.

From the foot of the bed, two dogs wag their tails at me. "Y'all ready to go out?"

More tail wagging followed by an excited sneeze from Sam. Becca decided to name her dog Rosie, 'cause that's how the little thing makes her feel. Personally, I think she should have left it Anarchy, but that's me.

I pull on a pair of sweatpants and a long-sleeved gray shirt, stretching as I walk toward the bathroom and, yeah, thinking about Becca. It was after midnight when she made it back to Charlotte. We talked on the phone as she drove, laughing about things I haven't thought about in years and talking about making more memories. It was a sweet call. Almost as sweet as our kisses on the terrace and the one I gave her before she slipped into her car.

Yesterday, we didn't speak as much. She had meetings to attend and a shit ton of people to placate. But she still called and I still heard her voice and her laughter. It's enough for now, but I'm still counting the minutes until she returns.

I open the sliding doors that lead out to the beach, allowing the dogs to race ahead of me. I get a good stretch in and start my run, kicking up sand and sending it to ghost in the air. The dogs chase after me, jumping up to play before falling into a steady pace beside me. I don't know if there's a leash law or a license these dogs are supposed to wear around their necks. I'm not even entirely sure they won't run away. But they seem smart enough to stay beside me.

I chuckle as I run. From the day we returned to Kiawah, I started moving full speed ahead with Becca. I haven't been down here ten days and here we are, making out like real lovers should, adopting dogs, and talking about having a future together. I won't complain, although at times, it feels too good to be true.

The dogs and I are out of breath when we decide to turn around to head back. Sam keeps up just fine, but the run was too much for Rosie's little legs. I scoop her up, carrying her all the way back to the house.

I feed them more chicken and fill the Tupperware bowls I scrounged up with more water. I'm just starting on making breakfast when the phone rings and Becca's face lights up the screen.

I answer the phone and turn up the volume. "Well, hey," I say.

"Good morning, baby," she says.

"Mornin'," I reply. "You all right? You seem tired."

"I was up late," she says. "How're Sam and my precious Rosie doing?"

"They're missing their momma," I say.

She laughs. "I miss them, too. They're cute. Oh, how did we end up with them again?"

"We really didn't. We were actually accused of kidnapping."

She pauses. "Are you serious?"

"Yup. Turns out you're a wanted woman, Becca. Miss Silvie was out with Trin and the grandbabies all day yesterday. She didn't get your message until late and had to track down the shelter owner to assure her that, no, we hadn't eaten the big one and sent the little one to kick ass in the dog fighting ring."

"Oh, no. What a mess!"

"Expect wanted posters with your face on them upon your return."

She laughs. "Just make sure it's one of my windblown shots. Those are my favorite."

"They're mine, too," I murmur. "But them nudies are a close second."

"Mm," she groans. "I wish I was there with you."

"Same," I say. I toss Sam a slice of bacon he's more than happy to catch. The little one shuffles over to me, evidently still tired, but not too tired to scratch at my ankle and remind me I forgot to feed her. I hand her a strip, watching her floppy ears bounce as she returns to her spot on the floor.

"When are you headed back?" I ask. I wash my hands and pop in a piece of bread into the toaster, pausing when Becca doesn't answer right away.

"I'm hoping by Thursday night."

"Thursday?" I ask. "That's three days away."

"I know. Things aren't great here. Don't worry. Tootles and I are working on the spreads online. We already went through the one for Forbes."

"I wasn't worried about that. I'm worried about you." I add cheese to the eggs and stir, noting the strain in her voice. "What's going on?"

"You don't want to know."

I scrape the eggs onto the plate. "Yeah, I do."

"I'm getting a lot of pressure from Mr. Singleton to become re-engaged to Denver."

"Ah, why?" I ask, wishing it didn't come out in a snarl.

Becca groans. "He's in trouble again."

"Because he's a dumbass," I helpfully add.

"And narcissistic," she mumbles.

I fill my glass with water a little too aggressively and slam it down beside my breakfast. I take a breath, trying to cool down. I have to remember this isn't my home or my things. I need to respect them, just as I need to be respectful of Becca and not drive to Charlotte and break Denver's neck.

I grip my fork, although I can't seem to take a bite. That doesn't stop me from gritting my teeth. "What are you going to do?"

It's a nice question. A decent one. And a hell of a lot more polite than telling Becca her asshole boss and his even more asshole son can fuck off. See? This here is what's called growth and maturity.

"I'm trying to spin what Denver did as a man with a broken heart acting out."

I roll my eyes. "And how exactly did he act out?"

"Oh, another accident in his Lamborghini. But don't worry. He wasn't drunk. He just lost control, because the young, naked woman in his passenger seat was giving him head."

"As a man, I can respect that." I manage a decent chew and swallow when a thought occurs to me. "That young woman wasn't of age, was she?"

"He's not *that* bad. She's twenty-two, I think. In fact, blow jobs are one of her specialties, given she's worked as a high-priced prostitute for quite a few years now. That blow job cost him ten grand and a three-inch gash below his crown line."

"Nice," I say, wondering just how many times Denver was dropped on his head as a child. "So, tell me. How are you equating prostitutes and blow jobs to a grieving and jilted lover?"

"Funny you should ask. We weren't willing to pay off the prostitute this time."

"We weren't?" I ask, finishing up my eggs.

"No, because by the time she was released, she'd already contacted several magazines—the less reputable kind, mind you—and offered an exclusive for her near-death experience at the hands of Denver Singleton the eighth, or whatever the hell number he is, for two million dollars."

"Two million for ten minutes of head?"

"Three minutes. She's that good."

"Damn," I say. "I should've been a prostitute."

I'm trying to get a laugh out of her, given that the more Becca speaks, the shriller her voice becomes. "You know, it's bad enough this fuck-up got into yet another car accident, ripped through a park the Boy Scouts had cleaned that day, and attracted the attention of a crowd of two hundred seniors who were attending a symphony mere yards away. He had to go and hire a prostitute."

"No kidding," I agree.

"If she was smart, really smart, I could have hired her to play the new girlfriend and Charlie Sheened the shit out of all of it."

"Oh, don't go bringing Charlie into this. That boy's been through enough."

Becca is not laughing. Not even a polite chuckle. She's *pissed*. I grin, thankful she's not pissed at me.

"Charlie Sheen has made mistakes. Lots of them. But you know what? He owns his mistakes and all his crazy antics. So, instead of the world coming down on him, they excuse it away as part of his entitled Hollywood upbringing. Every last indiscretion Charlie was a part of never touched his father. Martin Sheen continued on as a well-respected and revered actor."

"I get it," I say. "So, if the prostitute had sense, she would have made big money. Denver would be able to embrace his inner bad boy without consequence, thereby permitting his father to keep his good name. In time, the elderly folks that Denver exposed his genitals to would forget the scandalous and cringe-worthy incident and chalk it up to another sordid tale of youth gone wild."

"Exactly. Damn, Hale, you're getting pretty good at this."

"But nothing went according to plan," I say. "So, what now?"

"Now, I have to try and make Denver look like the victim," she mutters.

I rinse my plate, not loving where this is going. "A victim of a broken heart, because you dumped him?"

"Yes."

"This doesn't make him look good, Becks. It makes you look bad."

"I know."

"Then, why do it?" I ask. "It's not like he's going to give up snorting his daddy's money up his nose and sign up for the priesthood."

"You're right, but . . ."

"But what, Becks?"

"Hale, I shouldn't be talking about this, but I'm so tired of looking bad."

"What are you talking about?"

I pad outside with a fresh glass of water. The dogs follow. Sam rests dutifully at my feet. Rosie jumps onto my lap, something I'm sure she wouldn't do if Becca was here. I stroke her ears, wishing like this pooch that Becca was far away from everything Singleton.

"Becca, what did you mean by what you said? From everything you told me, the public adores you."

"The public associated with the Cougars does."

"What?" I ask. "Becks, you have to tell me a lot more than this if I'm going to help." Becca makes this little sound. I barely hear it over the fuss the gulls are making and the increasing sound of crashing waves. "Are you crying?"

She doesn't answer, which is answer enough.

"Baby," I say. "I don't want you sad. Come home. Be with me. I'll make you happy."

"I know you will," she whimpers. "It's just . . . being in Kiawah with you has brought up a lot of memories. The ones surrounding us, and our friends are wonderful. The others, though, the ones outside our small group, they're just *awful*."

It doesn't take a smart man to guess what she means. "You mean the ones with your family?"

The silence that follows is deafening and so are her words. "Hale, Daddy's dying."

My hand stops over Rosie's head. She looks back at me, but I barely notice.

"He has colon cancer," Becca explains. "It spread, even with the experimental chemo he was receiving. Momma called me this morning to say he doesn't have more than a few weeks left."

"She wants you to come home, doesn't she?"

"She does."

"Is that why you're staying in Charlotte?" I ask.

"No. I have to fix this thing with Denver, somehow. But I won't lie. Momma telling me what she did is a good reason to stay away."

Jesus. She can barely bring herself to speak the words.

"It took a lot for me to leave my family. As much as it brought me tremendous relief, I couldn't just disappear. I'm the daughter of Wilton Shields, among the most revered and wealthy men of Kiawah Island. He couldn't let me go on my terms. Not the original King of Spin."

"What did he say about you?"

"It wasn't just him. It was everyone who carries the Shields name and wants to keep it. They started circulating rumors about me whoring around. That I started using cocaine. Don't you worry none, they tried to get me help. But being the spoiled, drug-addicted ingrate that I am, I refused. They tried everything to put me back on the right path. When they failed as a family and right-proper Christians, they had no choice but to let me go."

I rub my eyes. Becca went through hell and I wasn't there to see her through it. I drop my hand away. "Those rumors didn't stand a chance. You made a name for yourself working in PR and with the Cougars."

"You're forgetting, that took years," Becca says. "The family attributed my eventual success to their tough love tactics. It was only when word reached them how well I was doing that Momma finally contacted me."

"She was proud of you," I say, already knowing I'm giving her momma too much credit.

"We both know that's not true. It was *acceptable* for her to reach out to only because I hadn't screwed up like they'd expected, and because people were reaching out to her, making a big fuss. 'We saw Becca,' the ladies of the auxiliary gushed. 'So good to see she turned her life around.' They talked about me so much, Momma had no choice but to take credit and talk me up like she knew everything about my life. Like we were the best of friends, even though she never once tried to help me or see if I was okay."

"I know, darlin'. But even if she wanted to, your daddy wouldn't have let her."

"She still should have tried, Hale. I'm her baby. Her only child. And she didn't even know whether I had any food to eat."

She breaks down. I let her. Tears, especially Becca's tears, stab me in the heart and give a merciless twist. But those tears are needed to cleanse all the mud-slinging her family did. They're there to heal. I only wish I was there to hold her.

"Your daddy controls your momma," I remind her. I don't want to defend Becca's momma. But I also don't want Becca to hurt as much as does. "She was being a good wife by obeying and portraying herself as a Southern lady, one of prestige who keeps her husband happy. That didn't make her a good mother. It just made her a good wife in all the right social circles."

"I wanted her to be a good momma," Becca admits. "I can forgive her, to some extent, because she was an abused woman. I just wish I had one memory, *just one*, Hale, where she tried to protect or defend me. But she never did."

The sound of a tissue being pulled from a box echoes on the other end of the line. "Do you remember the night Daddy withdrew from the election?"

"When he was running for mayor?" I ask, shaking the memory awake.

"He told everyone he withdrew because a business opportunity had come up in France and he wasn't certain how available he'd be. The real reason was Momma's cousin was running, too, and Daddy knew he wouldn't be able to beat him."

I didn't know Becca's cousin well. But he was young and eager and loved by many.

"Daddy was in a mood and looking to take his anger out on someone," she says, continuing. "He didn't like that someone he considered less than him could possibly be better or beat him."

I pinch the bridge of my nose, knowing something bad is coming. "What did he do to you, Becca?"

Her voice shakes. "I'd gone out with you, Trin, and our boys to that festival in Charleston. Do you remember? It was our freshman year of high school. Landon had his license and drove us into the city."

"Yeah, I remember." I'd won her a giant bear. It was brown with a pink nose.

"He called me into his study the moment I came home, claiming I hadn't done my chores. I told him I had and he smacked me, accusing me of talking back to him. He hit me so hard, I crashed into the bookshelf."

"*What*?" I say, unable to get past the rage at hearing Becca had been attacked.

"Nana June was very frail and weak at that point in her life. But do you know what? She threw herself on Daddy's back when he came after me, scratching at his eyes and telling me to run. I ran up to my room. I didn't know where else to go. I heard Nana June, Daddy, and Momma going at it. Momma took Daddy's side and yelled at Nana for interfering." Becca sniffs. "Nana June came up to my room to check on me. She promised me Daddy would never hurt me again so long as she was around."

Becca doesn't remind me that her loving and feisty Nana June died a few months later. Nor does she acknowledge that when her safety net and protector was gone, she was left to defend herself. She doesn't have to.

"Nana June could have been seriously hurt and all Momma did was blame me for upsetting my father."

There are many words I have to describe Becca's parents. None of them are good. I keep them to myself. Becca doesn't deserve to hear them. No matter how bad, these people gave her life. For that I'm grateful. It's the only reason I'll respect them as much as I do.

"I get it," I say.

"Sorry?" Becca asks.

Lord, she seems so lost in her thoughts. "I'm letting you know I understand. You don't want to look bad in front of those who think so highly of you."

"Working for the Cougars has been the one place I've always looked good," she agrees quietly. "When my father goes, I'll look bad again. Even if I go to be by his side, my family will never paint me as the devoted daughter who returned home to dutifully hold her daddy's hand when he left the earth."

"Does this mean you're thinking about seeing him?" I ask. Shit. I really don't want her to.

"Only because I think I should."

"Why do you think you should, Becca?" It's a lousy thing to ask someone whose father is dying. But this man shaped her into the woman she is, not with a kind hand, but with a twisted and cruel mind. Wilton Shields was never a real daddy. Not like the one Becca deserved.

"Because, no matter what, he's still my daddy." She swallows hard. "Do you want to know something terrible about me? Something only Trin knows?"

"I want to know everything about you," I promise.

She makes a sound, this one more reminiscent of a choked sob. I loathe it. She doesn't deserve this agony.

"I've wished my daddy dead more than once."

Her words are final, like the door being slammed hard in a rude stranger's face. Except, I understand why she says them.

"He is a sick man. So angry at life. A man who's ignored all the good around him, because nothing was ever good enough. I thought his death would be the only way to free myself from this disgusting hold he has on me. But now, I don't know what to think. It's easier to turn my back and walk away. Goodness, Hale, it's probably the healthiest thing to do. But now that his death is quickly approaching, I don't think I can."

"Then don't. We'll go together."

Her breath trembles. "Baby, you know you can't come with me."

"I don't know that. I want to be with you, Becca. No matter what happens, I don't want you to go through this alone."

"Hale, it may be too soon to tell you this, but with you at my side, I feel like I can do almost anything. But this . . . this is the one thing I can't do with you."

I drag my hand through my hair, wrestling with what to say. "I'm not going to push you. I won't be that man. But I'm here for whatever you need, with your family, with all the shit out in Charlotte. Whatever you need, I'm here for you."

"Thank you," she says. "I . . . I miss you."

"I miss you, too." I almost say I love you. Almost. As much as I'm feeling it, I'm worried it's too soon for us. But given the years I have with this woman, it's not too soon to feel it.

I love Becca. I'm not sure when it happened but it did. I loved her first as friend. But I loved her as something more from that night we first kissed and our bodies fell against the sand.

I disconnect and call Mason. "How are we doing?"

"Really good," he says. "I was just about to call you."

"Yeah?" I stop in the middle of pacing. After my conversation with Becca, I thought I'd have to run a marathon to keep what she said from eating me alive. "How good?"

"Neesa was cleaning up some files, skimming through your contacts, that kind of thing. She saw something suspicious on an account and alerted the team. Turns out, someone broke into your system and altered your records."

"Who?" I ask. "Don't tell me it was the Feds."

"It wasn't them, because we're the ones who brought it to their attention." I can't see Mason, but I can picture him smiling. "Neesa, this amazing woman you call your PA, looked back at your schedule the day the file was uploaded. You couldn't have possibly done it. Turns out, you were attending some dinner at the Met."

"Are you sure?" I ask.

"No, but Neesa is. She keeps a detailed log of all your calls to her. She's produced copies going years back to when you first hired her."

I grin. "I told you she's the best. Now, tell me about the log."

"Neesa doesn't just write out what you say, she writes specifics surrounding the conversation. The log indicates you called her right before the sit-down dinner, complaining about all the dickheads that where there and asking her to set up a meeting with Tim Bradly from the Giants, since he was looking to invest. She wrote down the date and time and then set something up in your calendar. When we went back to look at the time you called and what you wanted—"

"It was the same time someone broke into my system," I finish for him.

"Exactly."

"Motherfucker," I mutter.

"That's right. We just have to pinpoint who the motherfucker is. My guess is that it's that little bitch informant and that he works for, or has worked for you."

Which narrows the playing field. "That's my best guess, too. Make it happen, Mason."

"Hale, we've got you."

I disconnect, racking my brain for who it might be. There were a lot of new hires looking to prove themselves and none too happy about the constructive criticism I was hitting their ivy league educations with. There were also a few I'd let go, because of poor work ethics. If we can figure this out, and figure it out quickly, I can get back to my life and start my new one with Becca.

The doorbell rings. I assume it's Trin with more food, and possibly Miss Silvie with real food for the dogs. I'm not expecting who I see.

"Hello, Hale," Pris says, smiling. "Aren't you going to let me in?"

What the fuck? "What are you doing here, Pris?"

I should shut the door. Right here, right now, and barricade it with furniture. I would even offer her a whole rotisserie chicken if it would make her go away. But for all Pris and me weren't good together, or for each other, I owe her a little courtesy.

She scoots under my arm before I've decided whether or not our conversation should take place indoors or outside where she can't throw anything at me. Never mind. There are decorative stones along the front yard. Besides, I've pretty much determined I can keep her away from the knives.

I follow her in, smirking when I see her stop dead in front of Sam and Rosie. I wouldn't call them watch dogs. They didn't even bark to tell me Timmy fell in the well, or even offer so much as a run for your life warning bark. Hell, with Pris here, trouble's definitely afoot. Can't they see that?

They scoot forward slowly. "Are you dog sitting?" Pris asks.

"Nope. They're mine." I almost said "ours," but I haven't had time to hide the knives.

"You bought a dog?" She takes a gander at Sam. She raises her eyebrows so high, they almost disappear beneath her mound of hair. "And then this other thing?"

She sounds pretentious, I know. Believe it or not, this is Pris at her kindest.

"Yup, two of them." I ruffle Sam's fur. "Isn't that right, buddy?"

My affection and easy way earn me a tail wag that quickly fades when he glances back at Pris. Sam doesn't strike me as the judgmental type, seeing what he's been through. That doesn't stop the judgmental stare he passes from the top of Pris's platinum hair to her leopard print dress and matching shoes.

I scratch the back of his ears. "Don't worry, boy. It's not real leopard," I assure him. At least, not this time.

Rosie seems to have a super power for charming the ladies. Don't get me wrong, I can picture her suffocating Pris in her sleep if she gets the chance. But for now, she gives her a small wag. She's not a pedigree like Pris is used to, but Rosie is damn adorable.

Pris scoops Rosie up, her Fendi purse smacking against her side as she looks around. "This is . . . cute," she says.

It's awesome, as far as I'm concerned, but Pris isn't here to shoot the shit. "You didn't answer my question. What are you doing here, Pris?"

Her shoes tap against the dark floors as she makes her way in. "What are you going to do with these creatures when you're locked up for twenty years?"

I rub my face. "Pris, you don't know what you're talking about."

"Yes. I. Do. I spoke to my attorney. You're too pretty to go to prison. Some asshole with a tattoo of his mother on his face is going to make you his bitch."

"That's the spirit," I mutter.

She sighs dramatically and walks away with my dog. I storm after her, visions of a new fur coat for Pris dancing eerily before me. "Pris? Where are you going with Rosie?"

"Who?"

"The dog, Pris."

"To the living room," she announces. She turns around, scowling just like she always does when I piss her off. "Why?"

"No reason," I say, keeping poor Sam behind me. He whines. I don't. I'm too busy eyeing the block of knives just a few feet away.

Pris lowers herself onto the couch, flips Rosie onto her back, and begins to rub. "You named her Rosie?"

Sam places his head on my lap when I sit across from her. I almost say, no, my girlfriend did. Except there are two very dangerous things about those words. One, Becca technically isn't my girlfriend. Not really. We've talked about giving us a chance. We've kissed a lot, one time naked, the other times with the promise of sex. But we've yet to make it official.

The second reason, and maybe the most important, is that Rosie is on Pris's lap. Uttering the words "my girlfriend" would result in Pris snapping Rosie's ears off with her teeth, barrettes and all.

"Hale," Pris says, growing impatient. "Why did you name her Rosie?"

"It fits her?" I offer, my statement sounding too much like a question given Rosie's predicament.

"I suppose it does," Pris says. Whatever I say placates her enough. Her belly rubs turn less meat-tenderizing and more tender.

"You never wanted a dog with me," she says.

"Huh?" It takes a while for what's she says to register. "Oh. That's not true. I almost got you a Golden Retriever once."

She stops petting Rosie, her hands dangerously close to the dog's throat. "You did?" At my nod, she shakes her head. "Figures. My preference is for lap dogs. Not that you'd know. And if you were truly getting me a dog, it was probably to shut me up for something that annoyed you."

Okay. I'll give her that one.

Pris scoffs, scanning her surroundings. "Damn it, Hale. What are you doing here?"

"I think the better question is, what are you doing here?"

Pris seems ready to cry. "I'm here for us."

"Don't do this, Pris," I say. "There was only ever an 'us' when you needed the company."

Her eyes darken, just as they always did when she thought we should get naked. I don't like it and it's not going to happen. "You seemed to enjoy my company in bed."

"How many?" I ask.

"How many what?"

"How many men enjoyed your company in bed while we were together?" I ask.

She laughs, bitterly, as if I somehow wronged her. "You first. How many women did you fuck when you were with me?"

"None," I reply, leaving no room for argument.

Her eyes widen. "You're lying."

"Nope," I say. Pris and me were always there for each other physically. That emotional piece never came, especially when I realized neither of us had it in us to give.

"Are you telling me the truth?" she says, her lips tightening into a line.

"Why would I lie?" I ask. "I know there were other men in your life. You took the time to shove them in my face every chance you had. It was the perfect excuse to fuck someone else. But I never did."

Her features turn sour and I almost expect one of her loud tantrums. Instead, her eyes well with tears. No crocodile tears this time. The real kind I've never seen.

"I just assumed that when you didn't want me, you wanted someone else."

"The only thing I wanted was to build my business," I say. "It's the only thing I ever wanted when I was in New York."

I pause, a thought occurring to me. "How did you find me?" I ask.

She wipes her eyes. "I have my ways."

Yeah. She does. She also has her fair share of connections.

Most of them on Wall Street.

Chapter Fifteen

Becca

I rub my eyes. I look like hell and I didn't bother with makeup. But maybe Hale will let me freshen up at his place. I smile. Despite all the horrid things I've dealt with in Charlotte, that smile is always there when I think of Hale.

My Bluetooth rings, but I'm too tired and unfocused to listen to who's calling.

"Becca Shields," I say.

"You left before we could talk."

I will not scream. I will not scream. I will *not* scream. "Denver, we've said enough."

"You don't get it." His voice changes from gruff to one I don't quite recognize. "I love you."

I roll my eyes. "You do not, Denver. And, Jesus, how many times have you used that line on a woman?"

"Look, I've made mistakes and I've been with other women. But only because you rejected me. You hurt me, Becca. No one's ever hurt me this bad."

If there was a wall within the confines of my vehicle, I'd beat my head against it. Better yet, I'd take it apart and throw a brick or two at Denver. "Denver, those women you've been with, especially the one taking you to court for whiplash or whatever the hell happens when you're giving head and take out a few trees, may swallow all you give them. I don't. This was all a charade."

"A charade you came up with," he barks back.

"No, shit," I snap. "How the hell else was I going to save your sorry ass? Those good people of Charlotte were kind enough to love me. To give me a chance. As the son to one of the most successful and popular teams in the league, you could have been a hero. I would have posed you with the team at every game—"

"Waving the team flag like some kind of trained monkey? Fuck that."

"No. Fuck you," I tell him, flatly.

"You have no idea who you're talking to," he warns.

"No. *You* have no clue what you have. Where you talk about being a trained monkey, I talk about supporting a team, making a name for yourself, molding you into a Mark Cuban."

"I'm not him!" he yells.

"You're right. He's a successful businessman who built that success from nothing," I snap. "He not only owns an incredibly popular team, he's brilliant and renowned. You could have been respected and admired like him, Denver. A few years of doing what I tell you, learning from your daddy, and keeping your nose clean, would be all it took. You could have been Mark. Your daddy would have given you the team and not thought twice. Now, what are you going to do? Spend whatever piddly inheritance he leaves you? Is that your grand plan?"

"I don't like being told what to do," he snaps.

"Neither does Mark, jackass. But he listened when he needed to. Learned everything taught to him and asserted himself when necessary. He's outspoken. He calls the shots. Everyone listens when he says jump, because he earned that right. All you ever talk about is everything you're owed and how life has been unfair."

"Is that why you never gave me a chance? I tried with you, Becca. Yeah, yeah, this whole engagement thing was a stunt, and one I was forced to be involved in. But then I got to know you and everything changed."

Jesus, take the wheel. "The only thing you tried to get to know about me was my body. Those dinners we attended? The events we appeared together? You were either leering at my figure, criticizing me for not dressing sexier, or looking at someone else."

"Daddy is going to fire you," he says.

He's no longer yelling. He's speaking the truth. I've pushed my agenda too aggressively with the Singletons. I know it and Denver does, too.

"Please, Becca. He doesn't want to humiliate you. But he will." He huffs when I don't reply. "If you don't want to do it for me, do it for the team and everything you've done to make it what it is."

I blink several times. This isn't Denver talking to talk or attempting to manipulate me. He's serious. Mr. Singleton will fire me if I don't do what he wants. I heard it straight from the big boss himself.

The first sign for Kiawah comes into view. I should feel a sense of elation, knowing I'll be in Hale's arms soon. But I'm no longer coming home a winner. If Mr. Singleton fires me, I'll be disgraced, just as I was when I first left. And with Daddy being as sick as he is, the last laugh will be on me. He'll leave this earth believing I failed without him.

"Becca. Come on," Denver says. "Just one chance, baby."

"I'm not your baby," I say. "And I need to do what's right."

I disconnect with him and wipe a tear. The large oaks stretch their long limbs, threading their branches to create an arch veiled with Spanish moss. I can maneuver blindfolded through these roads. I chuckle when I pass the fishing hole we'd visit as kids. Damn those gators. Poor Sean could have lost an arm.

My phone rings again. I only answer when I see it's Trin. "Hey, Becks. How are you?"

I try to keep my voice even. "I'm almost home." It's an odd thing to say, but it's my best answer.

"Oh, sweets, you sound tired."

"I am," I admit.

"Are you hungry, too? We just had brunch with Landon and Luci. We told everyone not to bring anything. Of course, both Momma and Luci did. It turned into a feast and I'm bringing leftovers to Hale's." She pauses. "Maybe you can eat together?"

I smile. "I'd really love that."

"All right. We'll be there as soon as the baby wakes up from her nap." She sighs. "Becks, you don't sound good. I know there's a lot on your plate. Is there anything you want to talk about?"

My voice breaks. "Not right now. It's just that, sometimes, it's really hard to do the right thing."

"I know," Trin says. "But even the hard things pass. Until they do or when they're at their hardest, you have me."

I ignore the tears that stream down my face. "I know."

"And don't forget, now you have Hale, too."

I laugh a little. "Yes. At least one thing is going right."

I disconnect with Trin with a promise to see her soon. This morning began at the crack of dawn. I managed a shower before I received a text from Mr. Singleton demanding I reconsider pulling off the fake wedding or, at the very least, another fake engagement.

The press isn't buying Denver's broken heart. They would have, if he hadn't gone out the night before and been photographed arriving at his million-dollar condo with yet another questionable woman. I told Mr. Singleton as much, slipped on a simple maxi dress and told him I was returning to Kiawah for the next few days.

He wasn't happy. Neither was I. Goodness, I was so worked up, I didn't even bother with decent shoes.

My spirits lift a little as I pull into the now familiar driveway. I tilt my head when I see a Porsche parked in front of his house. Mason. He must be there. He must have good news!

My sliders slap against my heels as I hop out of my car and hurry toward the house. Hale has seen me in worse, but if anyone can see past my disheveled appearance, it's him.

I ring the doorbell, practically jumping in place and ready to throw my arms around him.

The door opens and—

A woman. A blond woman. Wearing panties and my dog pressed against her breasts answers the door. Her hair is tussled, as if she tossed and turned all night and in every position possible.

Her very perfect eyebrows lift, revealing very perfect makeup and a face Denver would be more than happy to introduce to his lap. "Yes?" she says.

"Ergah?" I respond.

She laughs. "My apologies. You must be the maid." She walks merrily away, her bouncy butt cheeks poking through a semi-thong. "Don't mind me, feel free to get started."

I'm not sure how I walk in or if I walk straight at all. Never mind. I'm not walking. I'm storming, the door slamming hard enough behind me to rattle the windows.

I see red. No, this isn't red. It's a strobe light of magenta, orange, purple, and okay, red, too.

Like a queen, the blond falls into the comfortable couch. "Coffee?" she asks. "Yes, that sounds lovely. I take mine with just a splash of almond milk."

My pulse pounds through my head. "Almond milk?"

"*Yes*," she snaps, as if I didn't hear her the first time.

Oh, my God. I'm going to kill someone and I know exactly who to start with.

Hale bounces down the rear staircase, the black athletic pants he's in just barely staying at his hips. He scratches his head, his eyelids heavy as if he's barely slept. My, I wonder what in heavens he was up all night doing.

I toss a glare at the blond. Never mind, I think I know.

"I'm going to work out," he tells her. "Help yourself to . . ."

His steps slow when he sees me. Oh, he's wide awake now. His large eyes zip from me to the blond. He does a double-take when he sees she's wearing my dog and not much else.

"What-what?" he says.

The blond giggles, because why the fuck not? "Hale, you know I get hot in bed."

Hale races down the stairs, holding out his arms when I march toward him. "You weren't supposed to be here until Thursday."

"Is that all you have to say to me?"

"Hale," blondie says. "Who's this?"

"Who am I?" I practically hiss. "Who the *fuck* are you?"

To the public I serve I'm a right-bred Southern lady, as sweet as nectar dripping from a bumblebee's chin, and as poised and refined as a seasoned ballerina. In my defense, we're not in public and there is a naked woman holding my dog in my almost lover's house!

I veer on Hale, my finger out, pointing it like a weapon. "*You*. Speak. Now."

My semi-possessed demon voice does absolutely nothing to ease the tension. Hale's jaw slacks open. "I know this looks bad," he begins.

"You think?"

The front door opens. "Hey," Trin's voice sings. "Y'all decent?" She skips in, her baby tucked against her chest and her little boy's hand held gently in hers. Callahan follows, balancing several casserole dishes in his arms.

Everyone stops in place. A naked woman wearing a dog has that effect.

Trin's mouth pops open, her attention bouncing from Blondie to Hale to me. Callahan barely blinks. He places the dishes on the counter and turns around, scooping his son up in his arms. "We'll be outside," he says. "Trin?"

"You may be outside," Trin tells him. "I'm not going anywhere. Take the baby, will you, love?" She narrows her eyes at the blond. "She might not like the sight of blood."

Callahan reaches for his daughter. "Nice," he tells Hale, not meaning it.

Hale covers his face, looking up at the ceiling.

"Who are you?" Trin asks, so livid she barely gets her mouth to work.

Blondie flips back her hair and smiles. "Hale Wilder's fiancée."

"What the fuck!" I say.

"That's not true," Hale says. "Becks, please, I know this looks bad."

"No shit!" I reply. I'm not someone anyone would call a screamer. But my voice is no longer a voice. It's taken on a life on its own and is about as murderous as I feel.

Hale curses, rubbing his face as if annoyed. Oh, *he's* mad.

"I can't believe you did this to me," I say.

"Becks, you don't understand—"

"I can't believe I fell for all your 'I miss you' shit!" My eyes sting with tears.

"You're not the maid?" Blondie asks, cuddling Rosie closer.

"Bitch, get away from my dog!" I yell.

"Your dog?" she asks, like *that's* the problem here.

"You heard her," Trin says, her chin out and her hands on her hips where they belong. "Drop the dog and get the hell out of my house."

"Your house?" Blondie asks, ignoring Hale and his pleas for everyone to calm down.

"Did I stutter?" Trin demands. "Leave the dog alone, put some clothes on, and get out."

Blondie adjusts Rosie, her focus drifting to Hale. She's not afraid of me or Trin, but she should be. "What exactly is going on? Who are these people?"

"These people?" Trin says. "Ma'am, are you messing with me right now? I hope not. Just 'cause you saw me holding a baby doesn't mean I won't smack you all the way back to New York if you keep gettin' lippy."

"How dare you?" Pris says.

She rises, dog and all and takes a step forward. I take a step, too. "Oh, sugar," I say. "No way in hell are you getting anywhere near her."

Hale shoves his way between us, cursing as Trin and I lay into Blondie. Blondie puts Rosie down, screaming, waving her arms *and* breasts.

"Stop," Hale says. "All of y'all just stop."

The fire burning within me surges, blurring my vision. "You cheating, *whoring*, little—"

"I didn't cheat," Hale says, his sharp tone instantly silencing me. His expression is weary, but it's the guilt that stills me in place. "I wouldn't do that to you."

"I don't know about that," Blondie says, fluffing her hair.

Blondie's words are a rough strike upside my head. I jerk away from Hale when he reaches for me, feeling more emotional than I want to be. He hurt me. My God, all I did was leave him a handful of days and he did this to me.

"Don't touch me," I tell him. "Don't you ever put your hands on me again."

Chapter Sixteen

Hale

This morning wasn't supposed to happen. I wasn't supposed to come downstairs to find Becks here and I especially wasn't supposed to find Pris naked with Becks. I shouldn't be surprised. Pris did her best to drag me to bed.

If I hadn't spent most of the night grilling her about what she knew, and if it wasn't too late for her to find a place to sleep, I never would have let her stay here.

Becca doesn't know that and neither does Trin. Both are plenty pissed, but it's the hurt and disappointment in Becca's eyes that just about tears me apart.

"Nothing happened," I say. "Priscilla's not my fiancée." I pause. I don't want to admit what I do next, but I need to be honest. "We dated for a time."

"We did more than that, Hale," Priscilla purrs.

She smiles, enjoying herself. Pris has always had a mean streak, but I'll damned if I let Becca bear the brunt of it.

I meet Becca's gaze. "What Pris and me had has been over for a while. She came here yesterday, unannounced, and spent the night."

"I certainly did," Pris says.

"In the guestroom, by herself," I snarl through my teeth.

Trin races into the guestroom. "Someone slept in here," she calls out.

Becca swallows hard. She doesn't appear any less relieved, nor does she seem to believe me. But I think she wants to. Trin bounces out of the bedroom and tosses—never mind, "tosses" is too mild a word. She *throws* Pris's clothes at her, shoes and all. If Pris didn't duck, Trin would have taken out an eye with a leopard print shoe.

"You might need these," Trin says, happily. "In fact, you really do. Get dressed and get going before someone gets hurt, and when I say someone, I mean you."

"Hale?" Pris says.

"Pris, just get out. I'll be in touch."

Damn. Those weren't the right words to say around Becca. She gapes at me, devastated.

In the quiet, all I hear is Pris tugging on her clothes and the distant lull of the ocean. It doesn't take Pris long to dress. She didn't have much on to start with. But when she starts to leave, it's as if nothing I said matters and she's leaving on her terms. She stops beside me, wrapping her arms around me to kiss my lips. I turn away fast.

She barely grazes my cheek, but I'm not giving her another chance to make up for it. I pull her hands off from around my neck. "Not happening," I tell her.

"I see," Pris says. "You don't need me now. Do you, Hale? You got what you wanted last night."

Becca gasps. "It's not like that," I say, yet again. But it seems nothing I say is good enough. Dark circles ring Becca's eyes. She seems tired, defeated, and I'm only making things worse.

"I thought things were going to be different," Becca says.

"They are, baby," I assure her.

"Baby?" Pris repeats, her head jerking between is. "Don't tell me she's the reason you wouldn't commit to me?"

I think back to the women I dated before Pris, and all those times Pris and my life in New York never seemed like enough. With everything I had and built, my loneliness never made sense. It does now.

"Becca is the reason I never committed," I admit. I meet Becca square in the face. "I never forgot you, Becks, and you never forgot me, either."

Pris plays with her hair, trying to save face. "You say that, but you always did know what to say. Didn't you, Hale?"

It was more like I knew when to duck and stay out of Pris's way. She has a different memory than I do and is doing her best to stir the pot.

"Pris," I say. "It's over. I told you that a few months back when you demanded a ring and I wouldn't give it to you." I'm looking at Pris now. I have to. I owe her as much. But I feel Becca. The hurt and anger she's experiencing slides across her skin like the first drops of rain before a major storm. "I also told you as much last night, Pris, when you tried to kiss me and asked me to join you in bed."

Pris could easily lie. It's something she's good at after years spent getting what she wants. She's also good at taking jabs and kicking those who are already down. But this time, she doesn't. Something she sees between me and Becca keeps her quiet, at least as much as her personality allows.

"This is what you want?" she asks.

I almost reach for Becca's hand, but I don't want her to deny me again, especially when I lay it all out there. "She's *who* I want." I capture Becca's gaze. Not with my words, but with my heart. "I never got over you, Becks."

There have been times in my life where everything stops. There's no air. There's no need for breath. There's nothing but you and that other person. The first time I felt it was back in high school. It was a Monday and Becca had found out she'd been accepted to Duke. She flounced toward me in her uniform, her sunny hair fluttering behind her as she leapt into my arms. She was so excited for the opportunity and to be so far away.

I held her, no longer as the beautiful girl I was friends with, and she saw me as more than they guy she joked and laughed with. It was the same look we exchanged the night we first kissed. It's the same look she gives me now. There's no air. No need to breathe. There's just us.

"*Fine*," Pris says, dissolving this brief wrinkle in time before I'm ready to let it go. "I just don't see how she'll ever be enough, Hale. I don't see how any woman will *ever* be enough." Pris was always struttin' around like a peacock, telling the world that she was the best and that anyone who tried to match her would end up cowering in the shadow of her plumage. Still, despite her nasty tone and superior attitude, I catch the barest hint of hurt. That doesn't mean I'll allow the snub against Becca.

"Don't," I tell her. "You don't get to disrespect Becca, especially in front of me."

Pris's expression crumbles. It's brief and if I wasn't staring directly at it, I'm not sure I'd catch it.

"I need you to go, Pris," I tell her as gently as possible. "Either me or Mason will reach out."

"That's it?" she asks, her voice quaky.

"That's all it's going to be, Pris."

She opens her mouth, but doesn't say a word. I think she needed to see me with Becca to accept that what we had is over. It still bothers me. I never wanted to hurt Pris, and wish she didn't have to see me like this with Becca to believe I'd moved on. Whatever Pris imagined we had convinced her that no one could take her place. So, as much as this moment is hard, she needed to witness it firsthand.

Without another word, she steps away.

The door opens and closes seconds later. Becks and me just stare at each other. I want to tell her something, anything to erase her lingering pain. Instead, I leave her to her thoughts, permitting her to work through them.

It takes Trin walking toward us for me to finally look away. "I went upstairs," she tells Becca. "That bed has been slept in as well and there's no evidence anyone has been there except for Hale."

My hand passes over my jaw where my stubble is turning into a beard. "You don't trust me, either?" I ask Trin.

"I didn't trust her," Trin replies. "And Hale, as much as I love you, none of this looked good." She smiles softly. "Except what you said to Becca."

Trin is trying to soften the blow. I nod, letting her know I understand where everyone is coming from. I don't know what I would have done if I'd caught Becca with another man. Forget it. I do know, and it wouldn't have been anywhere near this polite.

"I'll let you guys talk," Trin says. "Food's on the counter."

The front door opens and closes again. One vehicle drives away. Then another. Still, we don't speak.

She covers her face. I think she's going to start crying. I want to hold her, tell her I'm sorry for all she found. I also want to apologize for Pris's presence and for allowing her to spend the night. But she doesn't want me to touch her. That anger and hurt keeps me at arm's length, building a wall between us and keeping me far away.

When it seems like too much time has passed, I finally speak. "I wanted to say all the right things, but none of them came out."

She drops her hands away. Her face is red and blotchy, but I don't see a single tear. "I'm going to start your interview. The audio to dub into the beginning of your ABC special."

"What?" I follow her when she stomps away. "Becks, I don't want to do this now. We need talk this shit out."

"I'm doing your interview," she says. She throws the office door open and gets to work. I stop in the hall, watching her move fast. She pulls out the camera equipment she special ordered. The mic, the tripod, the little cameras that clip on clothing, they're all there.

She stops when I step in and shut the door behind me. She didn't expect me to follow, too caught up in what she saw and how it made her feel.

Fresh tears trickle down her cheeks. She wipes them awkwardly away, fighting to make them stop only for them to run faster.

"The last time we spoke we talked about making love, what it would be like now that we were together. How it would feel not to be rushed."

She wipes her eyes with the edge of sleeve, watching me closely instead of answering.

"I still want us to make love. I still want you to fall asleep against me and wake up with your face being the first thing I see. But there's more. I want to travel with you and see your smile light up when we watch the sunset from a castle in Ireland, or while shopping in those little stores you find only in France. I want to swim the Dead Sea with you and watch your cheeks flush as we hike through the forests of Austria. I look forward to laughing when you fuss with Trin's babies. But I also want you to know, I've thought about making babies of our own."

She gasps, in shock and more. I don't mean to pressure her. I only want her to understand what she means to me, what she's always meant to me.

I walk slowly to her, carefully taking her hands in mine. I look at how they fit across my palms. My hands are large, calloused, and marred from all the years I played ball. From all those times I scraped them, doing everything I had to do to make that winning touchdown. Until I made the final play, the impossible one, the one that made USC national champs. The one that blew out my knee and ended my NFL dream.

Becca's hands don't share my scars from the too-long practices in the rain and mud, and from men far bigger than me mowing me down. Her skin is delicate and her scars are emotional, buried deep beneath long, slender fingers, and skin so soft, all she needs are wings. Our hands are different sizes, shaded in different tones, toughened with different memories, but somehow they fit. *We* fit.

"You say all these things, all these pretty words that I want believe," Becca says. "But what you didn't explain was why that woman was here?" Her irises shimmer as she waits for me to answer. "I need you to tell me the truth or I swear to God . . ."

Becca doesn't need to say what she'll do. I already know she'll leave and this time not look back. We've had our share of trouble. But like me, cheating isn't something she'd tolerate no matter how much it would kill us to walk away.

"Neesa discovered some activity in my private accounts one of those nights I was with Pris. We were at a special event. There were a few big-wigs from Wall Street, many who Pris would cozy up to when she didn't think I was paying enough attention to her."

Becca's lips part slowly. "You think they used her to get information?"

I nod. "I didn't trust Pris with anything private. We never shared bank accounts, passwords, nothing personal or any delicate information. For the most part, we led completely separate lives."

"Unless you needed company?"

Becca isn't being petty or nasty. Her voice is soft and reasonable. She can accept that Pris and me weren't serious. But she won't easily forget we were physically intimate.

"Pris and me were never friends. Not like you and me," I stress. She dips her chin. "We never talked about anything worth talking about. But she was with me long enough to overhear some of my business interactions and dealings. I was on the phone a lot. I'd take calls in my office and also after hours, making deals, strategizing with my clients. Sometimes, others in finance would call me, trying to cozy up by offering inside information."

Becca's eyes widen.

My thumbs slowly pass over her knuckles. "I never took them up on it," I insist. "I never wanted to be a part of all that bullshit. Once you start, you don't stop. Before you know it, you owe a lot of people and they're looking to collect any way they can."

"I believe you. But do you think Priscilla would take inside information?" she asks.

"Nothing was ever said, but if you ask me, the majority of her family's fortune was made through embezzlement."

Becca tilts her head. "You think Priscilla is the key to all this?"

"In a way, but not directly," I explain. "Pris is a lot things. But she's not one to get mixed up in illegal activity." I sigh. "But she is one to share what she knows. She knew a lot just from being around me, and while she's not stupid, she can be manipulated under the right circumstances."

"In bed?" Becca offers.

I shrug. "Most likely. She craves attention and everyone within the social circles she frequents knows it. It would take the right person, needing the right information, to play along with what she needed."

"Someone who didn't have much in the means of scruples?" Becca guesses.

"And someone who wouldn't think twice about eliminating the competition," I agree. "Pris and me had a long talk last night. We discussed some of the things she's learned being around men in finance. Many of my competitors and people I've associated with through Wall Street were her lovers and frequented her bed."

"That didn't bother you?" Becca asks.

"Of course, it did. I hadn't realized how much business I'd conducted around her."

"That's not what I mean." Becca scans my face, trying to read me. "I meant her discussing men she'd slept with while she was with you."

Becca still doesn't get it or maybe can't understand the relationship I had with Pris. "What happened between me and Pris isn't something I'll ever look back on fondly, Becks. At worst, it was toxic. At best, we met each other's needs."

"I'm sorry," I say. I lift her chin when she bows her head. "It's nothing I'm proud of. But the way you and me left things screwed me up."

"I apologize," she says.

"I'm not trying to blame you, Becks. I was a hot mess. Not just because of what kept happening between us, but everything that happened with my family. I didn't want to care that deeply for anyone anymore. I distanced myself from Trin. For a time, I wouldn't even talk to Mason or Sean. When Pris came along, I knew this wouldn't be a woman to love. This would be a woman I could have, who'd have me, yet not in a way that mattered or could hurt me."

Becks nods, residual tears leaving her eyes. What I tell her isn't pretty and not something I'll ever be able to atone for. It's simply the truth and the ugly side of what I've done.

"Tell me more," Becca says quietly.

"There's much to tell," I say. "With all the men Pris had, I never imagined she'd want me to propose."

"Not about you and Priscilla," she says. Her hands squeeze mine. This time, she's the one reaching for me. "I don't want to hear about what you did with other women, okay?"

"All right," I say. "I'm just trying to be straight with you."

I give her a second to settle before I continue. "There were two names that kept coming up. She slept with both men quite a few times. She didn't know they knew each other, since they never seemed to attend the same events. When they did, they appeared to keep their distance. One night, when she was out with her friends, she saw them in a bar uptown, drinking like they were old friends. She left before they could see her. Mostly for her sake, not theirs."

"She didn't want to approach two men she was sleeping with," Becca presumes.

"No," I clarify. "She was trying to save face, so she could continue seeing them when she wanted to."

"Who were they?"

"Walter Cooling and Aston Malroy. Ever heard of them?"

"No," Becca says. "Should I have?"

"They're big in finance, but nowhere close to where I am."

"I see," Becca says.

So did I, which is why I woke up Mason around two in the morning. "There's more. Clark, my intern for the past year, was a young man Pris suggested I hire."

Becca eyes widen. "Was she sleeping with him, too?"

"No." I laugh, although I shouldn't. Pris would have sex with anyone to get back at me, especially if she was mad enough. "Walt introduced him to Pris as his nephew. Made him up to be a good kid and a good resource for her in case I started seeing anyone else."

"That doesn't make any sense," Becca states slowly.

"It does if you know her. Our inner circles saw us as a couple to some extent. She always took me to the parties and events that most mattered to her. To my knowledge, she never took those other two. Walt therefore knew Pris cared about me as much as she was capable of, just as he knew she'd come back to warm his bed when she was mad at me."

"So, having this intern was supposedly a win for both Pris and Walter. Clark would spy on their behalf, informing Pris if there was another woman and reporting to Walt about your business?"

"That's right. He told her he didn't know me well enough to ask me to hire Clark, which is true. But he asked her if she could help his nephew. In exchange, Clark would help her, too."

"Wouldn't Pris question why Walter didn't hire Clark himself?"

"Sure. Walt's answer was simple. He had taught him all he could." My hands slide onto her hips. She lets me, listening closely. "Want to hear the best part?" She nods. "Walt doesn't have a nephew, only nieces."

Becca shakes her head. "The intern was only there for Walt and Aston."

"Exactly. It's the same thing I told Mason this morning."

Becca leans back, analyzing me closely. "How did Pris know to find you?"

I smirk. "That's a good question. Guess who told her?"

"Oh, my God," Becca says. "Clark—the intern—because he was supposed to be keeping an eye on you for her."

"Yeah. The kid screwed up without even knowing. The only ones aware that I'm here are my legal team and the courts. Unless you have access to my files."

"Which Clark apparently did," Becca says. "*He's* the informant."

"Yup. The team and feds are already on it. So long as Pris keeps quiet about our conversation, they should be able to snag him before he can leave the country."

"Do you think she will? For your sake?"

I think back to Pris's mean streak and exactly how mean it can be. "I don't know. When she's mad, she can be a little vengeful."

"A little vengeful? Hale, why on earth would you ever be with someone like that?"

I speak long before I think about everything I'm saying. Becca still doesn't get it. "Because she wasn't you, Becks. This wasn't a woman to befriend or even someone I always got along with. Unlike you, she was someone incapable of breaking my heart."

Becca breaks down, crying all at once. I press my head against hers. "Priscilla wasn't you," I repeat. "She couldn't hurt me and I knew that I could never love her."

Becca lifts her head, gulping with how hard she's crying. "Do you think you could ever love me?"

This is the moment I always told myself I'd run from, except that I don't. I'm done running.

"I've always loved you, Becks. You just never fucking loved me enough to tell you."

"Oh, God."

I silence her with a kiss, pulling her so all she knows is my body and how bad I want her.

Forget the lead Pris gave me.

Forget that I'm still fighting for my reputation.

I want Becca. This beautiful woman life never made sense without.

My mouth claims hers. I lift her, gently squeezing her ass as I prop her on the edge of the desk. Her nails drag up my back, her arms hooking underneath mine, her long fingers cupping my shoulders.

Fuck. She tastes so good. I don't want to stop, but I won't make her do something she's not ready for. She grunts when I pull away.

"What are you doing?" she asks.

"Giving you moment to tell me no."

Her tears fall slowly. "We've already had a lifetime of no and not yet. I don't want to wait anymore. Not when I've loved you before I understood what love was and not when I've been so alone without you."

"What did you say?"

She smiles, her eyes shimmering. "That I love you, Hale. I always have."

She *loves me*.

I love her.

And now, there's nothing here to stop us.

Chapter Seventeen

Becca

Hale effortlessly carries me in a straddle, yanking a blanket from the family room before racing us outside. I can't stop kissing him or keep my hands from sliding all over his bare chest. He curses when I give his ear a teasing flick, banging the sliding glass door a few times before he manages to shut it.

I want to laugh and squeal with happiness. Kiss him until my lips bruise from the effort. He loves me. The man my life was empty without loves me!

We're alone. The only sound, the gentle ocean waves beating against the sand and the squawks and chirps of birds soaring across the bright blue sky. So, instead of delighted squeals and simple kisses of affection, it's time for us to share more.

He groans when I rub against him, clumsily flapping the large blanket to lay across the sand. It's a gorgeous day, warm, the small lingering clouds no match for bright sun. It's too early in the year for tourists, but it's perfect weather for locals to wander and fish. It doesn't matter to me and I don't think it matters to Hale. Between the dunes and the vegetation, we're well hidden should someone pass, and I'm done being shy.

He lowers us to the blanket onto our knees, placing me somewhere in the center. I yank down his sweats. He's not wearing underwear. That's good. It would only get in the way.

I reach for his long, thick shaft. He's fully hard, the tip rigid and throbbing. I take my time, playing, starting at the base and stroking him from base to the tip, my grip tight and slow.

His fingers thread through my hair, kissing me, his breath hitching the more I tease him.

I lost my shoes somewhere between the house and here. The tops of my feet slide across the fleece blanket as I remove his pants completely. I watch him as I lower myself and take my first taste of his hardness. My tongue swirls, moistening the tip several times before my wide mouth descends down his length.

"You don't know what you're doing to me," he rasps.

I didn't think he could become more aroused. But the deeper I take him, the more he proves me wrong. He fists my hair to better see me, gasping and cursing when he passes the back of my throat.

I'm more than happy to finish him this way, the surge of his lust accelerating mine. Hale has other plans. He lifts the skirt of my dress, ridding me of my panties and spinning me in the air. His swiftness and agility catches me by surprise, as does the care he uses so he doesn't hurt me.

He lands on his back with me on top of him, my knees on either side of his head. He shoves my skirt away, yanking my hips down toward eager lips. I hiss every cuss word I know through my teeth when he suckles, pulling off my dress and partially tearing the fabric in my haste to remove it.

I strip out of my bra, carelessly tossing it away. I reach for Hale's erection, wanting to get back to his needs, but barely able to do more than stroke him. I whimper, my wanton needs turning my brain to mush and urging me to rock my pelvis.

My back arches, exposing my taut nipples to the sun and the sky above. Heat and sunlight beat against my breasts, their heavy weight slapping against my skin the faster I move.

My orgasm builds in a rush I'm not prepared for, crashing harder than hail over granite. I fall forward, unable to stop my thighs from quivering or my pelvis from tilting up and down. Deep moans thunder through Hale's generous lips when I take him into my mouth again and create a firm seal. I meant to take things slow, to find out what he likes. But like me, once we started, neither of us could do anything slow.

I just finish my next orgasm when he flips me once more, placing me on my side with his chest pressed against my back. I crane my neck, trying to see Hale. He cups my jaw, holding me in place as he kisses me.

It should be a sexy, aggressive kiss, seeing what we just did to each other. But somehow Hale keeps it tender, the love he feels for me warming my heart with each gentle pass. "I love you, Becca," he says.

"I love you, too." I almost say, I love you more. Only because he can't imagine how much I've waited for him.

His tongue drags down the curve of my neck. "Are you ready for me?" he murmurs.

I shudder when he slides the tip of his rigid staff between my legs. "I've been waiting for you for years," I confess.

Hale slips his hand away from my face. My head sags from the weight of my anticipation. He reaches between us, positioning himself so he can push inside me.

I expect him to get down to business. He is a man, after all. Instead, he kisses me, his other hand tucking under me to play with my breasts, rolling and pulling the tight centers, making me whimper and sky-rocketing my desire.

Hale is well-endowed and I haven't had sex in many years. It takes him a while, every upswing of his hips pushing each inch of him inside of me. I'm almost crying with how good it feels, but when he starts, no tears come. Those groans and screams he craved from me begin.

I'm no longer that professional I work hard to be. I'm no longer me at all. The woman who takes one methodical step at a time to get the job done has disappeared and I bid her good riddance. I'm done being lonely and going without Hale's touch. What's remains is a crazed woman whose lover is more than happy to oblige her.

Hale lifts my leg, hooking it over his neck, watching me as he thrusts hard. He morphs from gentle lover to voracious male bent on pleasing me. He attacks with each ram of his hips, his greedy hands and lips capturing every part of my body.

I don't own my body anymore. It belongs to him just as his body is now mine. I bear down, meeting each excited slap of skin with one of my own.

I'm losing my mind. But my heart, that's something I lost to him a long time ago. I can't slow down. Our rhythm is outrageously fast.

Hale grunts, biting out my name, telling me how good it fucking feels. He's close. I can sense it.

Instead of allowing himself to finish, he flips me onto my back, sending a stream of sand into the air and onto our bodies. He folds my legs so they rest over his shoulders, my heels drifting over his back. His thumb rubs my throbbing center.

"Do you have any idea what you're doing to me?" he asks, his eyes glazed with desire.

I shake my head, out of breath with how turned on I am.

"Let me show you," he says.

He doesn't quite finish talking before he circles the center of my delicate flesh, electrifying me and sending jolts shooting out toward my thighs. I reach for my breasts and pinch my protruding nipples. I've never been this exposed or enlivened. But Hale is experienced. He's proving his prowess and I don't want him to stop.

I see his eyes. How he watches me as his hips continue to pound. Primal moans escape my mouth, my whimpering and grunts of bliss begging him to go harder and ram faster.

I orgasm at least twice, my body convulsing, my feet kicking out wildly as the wind picks up and the waves sing their sweet lullaby.

Another orgasm begins when Hale hauls me up, pulling me forward for another long kiss. My legs fall on either side of his. I move quickly, not yet ready to stop.

"It feels so good," I choke out, my voice trembling.

"Hell, yeah, it does," he assures me, gripping my hips and helping me to go harder. Sweat drizzles down his chest, slicking my breasts when our skin connects. His heady stare latches on mine. "Jesus, Becca, you're so damn beautiful."

My breasts lift and fall with each drag of my hips. "I want you so much, Hale."

He places me back on the blanket, thrusting wildly and filling me. We're loud as we reach the end, our mouths and lips seeking more of each other, and our voices crying out with pleasure. God help me, I could give a damn.

Hale falls back on his knees, clasping my ankles and spreading them in a "V." The cords of his neck strain and his teeth clamp. He comes, brutally, like a beast that was caged for too long.

I haul him on top of me as he finishes, kissing him until his movements slow and he stops.

The sun intensifies as he lowers himself beside me. He kisses my palm when I stroke the scruff along his jaw, his irises reflecting the joy I feel. "I'm never letting you go," he rasps. "You and me, we're infinite."

I smile, unable to stop my eyes from blurring. "We always have been, Hale."

I position myself across his chest, trying not to think about all those wasted years.

Hale kisses me, longingly and sweetly. It doesn't take long for our kiss and touches to turn to more. He pulls me on top of him, my spine bowing as I move and bounce my hips.

Hale encourages me to go faster, his hands on my backside, grazing my nipples with his teeth between sucks and seductive licks.

We're outside a few hours and spend several more in our bed.

We are infinite. We are in love.

But life isn't perfect. We're reminded of such in the coming weeks and in all the worst ways possible.

Chapter Eighteen

Hale

I stare at my childhood home for what seems like too long. The wraparound porch is exactly that, curving around the modern Victorian as if hugging its beauty and refusing to let go.

My brothers, Daddy, and me spent the entire summer before my sophomore year of high school building that thing. It was a brutal summer, as far as summers here go. The ocean is less than a mile away. During the summers, the breeze skimming along the water does a lot to cool the harsh sun painting our skin a deep gold and soaking our skin with sweat. But not that summer. It was like the breeze took a vacation, leaving our skin to bake with the permanent taste of salt on our lips.

The sun bleached my hair almost white that summer. But it left my brothers' hair alone. Back then, I attributed it to the baseball caps they wore. Except, back then, I was still mostly in the dark. I knew I was a little different. In the way I looked and in the way I carried myself. I just never dreamed how different I was and how much I didn't belong.

Emer and Carson have light eyes like me. I remember Mrs. Stevenson from up the road coming up one morning to drop off fresh peaches from her grove so Momma could bake us a pie.

That's the excuse she gave for visiting. Mrs. Stevenson, being the busybody that she was, wanted to see how our project was coming along.

"Three boys doing all that work? I don't believe it," she said. "Even if they are Jacob Wilder's boys."

Well, she wasn't quite right about that.

Mrs. Stevenson did stop and admire our work, scrutinizing to see if all the boards were laid right, even though that woman probably never swung a hammer in her life. She also stopped to admire our young strapping bodies. Mrs. Stevenson was always like that, checking out the young men around the island when she thought no one would notice.

I remember that day so well. Ever since Becca started my interview about my upbringing, I remember things I hadn't realized I'd forgotten.

Becca and me are lovers, first and foremost. She's become the most important person in every aspect of my life. We haven't spent a night apart since the first time we made love on the beach. There are dinners with our friends, our share of meals on our own, and lots of work to repair my legacy and business. She cares about me and what happens. It's obvious by the way she touches me and fusses whenever Mason calls. Her love, her devotion, it shows in every way, even with respect to these interviews.

The questions she asks probe deep despite their simplicity, painting those memories of my time with my family in vivid colors, bringing back the good times I remember, but also the torment that haunts me to this moment.

That day Mrs. Stevenson arrived is so ingrained from all the probing into my life Becca's done, I can almost see Mrs. Stevenson standing before me. She had the basket of peaches tucked under her arm, their amber and red colors bright and luminous under the sun. Her head shifted from side to side, taking in the detail of the woodwork, her large sunglasses hiding most of her face.

"My, Jacob," she told Daddy. "What handsome boys you have. And they look so much alike. The girls are going to give you a hard time, fellas," she warned.

My brothers laughed, knowing how she was and how she used those large glasses to hide the blatant stares she'd throw our way. I started to laugh as well, even though at fourteen, she made me strangely uncomfortable. But my laugh didn't quite release as it should, not when I saw the look on Daddy's face. He bowed his head, staring hard at the ground.

"Hale looks more like his mama," he said.

Mrs. Stevenson paused, turning to him because Daddy was a good-looking man too. "Don't they all?" she asked, clearly confused.

"Not as much as Hale," he said.

I didn't understand what he meant then. But I recognized her confusion, even though I was still young and blissfully blind. I wasn't hurt, exactly. I still thought I was loved and one of his boys. But as I look onto the porch and everything I thought my family and me had built together, all I feel is a bite of pain.

The door swings open without much care and the screen slams just as rough against the siding. My brother Carson steps out. I don't think it's much past eleven yet, but here he is, taking a swig from the half-empty bottle of beer in his hand. I think he's pissed I'm here and that's why the doorframe hit against the house as hard as it did. It takes a few sloppy steps forward on his part for me to realize that he's not angry, he's just way past drunk.

His feet shuffle forward, coming dangerously close to the edge of the porch. His dark hair is mussed and his beard is long enough to brush against his stained white T-shirt. It's not one of those fashionable beards that are in style. It's tangled and speaks of a man who no longer cares about anything, let alone shaving.

"Well, well, well," Carson say. "Look who the fuck finally showed."

I'm sure he's talking to me until Emer, our middle brother, emerges from the side of the house. The gray shirt he's wearing is coated with dirt, and he's holding freshly pulled weeds in both hands. He has a beard, too, but his is neat and trimmed close to his jaw.

In New York, everything I wore cost a lot, right down my drawers. But here in Kiawah it's not about dressing for success. It's all about being comfortable. Today, I'm in a pair of jeans and light navy T-shirt. The way Emer eyes me from head to toe, you'd think I'd shown up in fur and diamonds just to fuck with him.

Unlike Carson, Emer isn't drunk. Very much like Carson, he's not happy to see me. There're no warm brotherly hugs, not that there ever were. Those touchy-feely kind of brothers, we were never them. Roughhousing came naturally for us and usually ended in blood and Momma ordering us out of the house to run a few miles until we "stopped acting like wild animals and more like the Wilders we are."

"Go walk it off," Emer tells Carson, his steady gaze never leaving mine. I expect a fight today. I'm prepared for it and I'm not afraid. Regardless, the next few steps I take to meet Emer are the hardest yet.

Emer tosses the weeds in his hands aside. I already know they're from Momma's garden. Like all southern women in the area, she used to pride herself on a garden that overflowed with grand flowers and tomato plants that produced fruit almost too pretty to eat.

Carson hobbles down the steps, missing the last two. I hurry toward him to help him up, but he smacks my hand away. It doesn't hurt like I think he wants it to. He almost misses me, the tips of his fingers barely connecting.

"Are you here for your birth certificate or something?" Carson asks. "Maybe some money you think you're owed from the will? Shit, I hate to break it to you, but I think all that's done and used up." He rises, barely keeping his balance. "Isn't that right, Emer? Didn't we up and spend that money together, *brother*?"

The emphasis on the word "brother" is supposed to hurt me. For all I'm trying to be that stone figure I was on Wall Street, the one nothing could penetrate, Carson accomplishes his mission. Pain boils my insides. I do my best to not reflect it on my face. I'll admit, it takes some doing.

"Shut up, Carson," Emer spits out. "Take a walk and sober up."

Carson is three years older than me, and two more than Emer. For some reason I never figured out, Carson has always followed Emer's lead. Carson is loud, boisterous. In the best of times, he was the life of the party. In the worst, he was obnoxious and the first to start a fight.

Emer is borderline mute. Born leaders don't have to say much. They don't have to beat their chests, demanding to be heard. The few words they speak just need to be the right ones for people to listen and understand this is who they need to follow.

Carson spits out a few curses under his breath, but ultimately obeys. He staggers forward, trying to shove past me by ramming me with his broad shoulder. He almost falls when I don't budge. I don't try to help him this time. I just watch him recover, struggling to come to terms with how much he hates me.

Ramming me with his shoulder is something he used to do all the time as a kid. He stopped doing it as much when he realized I was too fast, and regretted doing it altogether when I knocked him to the ground. Carson had four inches on me then. I think I have four on him now. But alcohol is like that. It gives you courage you shouldn't have, and makes you stupid in ways that embarrass you. Not that I'm expecting Carson to be embarrassed anytime soon.

Me and Emer watch Carson stumble off. He doesn't make it far, choosing to slump on the first step leading down to the reflection garden Daddy built for Momma. His beer slips from his grip and rolls with a *clink* down against the slate steps before it stops on the thick lawn.

"What are you doing here, Hale?" Emer asks.

It takes me a second to pull my attention away from Carson and the way he's curled forward and swaying.

"I wanted to see y'all," I admit. I don't mention the mess I'm in. He's probably heard and probably celebrated. I especially don't mention the interviews Becca has conducted and how they brought up too many memories of a family I no longer see.

"Why? Missing Momma? Her letters?"

It's a strange question he asks. It affects me all the same. Just like the trip down memory lane Becca takes me on every time the mic goes on and the camera rolls.

Momma was a bright woman. She knew the Internet, technology, and anything high-tech probably as much as the rest of us. But she always wrote letters by hand when she wanted to get our attention.

Rarely, it was because she was disappointed in something we'd done. More times, it was to tell us something personal following one of our accomplishments or something she was proud of that we'd said or done. It could be something as basic as a good grade we received in class or kindness she witnessed.

"Keep the letters," she once told us, when Carson questioned why she didn't just tell us how she felt. "When I'm gone, you'll understand why I wrote them."

It was the only time she'd mentioned writing them. For the most part, she'd leave them under our pillows, in our drawers, somewhere we'd find them.

"You have my letters?" I ask.

There's only one thing that hit me harder than Momma's death. It was realizing she'd never write me again. When I left for college, I didn't take the letters with me. They'd still make an appearance every month, celebrating my achievements on the football field or congratulating me on making Dean's List. Sometimes, they were just to talk about what was going on at home, how Daddy had received another few contracts or to gush about how her indoor plants were doing. Every time I came home, I'd place my new letters with the old ones in a box I kept on the floor of my bedroom closet.

When I left for New York a few months after graduation, I expected more letters, but they never came. Daddy got sick. He died. Then Momma followed him to heaven soon after.

The letters stopped long before I was ready to stop receiving them. It was like she said, I'd understand why she wrote them when she was gone.

"We have all the stuff you thought you were better off without," Emer replies. "Including dem letters."

I hate the way he says that. Like Carson, I've always admired Emer. I wasn't particularly close to either of them and always felt like an outsider long before I found out I wasn't full blood.

If I was a better man and a smarter son, maybe I would've figured it out on my own. Like most kids in the world, trying to find their way, all I cared about was that my parents loved me. I didn't go out in search of the truth. I didn't realize there was truth to find.

"They're upstairs in your room. You want them?"

"My room," he still calls it. Damn.

When I was a boy, I thought I lived in the best place on earth, taking advantage of the sun and surf with groups of friends too large to count. This place always felt like home. That all changed abruptly, leaving scars I swear I can almost see.

I shrug. It's mostly all I can do. "Yeah. I'd like them."

Emer doesn't move, watching me closely. He's not someone that's ever been easy to read, choosing to keep his trap shut good and tight, silently pondering his next move and comment.

Most people speak just to speak. Emer never says anything he doesn't have to.

He keeps still, barely breathing. I'm not sure what he's trying to do. He seems to be testing me. But this test isn't one I can pass. It's bitter, lined with questions that go without being asked. I start to think this is mistake. That I shouldn't have shown up like I did. But from the first moment I woke up, I felt I had to be here.

Becca lay contently against my chest. She's exhausted from all the work she's doing to help me, keep the Cougars on top, and that dimwit Denver from getting bitch-slapped by the press. I left quietly, trying not to disturb her and overpowered with the need to see my brothers.

I couldn't explain why I needed to see them, exactly. And by the hard and merciless way Emer continues to regard me, he sure didn't share the same sentiment.

When the seconds turn to minutes and Emmer remains silent, I know I have to say something. "If this is a bad time, I'll leave. You have my number. Just call."

A laugh erupts from Carson. It's neither vicious nor filled with good humor. It's maniacal, bordering on psychotic and enough to send a shiver peeling its way down my spine.

"You hear that, Emer? You should call. Maybe *we* should call? It'll be a grand old time, don't you think?"

I frown in Carson's direction, watching the way his back jerks and quivers as he continues to laugh in that crazy way. Emer doesn't sport the "what the fuck?" expression I'm currently wearing. He barely blinks, as if he's forgotten Carson is present. I'm not sure what's happening and I'm no longer certain leaving is an option. Not given Carson's fragile state.

"Let's sit on the porch," Emer says.

It's all he manages. I suppose it's enough.

His heavy feet march up the stairs and across the wooden floor. He reaches the porch swing painted a bright turquoise and takes a seat. I follow behind him, giving him plenty of room when I sit beside him.

There's a good amount of space separating us. Emer should feel even further away. There's not so much as a speck of warmth between us. But this is the closest I've sat to my brother in years. I welcome it in a way, but there are more ways that I dread it.

It takes a long damn while for either of us to say anything. I'm the one who speaks first. I suppose that's the type of relationship that Emer and me have always had. "You before me" so he can figure out the best way to answer, but only if he thinks I chose to say enough. It's how Emer rolls and one of the reasons I've always respected him.

I lean forward, resting my forearms against my legs and clasping my hands. "How are you?" I ask.

I think he expected me to press about the letters. Maybe I should have since it's what he brought up. Except, as much as I would love to retrieve that box stuffed with memories of my mother's love and vanish, I need him to answer what I ask even more.

Emer jerks his chin in Carson's direction. "Better than him," he replies. "Delilah filed for divorce. She took the kids and left. He hasn't seen them in almost five months."

"She can't do that," I say.

"She can if he's not willing to stop her," Emer counters.

Carson and Delilah were college sweethearts and those kids meant everything to him. I don't have children. But if I did and that was Becca trying to leave, I'd do anything to make it work. "Why won't he do anything? File an injunction or something?"

"Because he doesn't think he fucking deserves them," Emer responds like it's obvious. "Look at him, Hale. Look at what he's become. You think any of us have been the same since Daddy and Momma died, *and* we found out about you?"

It's not just what Emer says that cements me in place. It's the amount of words that come out of him. Emer is the type that shuts down when people are losing their minds, choosing to watch and listen, to take it all in, becoming invisible until it's time to act.

At Daddy's funeral, he tucked Momma against him, becoming her human shield and pillar of strength as they lowered the casket into the ground. He glared across the way to where I stood with Mason and Sean flanking my sides.

After learning I wasn't Daddy's real son, I no longer felt like I belonged with the family. The only place I felt I should be was with the family I'd made throughout the years. That family was Mason, Sean, and Trin's family, who stood directly behind me.

Emer didn't say one word to me during the service. Not one. But it's like everything he didn't say throughout the years, he makes up for now, spitting the words like fire from a dragon to sizzle against my skin.

"It wasn't just about you, Hale. It was about us, too."

"How?" I ask. I'm not trying to be an asshole or pick a fight. I honestly want to know. "How is me not being Daddy's blood ever about you?"

Emer presses his mouth into such a straight line, his lips disappear. His muscles tense like he's ready to take a swing, instead of separating me and Carson like he did when we were kids.

"You don't think you're our brother. Do you?" he asks.

I don't realize how much I'm clenching my jaw until I jam the words out through my teeth. "Is this a serious question? If it is, I have a serious response."

"Then let's hear it, bigshot," Emer says, leaning back. "I'm all ears."

Rage burns me from the inside out. I'm not sure whether to start hollering or to start punching. I'm pretty sure I'll do both before I leave. Hell, I have all day. Let's get this family reunion started.

I start with the hollering. At least, that's my intent. But for as loud as I want and think I deserve to be, my voice grows oddly quiet, despite its deepening tone. "The man I thought was my father died telling me I wasn't his son. All those games I played as a kid, the ones only Momma would attend since Daddy had to work. Do you remember those, Emer? The same games he never missed for you and Carson? You know the real reason he was noticeably absent, don't you? All those times I begged him to play with me, but he was always too tired? He never seemed too tired out when it came to you and Carson. I suppose it all makes sense now, doesn't it? He didn't want to have to love me. He didn't want to have to be there for me. Why would he? I wasn't his real son."

"Yeah, you were."

It's not the insult I expect from Emer. What it is, is the slap across the face I never saw coming.

The slow shake of his head follows the reddening of his eyes. "You're right about one thing," he says. "Daddy didn't want to love you. But he did."

Emer stands, walking to the end of the porch and walking back again. This time, it's me who's quiet and watching him closely.

"You weren't even two years old when you got really sick. Momma was up all kinds of hours, rocking you, trying to soothe you. Daddy was nowhere to be seen. I was just a little over five, but I remember looking for him and wonderin' where he'd gone."

I don't move, worried that if I do, Emer will stop talking. He doesn't.

"I walked into his office and found him in the dark trying to sleep. He couldn't, you know? All he could do was stare at the ceiling, listening to Momma pace above him, her soft voice trying to comfort you, and you crying like you were in pain. I watched him for a long while. Kept waiting on him to go up and check on you. It seemed odd for him to be hiding away like that, being as worried as he was and unable to sleep."

"Did you ask him?" I question.

"No," Emer replies. "Hell, even then, I didn't like talking much. But all Daddy did was stare at that ceiling. He knew you weren't his, Hale." He releases a breath. "And it broke his Goddamn heart, because he wanted you to be."

"You don't know that," I snap, my temper flaring. "That's just an excuse, something a kid would tell himself to feel better about what he felt or saw."

"Don't tell me what I felt or what you think I did or didn't see," Emer fires back.

"I can and I will," I grind out. "It's the same thing I did as a kid, Emer. Every time Daddy ignored me, every time he hurried away, I tried to justify why he didn't treat me the same, coming up with any reasonable excuse to explain his actions away. I didn't want to think I wasn't his or that I mattered less. But even then, I knew, Emer. I knew he didn't want me. Except there I was, trying to convince myself that

Momma's excuses were true. That he was just busy." I huff. "Busy for me, but not for the two of you."

"All right," Emer says. "You want more proof? How about everything he did show up for, you attention seeking whore? It wasn't enough to be a football star. You were an academic scholar, too. You were a lifeguard and saved lives. When that wasn't enough, you made All-American."

"Are you listening to yourself? How much I had to do? How hard I had to work to get a speck of attention? I killed myself so he'd notice me, Emer. I did everything and more so he'd see and recognize that I was worthy. I couldn't just be me. Not if I wanted his attention and love. I had to be better—"

"Than us?" Emer offers, cutting me off.

I don't want to admit as much as I do. But I won't lie. "Maybe," I reply.

"There is no 'maybe'," Emer shoots back. "You were better and you always will be."

I try to deny it, but Emer interrupts. "You couldn't just take one honors course. You had to take all of them. A 4.0 was never enough. You had to exceed that and duke it out with Trinity Summers for class valedictorian. Sports? Why only be good at one? Let's make you captain of the football team, captain of the basketball team." He held out his arms. "While we're at it, maybe you should co-captain the baseball team, too. All in one year. Splitting them apart would've been too much."

"You don't get it," I say. "All the things I accomplished and worked my ass off for had to be done. It was the only way I could get Daddy to see me. Do you have *any* idea how many times he turned his back on me? How many times I wish he'd just talk to me. Two words, Emer. That's about as much as he'd feel obliged to say to me for every twenty to forty he'd easily share with you or Carson. You had his attention. You had his love by simply breathing. By being his boys. I had to *earn it*."

"And you did," Emer adds, casually. "Not because you were the glory boy this entire town couldn't get enough of, but because you were the son Dugan Myers had the balls to touch."

That's a name I hadn't heard in almost twenty years. But it's a name I remember well.

"You remember good ol' Dugan Myers? Rich asshole, pseudo Christian, and mouthiest mother-fucker you'll ever meet? Four daughters, four sons, all scared to death of him?"

Hell, anyone with any sense was scared to death of him. Dugan wasn't just mean. He was crazy.

Emer laughs about as friendly as Carson did. "I remember him, too. Tonya Myers, his middle daughter and perfect princess, got knocked up. She couldn't tell him the father was Blane Rogers. Not when Blane's family barely had two nickels to their name and not when he worked at that shoe store. So, she up and told her daddy it was yours." He scoffs. "She probably thought you were the only guy Dugan wouldn't beat her ass for being with. She was wrong about that, wasn't she?"

I don't reply. I remember seeing Tonya not long after that sportin' a black eye. Everyone knew her daddy had hit her. Just like they knew I'd never been with her. Everyone except Dugan.

"Daddy could've easily believed Tonya's father and let him kick your ass when he showed up here. But he didn't, Hale. Daddy jumped on top of him the moment Dugan struck you and ran him off this land."

My eyes widen. Despite all the memories bouncing around in my head, this wasn't one I'd thought about, not really.

"You think it was all about sports and academics? Do you really think our father was that heartless? Then you don't know as much as you think you do and you sure as shit aren't as smart as you thought. Daddy couldn't fight worth a damn and you know it. But he did that day. He fought like a lion. He bled for you. And it wasn't because you had won us the State championship a few days before. It was because someone had dared to put his hands on his boy."

I don't feel myself rise or ball my fists. But here I am, standing and staring at the porch we'd worked so hard to build. A breeze sweeps in from nowhere, scattering small leaves across the wood boards. The porch needs sanding and a fresh coat of stain. I see it when a tear falls and permeates into the wood.

Emer's feet step into my line of sight. "I'm not saying Daddy didn't try to keep from loving you. Regardless of what you think of me, I'm no liar. He *wasn't* supposed to love you, Hale. You were the result of another man taking his wife. And, I think, if we'd known sooner, rather than later, about you, maybe we wouldn't have loved you, either. But we did. All of us, even after we learned the truth about you."

He motions toward Carson, the gesture barely perceivable like most of Emer's ways. It's only then I raise my chin. "Daddy needed you. We all did. But maybe you're not our brother, after all." He meets me square in the face. "A real brother wouldn't have left us like you did."

"You have no idea what you're saying," I mutter, my rage and disappointment slicing my veins like a blade. "The hardest thing I ever had to do was walk away and leave you behind."

"Then why did you?" Emer asks. "I get that you needed a few days, weeks, maybe even months to process what Daddy said. We would've given you that. *Years*, Hale? Who the hell do you think you are?"

"I don't know who I am," I answer truthfully. "But I can tell you who I became, a man without a father, trying to live a life that wasn't a complete lie. Everything I thought I was, I wasn't. And everyone I knew to be real was furthest from the truth."

"Except your friends, right?" Emer asks. "Mason, Sean, Trinity, and let's not forget her brother, Landon, and *their* folks." He looks like he's ready to break me in two. "And then there's Becca. Sweet as sugar, gorgeous as the rising sun, Becca." He shoves a finger at me, not quite touching me, yet hurting me all the same. "It was okay to stand with them. Be there for them when they needed you, wasn't it? But God forbid you stand by those who called you their own."

"Don't bring my friends into this." I was already pissed when he dragged my posse into this conversation, but when he mentioned Becca . . . that was a whole lot of rage I could've done without.

"Why not, Hale?" Carson drawls.

My head whips in his direction. I thought for sure he'd passed out on the lawn by now. "I would think we'd be worth as much as them. Then again, we're the ones who were never good enough. For you or for Daddy."

He rises from where he sits near the grass on wobbly feet. It's only when I see how red and swollen his eyes are that I realize he's been crying. Damn. I can barely recognize him. A beer gut has formed over abs that were once as flat and rigid as mine. The muscles on his arms are nothing more than loose skin and fat.

Carson was the brother with more notches on his bed post than seemingly possible. Young women would turn on each other for a chance to be his, if only for a few hours. Now look. He had his choice of women only to have the one he married leave him and take his kids with him.

"Daddy wasn't supposed to love you," Carson says, repeating Emer's words like I hadn't heard them. "But he did. Just like the rest of us. Just as Momma did from the start. You were our brother, Hale. Our blood. And you up and died on us. You think we lost our father that day in the hospital? And our momma soon after that? Well, we did. But I guess we should have dug another hole beside them, because we lost you, too."

Carson stumbles across the lawn, tripping over his own feet. "You think watching you on TV, reading about you in the paper, seeing pictures on the Internet of you beside whatever woman you were fucking was enough? It wasn't."

Carson stops short near the bottom of the steps, his face purple and his veins popping with how loud he yells. "Goddamn you, Hale. You should have been there for us." He chokes on a sob. "We would've been there for you."

My eyes burn as if dipped into acid and I'm not alone. Emer, our leader, the reasonable one, the one who never showed a hint of his emotions, looks away before the first of his tears can show.

"I'm sorry," I say, my voice cracking with how much I mean it. "I'm so fucking sorry."

I didn't come here to apologize. Knowing what I know about my family, I expected to fight, to yell and roll around the dirt as my brothers laid into me. It's what I've expected for years and maybe what they expected, too.

Except here we are, three tough as nails men, fighting back tears like three little boys. Boys that spent years running around this property, scraping their knees, climbing trees, and overall pissing each other off.

But maybe loving each other, too. No matter how much we all tried to fight it.

The wind blows again, scattering more leaves and bringing a fresh stream of ocean air. For a moment, I'm that young man again, tasting salt from sweat on my lips, carrying planks and hammering boards into place to make the porch what it became.

Emer isn't crying. He's too busy sawing wood. Carson isn't drunk, he's flipping through the blueprint, making sure we're following it to a tee and talking about heading into town to fetch more lumber. Daddy is reaching for the tray Momma hands him, topped with sandwiches and large glasses filled with the best sweet tea this side of the island.

I look toward the front gate, almost expecting Mrs. Stevenson to pop out of her brand-new Lexus with her basket of peaches. But Mrs. Stevenson died a long time ago. And my Momma. And my Daddy. And so should the bad memories.

"Let's go," I say.

Almost as fast as they arrived, Emer's tears stop.

I motion toward the house. "Inside, if that's all right."

Carson looks to Emer. Emer keeps his attention on me. He's wondering what I'm up to. I don't know myself. All I know is I can't leave them again. Not like this.

"We can order ribs from that barbecue place Daddy liked," I offer. "The one with the fried corn and homemade coleslaw."

Neither replies. "We don't have to," I add. "I just . . . I'm not ready to say goodbye is all."

"Brisket," Emer says. "Momma liked the brisket."

"The fried pickles, too," Carson agrees.

They don't flat out say yes, but they don't argue with me, either. We wait for Carson to walk up the steps. He gets to the door and plows through it. Emer follows quietly behind him.

I wait, unsure what to do. It's only when Emer holds open the door that I know I'm welcome.

And that maybe I always belonged.

Chapter Nineteen

Becca

It was hard waking up without Hale beside me. When I read his note that he'd gone to see his brothers, it was hard not to follow and make certain he was okay. But the hardest thing of all was leaving Hale's bed to return to my childhood home.

Momma didn't give me a choice. "If you ever loved me, Becca June, you'll come and tell your daddy goodbye."

That's the call that woke me from sound sleep and the last thing I wanted to hear.

My Mercedes rolls to a stop. I climb out, slowly, my heart heavy and chills racking my spine. I look up at the grand estate. I don't feel what I feel because my father is dying and the hours he has left are few. The cold taking up residence deep within me is due to fear. Fear of what he'll say and what his words will do to me.

At thirty-two years old, I'm still afraid of my father. It saddens and disappoints me, but it sickens me more than anything.

I ring the doorbell beside the heavy door that marks the entrance to my childhood home. The door looks new. It's not. It's a door capable of keeping a giant out and secrets and screams locked tight within. Momma has a thing about keeping up appearances with things looking fresh, no matter how badly they're falling apart on the inside.

The door was recently sanded to perfection. I slide my fingers over it, feeling the slickness of the wood as I wait. She chose a dark stain this time. It goes nicely with the ornate ironwork that decorates the windows. I wish I could tell her I liked it. I wish I could tell her a lot of things. But like the feelings stirring deep in my gut, my conversations with Momma have never been sweet ones.

Even as a child, I noticed the strain between us. I wanted to connect with her as easily as Trin and her momma so effortlessly did. Once, when I was nine and my birthday was just a few days away, I tried to mirror Trin to see if Momma would respond like Miss Silvie.

Momma pulled away, frowning. "What are you up to, Becca June?" she asked.

"I want to be close to you," I admitted. "Like the Summers are. Trinity and her momma hug all the time when she comes home from school, in the kitchen while making supper, anywhere, really, they hug all the time."

"Sylvie Summers?" she asked, her voice judgmental, as if seeing more than what was there. "Didn't I tell you she refused to hold the Confederate flag during our annual picnic last year at the club? Sweet heavens, you'd have thought we were asking her to hold up the building itself."

I knew that flag was offensive, even then. Miss Silvie herself had told me why. She was teaching Trinity and I how to make cranberry cookies. She explained why the flag was special to some and why it hurt so many others. She didn't judge, but she did make us understand. But me talking to Momma wasn't about what Miss Silvie did. It was about what she and Trin had that I really wanted.

"Momma, I want us to be close," I repeated.

"To spend time together?" she guessed. "Maybe go shopping?"

The annoyance in her tone already told me I was fighting a losing battle. My mother never made me cry like my father. But that day, my tears didn't want to stop.

Momma raised her small thin brows she'd plucked one too many times, her impatience with me growing at the sight of my tears. She motioned around the room, where the dining room was stuffed to the gills with traditional Southern men and their wives. The *clink, clink* of meticulously polished silverware tapped against the stark white dishes. "What do you call this, Becca June?" she asked.

There wasn't so much of a sliver of what I'd hoped for. Instead, there was only confirmation of what I'd always suspected. I was a burden to my mother. An obligation. I wasn't something to simply love and cherish. "Wipe your eyes, Becca June. People are staring."

I shake out my hands. These are the type of memories my childhood home stirs. I don't need them now. I've never needed them.

The door swings open, the motion so awkward I know it's not whom I'm here to see. I was prepared to find my cousin, Kirk, in the kitchen, complaining about liberals and blaming everything on the manipulation of the media, or perhaps in the billiards room shooting pool with my other cousins. I hadn't expected him to answer the door.

Age wasn't kind to Kirk. He's heavier, the little hair he has left thinning at the top. He doesn't bother saying hello. Neither do I. "Upstairs," is all he bothers with.

I try to relax my hold on my purse strap. I don't realize how hard I'm gripping it until I have to shake out my hand when Kirk turns his back.

The air inside the house is frigid, as my father prefers. In another house, all the wood paneling would provide a sense of hominess and small children would slide down the long winding banister. This house has no such things. I wasn't allowed to be "childish," even as a child. This is the place where happiness comes to die and where the dreams you have are quickly silenced.

Kirk hops up the stairs in his bare feet. Momma never allowed shoes upstairs. It's the reason Kirk glances over his shoulder and frowns at my feet.

My mint heels are high, but respectable, and my white cold-shoulder dress sleek, yet professional. "I'm not staying long," I say, before he can remind me to take my shoes off.

"Suit yourself," he mutters, caring about as much as I do.

We reach the second floor. Just as I didn't expect Kirk to answer the door, I don't expect all the people gathered along the east wing. Matthew is here with his wife, Lynda. Matthew appears relieved to see me and he almost smiles. "Hi, Becca," he says.

"Hi, Matthew," I reply.

Brent's drunk. The tangy smell of Wild Turkey seeps across the space with his sharp exhale. He never married. Neither did Parker, who, like Brent, is only standing because the wall is holding him up.

Both give me the once-over, as if barely recognizing me through their haze. I pass them and Sully, and his wife, Jerilyn, holding his hand, while her free one strokes her pregnant belly. I nod to her. She was nice enough to invite me to their wedding. I sent a gift, but declined the invitation.

I keep walking, my head neither high nor bowed. I try to avoid eye contact with Parker. He's on wife number four and it shows in every wrinkle on his face. Davey crosses his arms, his long hair covering his eyes as he leans forward. It doesn't quite conceal him. I know he's watching me. But like most of my family, he doesn't say anything.

I was the black sheep of the family long before I left. Nothing's changed. If anything, there's another coat of midnight dark wool covering my hide.

Momma waits at the end of the hall speaking quietly to Reverend Ellis. She abruptly quiets when she sees me.

"Hello, Becca June," Reverend Ellis says, smiling kindly.

"Hello, Reverend," I reply. "Thank you for coming."

He places his hand on my shoulder. "I'm here for whatever you need, child."

I tilt my head respectfully and turn to my mother.

The frigid temperature in the hallway drops several degrees when I look at her. She's not scowling. People are watching, after all.

I want to cry and it has nothing to do with my father. In my absence, my mother became old, small, and frail, and I couldn't help her.

My heart clenches. I try to be kind, wishing it wasn't so much of an effort and praying that awful feeling spreading like wicked wildfire across my chest will cease its torment.

"Hello, Momma," I say, bending to kiss her cheek.

She clutches my face gently, a gesture of tenderness she's never demonstrated before. It's brief, but it's there, a minute effort that took a great deal from the woman who gave me life.

I take that moment and tuck it away, deep within that space in my heart reserved just for her. She may not like me, and I may never have meant as much to her as I would've hoped, but she's still my Momma and I love her.

"You look well," she says.

"Thank you," I say, my voice strained and delicate enough to barely be more than a wisp of air. "You do too, ma'am,"

I meant what I promised myself all those years ago, that I'd never return to this house again. But my father is dying. By the way everyone has gathered, today might very well be the day.

That little piece within my heart I reserve for my mother always hoped she'd reach out to me in kindness. It prayed she'd someday find the courage to tell me that I'd made it, and that she was proud. But that would have gone against my father's wishes. Sick or not, she believes he rules and decides for the family.

It hurts. In many ways, I remain that little girl in the dining room packed with people, desperately trying to connect with a woman more concerned about what others would see than with the child who desperately needed her.

"Thank you for coming," Momma says. "He's been waitin' on you to arrive."

He has . . .

I follow her inside their bedroom. This was a place I'd only ever seen from the hallway. We weren't allowed in my parents' quarters. To them, it was sacred, not a place for nosey children with dirty hands and tendencies for destroying things.

One Christmas, my cousins and I dared each other to go into the room and retrieve one item as proof they'd been fearless enough to enter. Kirk made it out with my mother's silver hair brush. It was the same brush Daddy beat Kirk with when he caught him. He'd never officially adopted the boys when my uncle and aunt passed, but he disciplined them as he saw fit.

Dark, parquet wood covers the floor. More paneling covers the walls. The room is huge, the four poster bed near the window practically swallowed by its massiveness.

I look in the direction of the bathroom. I don't see my father buried beneath the thick burgundy and gold paisley comforter. But, apparently, he's there.

"He can't get up anymore," my mother says, guessing correctly that I didn't see him. "The medicine the doctor gave him robbed him of his appetite and he's lost some weight. But he's there."

"Is that Becca June?" A hoarse and unrecognizable voice calls to me from the confines of the bed.

I knew he'd call me by my full name. Still, the name pokes through me, swimming through my veins like a river of glass.

"Yes, darlin'," Momma replies, her voice louder than she would usually allow. "She's come to see her daddy."

For her to address him as such does a lot to me. None of it's good.

"Tell her to come closer," he says.

Momma motions me forward and turns to go. She doesn't wait for me to accept the invitation. She simply presumes that I will, shutting the door quietly behind her and leaving me alone to face my fate.

I no longer have feet; cinderblocks have replaced what my shoes once were. I no longer have legs, just long rods of steel making it hard to bend my knees. I'm sick. It shouldn't be this way. I should be throwing myself on top of my father, sobbing, begging him not to leave me, telling him to get better—pleading with him to *fucking love me.*

I shouldn't be so terrified of a feeble old man. But I am. Once more, I'm that little girl, wanting more than anything to connect with her mother, only for this awful and dark house to close in around me, reducing me to nothing but a fragile, petrified being.

I hate it here. I want to leave. I don't want to see him. I don't want to hear what he'll say or have him use this last moment to cut me down.

A small dining room chair is placed in front of the bed. The seat cushion is thick, black velvet, allowing those who've come to pay their respects to be as comfortable as possible. There're two more chairs by the window. But this seat is reserved solely for me.

I stop short of reaching the bed, stunned by the shell of a man my father has become. The round robust face that would flash fire engine red whenever he was angry is nothing more than loose skin and sunken cheekbones sharp enough to cut me. His wheat-colored hair, once peppered with traces of silver, is all but gone. Fragile pieces of silver poke through scattered places along his spotted scalp. The chemo destroyed everything except the cancer.

"Hello, Daddy," I say.

I'm not certain he hears me. My voice is softer than the way Momma spoke.

Dark rimmed eyes scan my face. My clothes are neither flashy like I wear out to dinner with Hale nor conservative enough for church. They speak of how young I still look and how successful I became, despite how badly my father wished for my downfall.

Because I was bad.

Because I was disrespectful.

Because I wasn't the boy he'd wanted.

Instead, I was a girl he couldn't submit to his will, who became the woman who'd never succumb.

"I always knew you'd come back," he says.

My entire body bristles, prepared for a fight I don't want to have.

Until he smiles.

The corners of his mouth lace with genuine humor. I'm not sure how to take it. I steel myself for bitter words he'll lash like a whip to scar me more, so I'll never heal.

He starts laughing, loudly. It's hard enough to cause him pain, and given his delicate condition, hard enough to crack his sternum.

He's trying to be funny. With me.

Regardless of how he treated me, there was a side of him that drew friends and made him popular. "Your father is the funniest man I know," Tim Robinson, our accountant, once told me.

My father was famous for being quick and clever, often bragging how his silver tongue was what had charmed my mother. It wasn't a side I experienced firsthand. Until now.

My *father* is joking with me on his deathbed.

That silver tongue was one of the many things I'd inherited from him. I don't think he noticed, unless it was directed at him. Then it wouldn't cause him to laugh, but rather spur his anger and vengeance.

I battle with whether I should come back with something just as funny or maybe something wicked. No one has to tell me my father's number is up. By the looks of it, death is mere hours away.

This is my final opportunity to be with him. I could leave on good terms or pound the last nail on the coffin, dramatizing the spoils of our horrible relationship. I can't stomach either. I can't yell at this frail man and demand to know why I was never good enough, why I had to be what he wanted in order for him to love me. I can't even bring myself to say I forgive you. So, I say the only thing I can.

"I'm here like you asked, Daddy."

"You're not scrawny anymore, Becca June."

It's an odd thing to say. I always had curves. But the last time he saw me, I still had a thin figure of an athletic twenty-two-year-old. Maybe, like me, he's struggling for things to say.

"No, sir, I'm not."

"What're you doing now?" he asks. "You married? Got yourself a husband and kids?" He gives me the once over only my father can. "Someone taking care of you?"

I almost mention Hale. But the only thing Hale takes care of is my heart and that's not what my father is asking. "I'm not married. I don't have children. I support myself, sir."

My tone is respectful, the same way it would've been when I was a teen and wanted to make a point or explain what I needed. Back then, regardless of how softly and intelligently I spoke, depending on his mood, he'd either grant me what I wanted or scream at me for asking.

Old habits die hard. It takes everything I have not to flinch, expecting those cruel words or an inevitable blow.

"No one would have you?" he asks, frowning.

I should leave in a huff right now, turn on my heel so my back is the last thing he sees. Instead, I laugh. This man is honestly stunned some prince on horseback hasn't picked me up.

"Sir, there were plenty of men who wanted me. I just didn't want them."

"You one of dem lesbians now, girl?"

My smile falters. "No. There just hasn't been anyone yet." That's a lie. But I don't want to bring Hale into this. I won't risk Daddy putting him down.

My gaze travels to the window, where the heavy curtains swallow any sunlight that dares to bleed into the room. Here, in my parents' room, only darkness welcomes darkness.

When I was little, I often looked away from my father, too scared to face him. When I stopped looking away, that's when things really changed between us and the resentment and tension soared to unstoppable heights, leaving everyone else walking on eggshells until the next battle began.

I turn back to him. Only a second or so passed. It wasn't enough for that feeling squeezing my chest to lessen. If anything, I receive an extra harsh churn when I look back upon his face. There's nothing left of the strong and imposing man I knew. But even though he looks weak and feeble, he's still that man capable of causing harm.

"Do you know the Cougars?"

Wrinkled eyelids tent over his hazy irises. "Of course, I do. They're the best team in the league. Some big shot went in a few years ago and shook everything up, cleaning up a reputation they'd all turned to shit." He frowns. "Why? You that guy's secretary or something?"

"No, daddy. I'm the guy who saved the Cougars. I'm the one who shook everything up."

He makes a face. "You weren't stupid with all that money your grandmother left you, were you? When you spent it all at once, I thought you'd gone and messed up everything she tried to do for you." He huffs. "At least you did right by her and what she gave you."

His comments confuse me. I'd used the money Nana June left me to pay for college. There was plenty left over. When I left, I turned it over to Momma. It was her mother's money, after all, and there was always a part of me who felt Momma needed it more than I did.

"I used it for my education," I say, not wanting to rat Momma out. She'd obviously hidden it from Daddy. "The rest of my success came from hard work." I cross my legs. "You never heard about me with the Cougars? Never read about me in the paper or saw me on TV?"

"Naw, I didn't want to hear about you. Nothing good, anyway, only the bad."

I frown, trying to understand how he can speak to me like nothing was ever wrong between us and then say something like that. "Why?"

His eyes moisten and it becomes the inevitable death of me. "So you could come back here, to me, to your family, Becca June."

A tear dribbles from his left eye, followed by another.

The sour taste leaves my stomach, crackling like a dying ember until it reaches my throat and causes my eyes to sting beyond measure.

"You don't get it, do you, girl?" he accuses. "You never have. You were *supposed to need me*. You were supposed to beg me for advice, seek me out so I could guide you—so I could make you into the lady you were destined to be."

He coughs, the cacophony of words too much for his weakened state. "You were supposed to need me," he says again. "I was supposed to be your hero. Just like every father dreams he can be."

Those giant pieces of cinderblock I'd protected my heart with each time we'd fought, that *beautiful* indestructible wall I'd created to protect myself against his next blow or terrible word, cracks, falling apart and littering the ground.

It's not an immediate destruction. No, my walls were stronger than that. But as they fall, piece by piece, behind it, the light bathed in forgiveness shines a brilliant light.

"You wanted to be my hero?" I stammer.

"Was that too much for a father to ask?"

"Then why did you treat me like you did?" I ask, my voice splintering. "Why did you hit me? Why couldn't you just be kind? Why did *everything* have to be so hard?"

"I was trying to make you into what you needed to be," he says, those awful tears falling with what remains of my walls. "The best way I knew how. Even if it wasn't your way."

"I was a good girl, Daddy—"

"Because I made you that way. Because you were too afraid not to be."

He was right, but the harshness he used and the way he went about it was so wrong.

"Come here, child," he says, his rusty voice groaning from the effort it takes him to speak.

I lean in, swallowing hard when his weathered and deeply wrinkled hand cups my face. His hands are cold, bone white, as opposed to bronzed by the summer sun. Blue veins run across them, sinking into the empty pockets near his knuckles where the skin sticks firmly against the bone.

I sob for all the years I missed that could've been good if we'd both tried a little harder. Had I not been so quick to judge and more easy-going, maybe he would have been more willing to listen.

Daddy lets me cry, allowing me to release my pain until I calm and his strength rebuilds enough to speak.

"Becca June, I've made mistakes. I'm not so proud to think I'm perfect. But when it comes to you, I did the best job I could." This time, he's the one openly weeping. "But it wasn't good enough, was it?"

"Oh, *Daddy*," I say. What's left of my strength falls away, just like my carefully constructed wall.

"You left me. You left your momma," he says. He shakes his head. "You're still that damn selfish bitch you always have been."

My tears evaporate from my eyes, my heart, from every cell of my being. The feeble old man I first saw, the one I pitied so badly I could barely meet his face, regains that rage I know and taps into that familiar cruelty.

"You're exactly the trash I always feared you'd become." He's yelling, as loud as his vocal cords will allow. "You're alone with no man, pretending to be something you are not. Successful?" He spits out. "If you didn't look like you did, if you weren't spreading your legs like you are, that football team would have nothing to do with you."

He's not done.

I am.

I stand on shaking limbs, almost losing my balance. I grasp the dining room chair to keep my feet and still my father screams.

"You're a whore," he says. "You're nothing. No matter how bad I tried to save you—you hear me, girl? That night, that was *me* leaving *you*!"

I abandon the room slowly, using the space separating me from the door to wipe my makeup smeared face. With all the care I can muster, I shut the door quietly behind me. It doesn't quite muffle his screams, his rants, assuring me that everyone in the hall hears and heard the nasty and vicious remarks of his farewell.

The standoffish and perhaps mocking expressions I expect are not what greets me. Everyone present is aghast, horrified by the encounter and the indecencies my father continues to holler. Even Kirk, whose attention skips between me and the closed door, regards me with sympathy.

Everyone heard him. My only reprieve is that the reverend is mercifully gone.

My mother steps out of the room beside theirs, an armful of carefully folded towels tucked against her and her thin lips pressed into a line. "You shouldn't have upset him like that. He needs his rest."

My family's eyes fly open, every woman present clasping her mouth. It takes everything in me not to lose my shit, my body quaking with the need to lash out. Matthew reaches for me as if fearing I'll launch myself at my mother and beat her with my fists.

I don't. Anything I do or say will harm me, not them.

If I scream at my dying father, no matter what vulgarities he throws my way, I'm the one who looks bad. I'll be the black sheep who kicks him one last time, who smothers him with her filthy wool.

I refuse to take the bait from him or from her. So, I walk away. It's the one thing I can do.

I don't plan to stop. I don't plan to return. They'll bury him and all the darkness without me. But when I reach the top of the staircase, my mother's final words hold me in place.

"He's still your father," she says.

Chapter Twenty

Hale

The dogs hurry to greet me when I open the door. Their tails wag as if it's been days, not hours, since they last saw me. I pop the bag of barbecue on the counter and rub their fur.

"What's wrong? Thought I wasn't coming back? Thought I was leaving y'all?"

I almost laugh. How did I go from big boss with a bite back to a country boy with two fur balls with no bite at all? But the laugh that stirs from greeting these pups and from finding a sense of peace with my family doesn't quite come. Becca's not answering my texts or calls.

"Our puppies," as we've grown to call them, prance beside me as I open the back door to let them out. I check my phone again. There's a text from Trin telling me Becca isn't answering her, either. It does nothing to ease my worry. If she was called back to Charlotte, she would have sent a quick text.

I start to pocket my phone when it buzzes. My brief relief from thinking it's finally Becca is quickly squashed.

It's a text from Mason, urging me to call him right away.

I let the dogs in and call Mason. He picks up just as I spot the note Becca left on the counter.

"Hey," Mason says. "I have incredible news for you."

I barely hear his voice as my eyes focus on the note.

Momma called. Daddy is close to death. I have to go.

"Hale?" Mason says. "Are you there?"

"I can't talk right now," I say. I snag my keys and take off in a sprint toward the mud room, the dogs trailing me like they know something is wrong.

"Hale, it's important."

"Becca's daddy's dying. She's with him now."

There's an abrupt silence and I almost think he disconnected. "Don't go there, Hale. A fight is the last thing you need right now."

I stop in the middle of setting the alarm. "Mason, remember what they did to her last time? What they put her through? Her father broke her nose and left her almost unconscious. Then he and her pussy cousins left her fucking bleeding on the sand. You think that brutality's going to end just because he's dying? With all her cousins there to do his fucking bidding?"

Mason hisses out a curse. "Take Callahan with you. Landon, too. Don't be showing up there by yourself, Hale. There's no telling what those fools will do when they see you."

I disconnect and give up on the alarm, slamming my hand against the garage door opener. I don't care what happens to me. All I care about is Becca and what they might do. Her cousins, I don't think they would physically touch her. But they don't have to throw hands to harm her. Her momma will be no help. And her daddy . . . just because he's dying doesn't mean he isn't that same mean son of a bitch.

I reach for my driver's side door when Becca's Mercedes pulls up to the front of the house. My heart just about tanks into my stomach. I jog toward her, what little relief her sudden presence offers shooting out of my lungs in a pained exhale when I see her.

Her face is beet red and swollen. I can't tell if she's bruised or if her skin tone is due to how hard she's crying. I've never her seen her like this. Those motherfuckers hurt her badly. I'm ready to rage, to find them.

I throw the door open the remainder of the way when she tries to step out and haul her to me. "What happened?" I ask.

She buries her face against my chest, gripping me as if I'm the only thing keeping her upright. I don't know compassion. Not now. All I know is the need to avenge her.

I'm so terrified of what they did to her, the tenderness I demonstrate stuns me. I stroke away her tears and sweat-drenched hair. "Did they hurt you, baby?" I ask. "Did they touch you?"

I don't ask if her father's dead. These aren't tears of pain that accompany grief. This is the agony of a battered spirit, something she didn't deserve.

She tries to speak, but all that comes out are jumbled sounds and syllables that make no sense. I kiss her face and tuck her against me. Then, with as much care as I can, I reach for her keys and purse and lock her car.

I should take her in through the front. There's more space there. But I go through the garage and close it, setting the alarm as fast as I can.

The need to secure her inside, to make sure she's safe from any possible harm, overwhelms me. Becca's hurt, broken. I'll be damned if I let anything else happen to her.

The dogs whine, circling us as I lead her inside and up to our bedroom. They're frightened by what they sense in Becca. I am, too. It's all I can do not to pay those people she calls her family a visit.

I sit her on the bed, kissing her head and wiping all the tears that fall. It takes her a long while to calm, long enough for the setting sun to crawl across the room and leave us with only a trickle of light.

Sam rests at my feet, quietly whining. Rosie alternates from hopping on the bed to jumping on the floor, until finally settling in front of Becca. It's a bad sign that Becca has barely acknowledged her sweet pups. It's also a bad sign that she can't seem to let me go.

"I saw my father," Becca finally says. "It was awful."

I knew anything involving her family would be. But in my wildest dreams, I never would have guessed how bad, until she tells me.

Every word is like a physical blow. Every detail of the event is like something from the worst of dreams. What Becca describes isn't an angry man. It's a twisted man. A man so hateful and full of spite, he had to cast the last insult.

Wilton Shields couldn't bring himself to leave this world peacefully with a kind thought or a chance at forgiveness. No, he used the moment to hurt his daughter and to make sure she'll never forget it.

Damn him. Leaving Becca with this last memory of him was her daddy's final 'fuck you.'

In a way, he's lucky he's dying. If he wasn't, I might kill him myself.

Mason had warned me not to go by myself. He wasn't really afraid of what they would do. He was afraid of what I would do in response. Like me, Mason knew Becca's daddy was incapable of gentleness, of thoughts meant to be kind, or a final act of forgiveness.

I don't realize how tight I'm clutching Becca until I ease my hold. She doesn't complain or struggle. She simply allows me to hold her in the way we both need.

"Did anyone help you?" I manage. "Anyone at all try to offer you comfort?"

Becca pushes her hair behind her shoulder. It's the first time since she arrived that she's let me go. "Matthew followed me out to my car. His wife, Lynda, too. They seemed sad." She sniffs. "Horrified, even. But they didn't say anything."

I shake my head. Becca could have been a stranger on the street. But if I'd seen what happened, I would have done or said something. Here, her own kin can't offer her so much as a sympathetic embrace.

"I-I told them that I wouldn't be at the funeral. That I was done." She reaches for a tissue and dabs her eyes. "They nodded, like they understood, even though they didn't make a sound."

"You should have called me." I lift her hands and kiss them. "You should have let me know. I would have gone with you. You didn't have to be alone."

Gratitude spreads across her pretty face upon hearing my words. Becca was alone. She recognizes I understand that's how she felt.

"You were a lamb," I tell her. "Walking into an arena filled with lions who cared more about pleasing their king than you."

"A lamb," she says, closing her eyes briefly. "Here I always thought I was the black sheep."

She's trying to lighten the mood and make us feel better. I do, in a way, but not because of what she says, but because of how she handled everything flung her way.

"The black sheep, the odd balls, the fuckups, they don't go out and accomplish everything you did. They don't stand up to the lions and win. They cower and willingly obey to save themselves. Your family are those lions, Becks. They wanted and expected to you to fail without your daddy's money and influence. Instead, you prospered and surpassed them all, proving you never needed them."

She smiles softly as another tear leaks down her face.

"You're a lamb, because of the gentleness you demonstrate to those blessed enough to call you a friend. That soft side you show to those who've captured your heart reflect in your beauty. You showed your family you're not afraid, Becca. No matter how bad they treated you or how hard things were, you didn't fear them. Never once did you crawl back, begging for help."

"No, I didn't," she agrees, that sense of pride I know so well rebuilding.

"What happened today was total shit," I say. "There's no shame in what you did or in the tears that fell in their presence. But there is shame in everything that man said to you and they know it."

"I don't think my momma would agree," she says. Anger and disappointment barely glaze her comment, but I still sense it.

"Your momma needs to believe what she believes to justify her life and why she stayed with a man who was not only brutal to her, but to her only child."

Becca watches me, listening closely. "From the start, your momma wanted what her friends had. What her momma had. The grand estate, the pretty clothes, and the handsome husband with money, so all she had to do is play the part of a traditional southern lady. An elegant woman, who belongs to all the right clubs and who is seen in the proper circles. The difference is the man she chose wasn't a real gentleman, not like your granddaddy was. He was one of the richest, best looking men in his day, but he was also a monster, Becca." I kiss her lips. "A monster my lamb defeated when she showed her teeth."

"Thank you," she whimpers.

Her head falls against my shoulder, right where it belongs. My knuckles glide against her arm, trying to soothe the pain that remains. But that pain should never have come.

"You should have told me, baby," I say. "We would have faced those fucking lions together."

"I didn't feel right pulling you away from your brothers," she says. "I know what it must have taken for you to see them. I couldn't rob you of that moment."

She looks at me, her expression carrying everything she experienced today, except all that hate doesn't stand a chance against the strength that remains. "I also couldn't risk anything happening to you."

"I could have handled it. I would've taken it all if it meant sparing you. I love you, Becca."

"I love you, too, Hale."

Slowly, her hands unravel from my waist and she rises. "Will you do something for me?"

I'm already on my feet, my heart thudding madly as I look at the woman I want to marry and grow old and weary with. "I would do anything for you."

She backs away, pressing her palm against my chest to keep me in place when I follow.

Becca leads the dogs out of the bedroom and shuts the door. With an exhausted sigh, her gaze melds with mine. "I don't want to think about all the bad things I lived through today. I only want to know you and how good I feel when I'm with you. Will you make love to me, Hale? Will you make me forget everything except for you?"

I tug off my shirt and let it fall on the floor. The rest of my clothes follow. Her large breasts lift and lower as her breathing increases. The lingering sadness shadowing her irises dissipated, replaced by wanton desire and the sex she begs me to give her.

She wants to forget what happened today.

And I know exactly how to distract her.

I surge forward, spreading my arms wide and pinning her to the door. The tip of my tongue glides between her lips until she opens wide, permitting me to kiss her deeply. She sways her hips as I rock back and forth, her hands clamping my ass, enjoying the feel of my body against hers.

My lips ghost over her throat, passing lazy kisses across her jaw. I nibble on her ear, her chin, and down her neck, as my hands slip behind her back to unzip her dress and pull it down until it pools at her feet.

I leave her shoes on and her lacey white thong in place. The bra I unsnap with two fingers, allowing her breasts to spill over my chest. I should be used to their weight and feel by now, but like the rest of Becca, I can't get enough of them. I knead her breasts and suck on the tips until most of the large pink areolas disappear into my mouth.

My tongue and teeth tease and stimulate. Becca shivers, her soft moans increasing as she clutches me tighter. "*More*," she pleads.

It's her favorite thing to ask when we make love and my favorite thing to give her.

I pull her off the door when she tries to kneel and take me in. "Not yet," I tell her, leading her toward the French doors that lead to the second-floor terrace. "Soon. For now, I want to play."

I lower her into the wide cushioned chair placed near the doors and just in front of our bed. She smiles impishly. "What are you up to?" she asks.

My grin and tone sizzles with lust. I spread my arms, giving her a very nice view of my naked form. "I'm already up and ready to go, darlin'. I'm just waiting on you to get going."

I sit at the edge of our bed, watching her, taking in every sweep and curve of her light golden skin. My eyelids grow heavy as I grip my erection, relishing the delighted surprise in Becca's features as I stroke.

My body shudders, inciting the raw hunger flashing in Becca's gaze. One leg lifts, the heel of her shoe digging into the push white fabric. The other leg follows, her attention never leaving mine as she parts her legs wide. I try to concentrate on keeping my strokes smooth and even. Becca tugs the crotch of her panties aside and exposes her supple pink flesh, interrupting my focus and making me harder.

"Damn," I rasp.

She passes her hand leisurely. "What's wrong?" she purrs. "I thought you wanted me to get ready for you?"

"I'm not complaining," I say, my voice hitching as we increase our speed. "Just looking forward to how hard we're going to go at it."

Becca's eyes roll and her lashes flutter. "Hale . . ." she whimpers.

From one breath to the next, I'm lifting her hips and lowering them down to my face. The back of my head rests on the cushy seat and I keep her close against me. Becca uses the rear of the chair to keep her balance as she pitches back and forth, struggling to keep her thong from getting in the way.

I end up tearing the thing off, not wanting anything to keep me from devouring her. She can't take all the sucks and swirls. She comes undone, falling forward. I hang on to her, circling her waist and continuing my eager taste.

My deep moans vibrate against her skin, making her gasp and whimper and beg for more. Her hair fans across my lap, tickling my legs. I almost laugh. But when she adjusts her position and sucks me deep, I'm no longer laughing, I'm two pulls shy of roaring her name.

Both of us lose our damn selves in what we're doing, each of us fighting to outdo and out-lust the other. This is a new position for us. But it won't be the last time we use it. I flip her up and over, bending her forward and taking her from behind.

Becca grips the arm rests, my thrusts so delicious, wicked, and forceful, her hair bounces in tangled waves. Becca swears, over and over, the dirty and sexy talk spewing from her lush mouth exciting me and encouraging me to pound faster.

Her orgasms peak and crash, one after the other. But I'm nowhere near done. I turn her around, falling into the seat and planting my feet on the floor. I position her so her soles rest on my knees. Becca bounces and turns her hips as I thrust, each slide in and out accelerating our frantic efforts.

I expect to last longer. But between this position, her cries of pleasure, and the way the sounds of our lovemaking echo in the expanse of the large suite, I don't. Not this time.

Becca wanted to forget about this day. I wanted her to only know the good we have and passion we're just barely touching upon.

I spend the night showing her that I only want her to know love and kindness, now, and forever.

Chapter Twenty-One

Becca

Hale is on top of me, gripping the headboard to pound harder.

"More," I beg. "*Please don't stop.*"

I fasten my ankles around his lower back and drive him deeper. He doesn't need my help; he's doing well enough. Three orgasms in and another one building, I can barely speak, my body swimming with raw desire.

His speed quickens, giving me more, and more, and more.

We smile wickedly. This sex is hot! I should be pulling away from him to taste his rigid staff. But I take the passion he's giving me and bask in it, enjoying the much-needed distraction and the unending bouts of pleasure.

He flips me onto my knees, positioning me so my hands grip the frame to keep me situated. His feet land on either side of my thighs as he crouches and increases the speed of his thrusts.

I unravel, allowing the tears of bliss to replace the ones that burned permanent scars yesterday.

I won't attend the funeral. That's what I told my cousin, Matthew, and his wife when they chased me out to the car. As much as Matthew wasn't there for me throughout my life, he seemed to care enough about what Daddy said and what it did to me. For the briefest second, I thought he'd try to talk me out of it or maybe even insult me.

Bitch move, right? Not going to your own father's funeral?

No, sometimes the bitch is the one dying bitter and alone.

They nodded. I drove away, wishing I didn't sob the entire ride back here.

I drove along the wooded road, with the emergency brake still engaged. I wish I cared enough to release it, but nothing mattered then, except reaching Hale. Like I hoped, he was exactly everything I needed.

He clutched me in his arms, kissed my face, and allowed me to spill every bit of my misery. As much as I cried, those tears I shed for him, when he told me about his time with his brothers, were more important.

No. Hale is more important. He always was.

My core clenches around him, the spasms quivering my thighs painfully delightful.

"Fuck," Hale curses, filling me.

The warmth and release he delivers makes me moan louder. "*Fuck*," he says, again.

He slows his pace gradually. I wait for him to harden again as he strokes in and out. As wonderfully tender as I am from all our love-making these past few hours, I'm not quite sated.

Trin once told me sex can be healing. I never quite understood her until now. And, my, couldn't I benefit from more healing?

I don't expect my arms to be as weak as they are. Hale catches me when he pulls out and my grip on the frame loosens abruptly.

He draws me to him, kissing my neck. "You okay?"

I watch the way his large hands cup my breasts, my skin slippery from the perspiration gathered beneath them.

"You're just what I needed," I admit quietly.

My head is heavy from stress and maybe from more than I care to admit.

"You're always what I need," he whispers.

"Don't make me cry," I whisper, biting down on my lip. "I don't want to do it anymore."

The tears Hale causes are the good kind of tears, those I need so I don't feel so vacant and alone. Maybe I should let them fall. But good and bad tears . . . I've cried them enough these past few hours. My well should have run dry by now. But there's that misery, blurring my vision and threatening to split me apart in all those painful ways I don't want it to.

Hale drags his tongue along my neck. He doesn't tease my delicate spots, those still tingling and begging for his attention. That's okay. The kiss that follows is enough and so is the way he touches me.

He lowers us to the mattress, straightening my legs when I can't seem to find the will or strength.

My fatigue isn't simply related to the past few hours, but perhaps to all those times with my family that aren't worth remembering.

Hale props himself up, arranging my hair to the side when I don't bother pushing it away from my face. Concern furrows his brow. He wraps us in a cool sheet and settles against me. It's only then he speaks.

"I'm worried about you," he admits.

"I don't want you to be." It's true. Worrying about me and what my family said isn't worth it. In time, with therapy and, possibly, medication, I'll move on. I have to. This dysfunctional relationship with my family has gone on long enough.

He slides his hand down, ensuring that the sheet completely covers my back. "Doesn't mean I'll stop," he replies.

"I know," I whisper, smiling. "Which is why I never want to know life without you."

Moonlight trickles in through the blinds, but dawn doesn't feel too far away. I'm not sure what wakes me. I'm not cold. All I feel is warm and safe.

Hale's arms cocoon me against him. His skin feels like silk, all the while possessing the strength of granite. I dip my head to press a kiss against his skin.

That's when I hear it. Footsteps.

I gently shake Hale, a little harder when he doesn't move. "Hale. *Hale*," I whisper harshly.

He rolls on top of me and immediately positions himself between my legs. "Hi, baby," he murmurs, kissing my ear.

I ignore pangs of need and the shivers his affections cause. "Hale, there's someone in the house."

His head lifts. "What?"

Something crashes downstairs. He leaps out of bed, yanking on his jeans. I gather the sheets against my breasts as he pulls out the gun he keeps in his nightstand.

"Stay here," he orders.

I scoot to the edge of the bed, bunching the bed linens closer.

The door bursts open and Sean steps in, munching on a bowl of cereal. "Hey y'all," he says.

"What the hell, Sean?" Hale hollers over the last bits of my screams.

Sean is clearly confused. "What?" he asks. "It's not like we don't know you're fucking."

Hale and I exchange glances as Rosie and Sam swarm in. Their tails wag and they're panting, evidently excited to see us.

"Dem nice dogs you got here. They didn't even bark when we came in." Sean sits on the edge of the bed and takes another spoonful of what might or might not be shredded wheat.

"We?" Hale asks.

"Mason's here, too."

"Hey y'all," Mason's deep voice booms from the hallway.

"He didn't want me to come in. Said something about it being rude or in poor taste. I don't know. Something like that."

Hale mutters a curse. "Are you out of your mind?" He houses the gun back in its case. "I could have blown your fucking head off."

I love Sean. I truly do. Those people you would give a kidney to if they needed one? Sean is one of those. But eloquence is not his forte, and there're just not enough chickens left in that henhouse. Once more, he blinks back at Hale, confused.

"That's not true," he insists. "You're a way better shot than that, Hale. Don't you ever let anyone tell you different."

What sounds like a little girl giggling in the hallway has me turning in that direction. Mason. Only Sean can make the big guy laugh like that.

Satisfied that his comments explained away his intrusiveness, Sean resumes his cereal eating duties. "I was real hungry, even after I ate that rotisserie chicken you had in there." He lifts his bowl. "I hope you don't mind, but I ate the last bit of your shredded wheat, too. It didn't suck, but I'm not going to lie, it wasn't great. I'm not gonna spend the rest of the day in the bathroom, am I?" He takes another bite. "That would really blow. There's a fight later tonight I want to catch on TV."

"Are you seriously going to sit there while Becca is lying here naked?" Hale demands.

"What? It's not like I've never seen her naked."

Hale squares his jaw. "Oh, yeah? And when did that happen?"

"It happened all the time. The five of us used to go skinny dipping back up at the lake."

"You boys promised you wouldn't look," I remind him.

Hale and Sean exchange glances, frowning. "We were young, teenagers, and boys," Hale says. "Did you really expect us to keep that promise?"

"Yeah, did you really expect that?" Mason calls from the hallway.

"So, then, why are you mad now?" Sean asks Hale. "Besides, she's all covered up. Aren't you, Becks?"

"I sure as shit am," I reply, pulling the thick blanket closer to me.

"Things have changed since we were teens," Hale points out.

"Because she's your woman now?"

Hale quiets. "Yeah, that's part of it."

I smile, even though my eyes have that familiar sting of tears. I'm Hale Wilder's woman. It sounds lovely. Sometimes, you need an inappropriate friend like Sean barging in while you're sleeping naked with your man to show you how lovely it is.

I gather my puppies as they inch closer, loving the sweet scent of their fur as I kiss their heads. "Hi, babies," I coo.

Hale slides back into bed, placing his arm around me. Sam immediately leaves me to spread out across his lap. "Sean, how did you sneak in here?"

"I didn't sneak. Trin and Callahan are in Raleigh with her family. Something about her father meeting with the governor about the state of affairs. Or maybe they're there checking out the local restaurants. You know how Callahan likes to eat. Whatever it was, they were worried and asked us to find you."

Hale rubs his face. "We forgot to call her," he says.

"I know," I reply, immediately feeling bad.

"Yeah," Sean agrees. "Trin was all beside herself when she couldn't reach y'all. She gave us the passcode to the alarm. We saw your cars here, so we didn't panic. We were both hungry from flying and decided to have us some breakfast."

Sean wipes his mouth with the back of his hand. "Me and Mason had bacon to start with. So did your dogs. They *really* love bacon. Especially the little one. I feel a lot better about that. I was starting to think she was some kind of vegetarian when she initially didn't take it. I don't know about y'all, but I don't trust vegetarians. There's something not right about turning your back on the meat God himself instructed to make into burgers. Hear what I'm saying? That's blasphemous, as far as I'm concerned."

Another little girl laugh from the hall. I throw back my head, laughing. Home sweet home, there's no place like Kiawah.

"Why are you here?" Hale asks.

"Oh, for two reasons." He holds up his spoon. "One is, we were worried about what was going to happen if you showed up at Becca's Daddy's place, so me and Mason hopped on the first flight down here, expecting to kick some ass."

Hale glances at me, worried, and likely thinking about everything I went through. The pain from yesterday is gone. Will it be there in the coming weeks? Maybe even months? Yes. But with Hale by my side and some work on myself, I'll be okay eventually.

"Is Trin still breastfeeding?" Sean asks. "I don't want her stressed. She might dry up or something."

"It doesn't work that way, Sean," I assure him.

"I texted her, anyway," Mason calls from the hall. "Let her know everyone's fine."

"Thank you," Hale and I say at once.

My head rests against Hale's shoulder as Rosie cuddles closer.

"Speaking of breast-feeding," Sean says. "Are you gonna do that?" He points to my chest. "I'm not an expert or anything, but I figured if Trinity could feed both those babies of hers with no problem, you—" He twirls his finger in a figure eight. "—and all that can feed a small village. Are you up to feeding a small village, Becca?"

"I think I owe it to the world to try," I agree.

"Thank you for your generosity to the world," Sean commends me.

"Yeah, thanks, Becca," Mason calls from the hall.

"Sean, sweetheart," I say. "You were saying something about there being two reasons you came down here?"

"You remember that don't you, Sean?" Hale says. "Up until you were distracted by something shiny, namely Becca's breasts?"

Sean sets his cereal bowl aside. "Oh, yeah." He frowns. "But maybe Mason should tell you."

Mason pokes his head in. "Is it all right to come in?"

Of course, he asks Hale. "Oh, sure," Hale says. "Why the hell not?"

Mason eases his way in, carrying a folder in his hand and trying to keep from looking at me directly.

Sean points to the floor. "You see that?" he says. "That's a thong. Torn off by a sharp set of teeth as near as I can figure."

"Sean," Hale warns.

"I think that's why women don't get the rashes I do," Sean says, as if Hale hadn't spoken. "They let their goods breathe, you hear what I'm saying?"

Mason pinches the bridge of his nose, as he often does in Sean's presence. As he lets go, he slides the folder across the bed.

Hale lifts it. "What's this?"

Mason meets him square in the face. "A major step toward ensuring all pending charges are dropped against you."

Hale turns on the bedside light and flips through the file. I lean in, trying to read as Rosie repositions herself on my lap. "It's a sworn testimony from my intern, Clark."

"Oh, my God," I say, scanning the document.

"He confessed to providing Cooling and Malroy access to your accounts and many others, as well as providing details on how he was placed in your employment, and how he was the one to contact the Feds," Mason explains. "It's amazing how the threat of incarceration for aiding and abetting will get a young man to sing."

"Shit," Hale says. "What's next?"

"A good amount of help from the Feds. The head of the agency is trying to save face, and his job, by fastening his jaws over the throats of Cooling and Malroy. He's secured warrants for their files, accounts, and businesses."

"That's amazing news," I say, turning to Hale and squeezing his arm.

He keeps his attention on Mason. "When will they execute the warrant?"

Mason smirks. "They did so last night and raided both offices. Cooling and few of his partners were caught destroying evidence."

Hale lets out a whistle.

"Yeah," Mason says. "They said someone caught wind of what was happening and panicked. About an hour ago, the Feds caught Malroy and his wife trying to flee to Dubai."

"Damn," Hale says.

"It's not official, but I've spoken to enough people at the bureau to know you're off the hook," Mason says. "The Feds still have to go through the evidence from Cooling's and Malroy's offices, but it looks good for you and really bad for them."

Hale flips through the folder and through stacks of what appear to be letters. "What's all this?"

"Becca wasn't the only one looking out for your character," Mason says. "Those are signed statements of support from your clients, praising you for what you did for them and how you always gave it to them straight." He points to the hand-written letter on top. "I think you'll find the one from Mrs. Valez especially touching."

I cover my mouth. Hale doesn't speak, holding the letter delicately in his hands. "Thank you," he says.

"My pleasure," Mason replies. "Come on, Sean. Momma's expecting us at her place." He looks at us. "We're not going back to New York until tomorrow. How about dinner later? Trin and Callahan are promising to be back. They want us over at Landon's. He and his fiancée have been so busy planning their wedding, they're missing their family and friends."

"Yeah," Hale says, taking in my grin. "It'll be nice to see all of y'all."

They leave, Sean still munching on his cereal as they quietly close the door behind them. "It's going to be okay," I tell Hale, kissing his cheek.

He meets my gaze. "Becca, my love, it has to be."

Epilogue

Hale

Summer arrived to lift our spirits and fall followed with almost as much enthusiasm. But winter was the best part of that year. All charges against me were dropped and I was given a very sincere and heartfelt apology from the new head of the FBI. The Feds destroyed Cooling and Malroy with all the evidence they discovered, along with eleven more of their associates, including my former intern, Clark.

The Feds assured Clark he'd get a lighter sentence if he cooperated, and he did. The little bastard barely received five years. Pretty good, given his pals received $5,000,000 fines and up to twenty-year terms.

Cooling and Malroy had flung mud on the wrong man. Not only did everything they attempted to do to me and the rest of their competitors turn against them, the investigation revealed there were a long list of victims. Cooling and Malroy had been doing this shit for years, placing pawns in almost every investment firm in the city and using their hard-earned research to make them rich.

It worked for a while, sure, as this sleazy shit often does, but then they got greedy and there's a reason greed is one of the seven deadly sins.

I scroll through my emails as the spring sun beats down on me, my phone pressed against my ear.

"Did the merger go through?" I ask.

"Yes, Hale," Neesa answers. "Every one of your clients who invested tripled the earnings on their stocks."

"Okay. I wasn't sure you'd get everything done, Jayla."

She sighs. "When have I ever not done everything you've asked?"

"I'm not saying you don't work hard, Martina," I assure her. "I'm just saying you're often distracted with my boy Mason's tongue down your throat."

"Don't be an asshole," she snaps. "It's Friday and I'm trying to get out of here so we don't miss our plane to Kiawah."

Like I can't picture her blushing. "Now, is that any way for my newest associate and potential future Vice President of Wilder Investments to talk to the big boss?" I ask. I adjust the blanket around me and Becca when the wind picks up. Yes, we're outside, and yes, we're very much naked.

The pause is almost as dramatic as I expect. "What did you say?" she asks.

"Aw, nothing'," I add in my thickest southern accent. "I'm just making you an offer, is all. Go to business school. I'll pay for it and spend the next few years grooming you to take over." I look over at Becca. "I have better things to do with my time."

"Hale, you're . . . I'm going to . . . oh . . . you *asshole*."

She starts crying. Neesa is cute that way. "See you tonight," I say.

Becca is still yapping away on her phone, giving her assistant some final instructions. I slip back into my black sweatpants and jog back into the house to do some prep work, including popping open a nice bottle of champagne.

Today marks the first full week Platinum PR has been in full operation. Those spreads Becca organized to save my rep? Anyone and everyone saw them, helping her become the most sought-after publicist in the country.

Now, instead of working for the Cougars, Becca works for herself here in Kiawah or back in our penthouse in New York.

I fill the flutes, set up the little plates of appetizers Trin dropped off earlier, and gather a few small things from the guest bedroom. I'm just about finished when Becca enters the house, the dogs skipping behind her. She shuts the door and drops her blanket away, reaching for the sundress I peeled her out of earlier.

"One minute," she mouths, holding out her finger and tugging on her dress. She doesn't bother with panties. Why should she? We still have a few hours alone left.

I pass her the champagne when she nears. It splashes on her breasts when I pull her close and take a nibble.

"No, *no*," she bites out to her assistant when I lick the champagne off her skin. "We need Tootles for this one. Let him know we'll work around his schedule. . . . alright, sugar . . . we'll talk on Monday, bye."

Becca disconnects, laughing. "Hale! That poor thing probably thought I was yelling at her."

"Hmm?" I ask, taking another lick.

She greets me with a smile. "You know, summer is starting back up in another few weeks. We won't be able to make love out there once the tourists start showing up again."

"We will if you're quiet." I kiss her lips and reach for my champagne, watching Sam and Rosie as they begin their daily round of tug of war. "Never mind. You don't have it in you. My super ability to please you won't allow your silence."

She laughs again, the sound sweeter than the waves announcing the start of high tide. "You've got me there."

I lift my glass. "What should we toast to?"

Becca strokes my chin, giving it some thought. "What about to the Anaconda of Wall Street giving Platinum PR one hell of a squeeze? Oh, and maybe our anniversary."

"It's our anniversary?" I ask.

She glances down all shy like. "It's what I'm calling it. Today marks one year to the day that you first kissed me."

"Does it?"

"Hale," she says, sounding disappointed. "It's the day we did that shoot."

"With Tootles," she presses when I stare back her. She sighs. "Never mind. I guess it's silly."

I take a sip of my champagne. "Does that mean you don't want your presents?"

She lifts her head slowly. "Are you serious?" She covers her mouth, gasping. "You remembered?"

My smirk dissolves. "Baby, how could I ever forget?"

I motion to the dining room table where a scroll tied with gold ribbon rests in front of a framed black and white picture of that now infamous kiss. There's Becca, her backside just barely covered, that black sheet pressed against her breasts, and me, my fingers tangling through her hair and my lips kissing hers.

My arm circles her waist as she lifts the photo. "You're going to make me cry," she says.

"Don't do that," I tell her, quietly. "Open the scroll. Maybe it will make you smile."

She does, taking care not to rip the paper. She unrolls it and looks up at me. "I don't understand. What is this?"

"The deed to this house." I keep talking, ignoring her sharp intake of breath, and shrug like it's no big deal. "We both love it so much I decided to buy it for you." I take another sip of my champagne. "Offered Trin and Callahan a sweet deal they were happy to take."

"I'm pregnant."

I think I misheard. That doesn't stop me from dragging my gaze down her belly and back up to her face. "What?"

Becca isn't smiling. She's glowing and beaming and doing all the things I'd expect her to do if she was pregnant with my baby. "I didn't have the stomach flu a few weeks back," she says. "My body was just, well, getting used to our baby."

"Our baby," I repeat. She nods. "You're pregnant?" She nods again, barely able to keep still. "We're having a baby?" She squeals and throws her arms around me.

I laugh and smile and lift her and just about stumble over every word I say, until I remember there's one thing left to do. I place her carefully on the floor and toss back the remainder of my champagne, catching the three-carat diamond ring I placed at the bottom of the flute between my teeth.

Becca's eyes widen as I fall to one knee. But then her tears start and my heart swells, and I can't remember all the words I meant to say. "I had a great proposal all planned out," I begin. "With these gifts, and food, and yeah . . . stuff."

Becca covers her mouth, crying.

"I have to admit," I say, my eyes stinging. "Your gift is better."

I let out a breath and slide the ring on her finger. "We talk about forever, Becca. About how we share something special that will outlast time itself. I want to mark this day when we started over and you told me about our baby growing inside you with this ring. Will you marry me?"

"*Yes!*"

I kiss her belly, then rise and kiss her for all I'm worth.

I'm promising to love her and our child forever. And, y'all, love has never looked so infinite.

This book contains excerpts from *Inseverable* and *Eternal* from the Carolina Beach Series by Cecy Robson. The excerpts have been set for this edition only and may not reflect the final content of the final novels.

Inseverable

A Carolina Beach Novel

by Cecy Robson

Prologue

Callahan

Three days.

That's all I have left until this shit ends.

Three days shouldn't feel like forever, not compared to the eight years I've bled to the Army. Thing is, good men have been killed in less time. In as quick as a blink, a squeeze of a trigger, or a small breath right before a grenade blows is all the time it takes to shove someone right out of life and well into death.

That's what makes three days as long as it is. Three days is plenty of time to die.

My eyes tear when the wind picks up and shoots grime through the small hole of my lookout point. This blown out piece of cinderblock is only big enough to allow me a view of the street below, but not so small I don't get smacked in the face with more filth. The tarp flaps above me as I spit out another layer of the dirt-sand mix spackling my teeth. Christ Almighty, I need a swig of the water resting near my elbow. But my thirst, like everything else has to wait.

I have a job to do.

I adjust my hips against the cracked cement of my bed, bathroom, and home all rolled into one, thankful that the agonizing ache stretching over the lower half of my body has settled into a now familiar numbness.

Out of all the points I'd scouted, and all the accumulated years spent in this position, I should be used to it. And in a strange way, it should almost be home. Yet nothing ever has been home.

But in three days, maybe something finally will be . . .

I shove my thoughts away and breathe as my fellow Rangers stalk along the street. It's then I see them, a mother and daughter walking straight toward my team. Less than one city block separates them from the men counting on me to keep them alive.

The hell? How did they get past the other sniper unreported? Rogers is new on watch. But the quick paces these two are taking should have clued him in that something's up. I train my scope on their faces; their expressions are blank, unreadable. 'Cept that's not what keeps my attention.

The little girl can't be more than five. So why the fuck isn't her mother holding her hand? I lift my radio and bark a warning, dropping it beside me as I lock my scope dead center on the woman's head.

The radio crackles and Modreski chimes in, yelling at his team to hold their positions. He asks me what my plan is, knowing if something's caused the short-hairs on my neck to rise, he and the boys damn well need to listen. But I don't hear him, with a breath and a squeeze of the trigger, I leave a kid without a mother.

Just beneath the sleeve of her *abayah*—the dress completely covering her body—I see it, a detonator that would trigger the explosives likely strapped to her chest. A few Rangers I know—Simons and Boreman, rush forward. I start to mutter a curse, pissed at her for making me shoot her in front of her kid. But the curse lodges in my throat when I see the kid isn't looking at her mother lying next to her dead.

She's watching my advancing team as she lifts the detonator clasped tight in her hand.

Chapter One

Trinity

"Trin! You coming?" Hale calls.

Even over the steady hum of the ocean, his deep voice cuts through the small opening of our lifeguard station.

"I need five more seconds," I yell back, my thick southern accent drawing out each of my words.

"That's what you said nine minutes ago," he complains.

"But I didn't mean it last time," I holler back.

I grin because even though I can't see or hear him, I know he's chuckling, no matter how much he's trying to hold it in. I hurry and finish writing the schedule on the white board and cap the dry erase marker, before tossing it in the small cup holder to join the rest.

No sooner do I reach for my beach bag and throw the sandy thing over my shoulder than the office phone rings.

Most people would run away, ignoring it, after all by now it's seven thirty and way after closing. But I've always been one of those goody-goody responsible types—you know the ones the teachers assign as classroom monitor and who always turned in her library books a day early? What can I say, I'm all about a good time.

I lift the receiver before it finishes ringing. "Magenta Groves Beach Resort, lifeguard station seven, this is Trinity speaking. How may I help you?"

"Trin. Screw the whiteboard and get in the damn car!" Hale yells through the receiver. I whip around as his voice echoes behind me, as well as through the phone. He hops up the steps as he disconnects, laughing like that was the best prank ever.

"Why did you do that?" I ask.

"Because I knew you'd stop to answer the phone, even though the rest of us have been waiting on you."

I pretend to scowl, but don't quite manage. Me and scowling don't go hand and hand. Life's too short to wrap your mind around everything that's wrong with it. So I grin, because that's something I can do and do well.

"You think you're so smart. Don't you?" I ask, placing the phone back on the charger.

"You forgot good-looking," he says. "But I'll let it slide on account of I'm modest, too."

I laugh, but don't argue—at least about the good-looking part. We've only been back at Kiawah for a week, but already Hale's wavy blond hair has bleached significantly and his skin tone deepened to a light bronze. His steps are slow and purposeful as he crosses the small space separating us and stops in front of me.

"Let's go, Trin," he says, hauling me along. "You've done enough for the day."

I readjust my bag over my shoulder, and follow him out of the office, the usual bounce to my walk kicking in despite my heavy bag.

"Here. I'll take that," Hale offers, reaching for my bag.

I step just out of reach, knowing he has his own stuff to carry. "I've got it, big guy," I tell him.

"You sure?" he slams the door behind us. I stare out to the beach where a young couple is chasing after their little toddler as Hale fumbles with the lock.

"I'm sure," I reply, my attention staying on the young family. "Hey, Hale, you know how I always mind my own business."

"Nope," he says, leading me forward.

"Well, this time I can't," I continue, ignoring his comment. "For your own good, I have to tell you that this maybe your last chance to do something about Becca. The summer hasn't quite started, but it won't be long before it's gone."

"Yeah. I know," he mumbles.

"And?" I ask, turning back to him.

He tugs on my long ponytail. Unlike Becca, my best friend in the world, I'm neither tall, blond nor leggy. My hair is as black as midnight in winter, and I'm just barely five feet three. And where her eyes are light and striking mine are a dull brown. But I do have something my bae doesn't have. Freckles. Y'all feel free to envy me at any time.

"Well?" I press. "You going to do something about that girl or aren't you?"

He shoves his key into the pocket of his long red lifeguard shorts and glides the sunglasses perched on top of his head back onto his face. "I guess we'll just have to wait and see," he tells me.

His smirk widens into that grin of his—the one capable of sizzling panties like coals over a fire. I shake my head. "Boy, between that smile of yours and that face it's a wonder Becca's not running to you rather than away."

He flings his arm around my shoulders as our feet dig through the sand. "Now, sugar, I'm sure I don't know what you mean," he says, keeping his grin in a way that tells me he's lying.

"Come on. You can have anyone you want. And if it's Becca, you need to act fast before those girls slapping each other just to lie their beach blankets near your post lead you astray and down a long dark path of sin, sex, and STDs."

"Is that so?" he asks.

"I'm just watching out for you," I say, stepping with him onto the gray weathered steps leading to the lot. "It's the kind of friend I am. You know, the kind who likes to pretend you're still a virgin and not the manwhore you've become."

He laughs hard enough to shake us both as we reach the edge of the pier. Ahead of us in the sandy lot, Sean, Mason, and Becca look up from where they've been waiting for us.

Mason's dark skin glistens with sweat, likely from having dragged all the heavy equipment we weren't using back into the shed. But he's got the muscle and the stocky build for it. Poor Sean has the endurance to swim a few miles and back, but his long-limbed body is better suited for reaching things the rest of us can't, and his personality is best for those who don't mind the occasional dip in the gutter and can appreciate his not-always brilliant remarks.

But of course it's Becca Hale hones in on.

I can't blame him. Becca is leaning against the Jeep, poised like Miss America and as alluring as Miss Universe.

"What the fuck's taking y'all so long?" she yells.

But that mouth of hers makes her all Becca, so does that smile that pulls Hale closer.

"You know how she gets," Hale hollers, hooking his thumb my way. "Had to get the floors waxed, the office dusted, and mend that sea gull's broken wing before setting it free."

"You did all that shit?" Sean asks, moving forward. "Man, and here I was thinking you were just working on the schedule."

Mason who tends to be the most serious among us just shakes his head and laughs, because that's what we all do around Sean.

Becca backs away toward the driver's side, keeping her grin as she points to our boys. "Alex Pettyfer, Nathan Owens, Channing Tatum, y'all got the back," she tells them. She grabs my bag and tosses it onto the floor of the passenger side. "You, get to ride with me, cutie."

I almost ask to switch with Alex Pettyfer, aka Hale. But I've known Becca long enough to know something's up. So I hop in the front, barely snapping my seatbelt in place before she shifts in gear and tears out of the lot.

We catch the road leading out of the resort. Mason tugs on my hair just like Hale had, just to say "hi". Like most men I meet, he thinks I'm cute. As in a kid sister or a BFF cute. Not cute as in, "hey how about you let me rip off your thong with my teeth?" You know what I mean? The kind of "cute" that really matters.

I've pretty much resolved myself to BFF status, even though I wish I could be more.

Hale, whether because of what I said, or because he realizes time is running out for him to make a move, leans in between the seats, his attention fixed on Becca. Unlike me, that's not sand filling out the cups in her swimsuit.

"Hey, Becks, how about we catch dinner Tuesday after work? Maybe even a movie?"

Becca's wild hair—highlighted in alternating shades of blond and blonder—slaps around her gorgeous features as she grins. "I don't know. The boss may not like me dating a co-worker." She looks at me then. "Isn't that right, Boss?"

I crack up. All my lifeguards can do whatever they want during their time off. But these four in particular? These four that have been my friends since before any of us learned to read, swim, or cuss. I know they're a good bunch. I know they have my back. For all we joke, the minute their toes dig into that smooth white sand, it's on.

I perch my legs up and over the dash and cross my arms behind my head. "As your fearless leader, I hereby let that be your call, ma'am."

Okay. Maybe I'm not so fearless. And "leader" is a pretty loose title considering all I do is run a few drills each day and make sure everyone has a shift.

"I'll think about it," is all Becca tells him.

Hale is a good guy. Good enough to slink back and give her space. Like all my male besties, he's had a crush on Becca since he hit puberty and his male parts saluted her in celebration. Capable of stirring erections with a single glance was Becca's super power. Mine is the ability to make people snort drinks through their noses at my jokes. I adjust my head beneath my hand after another glance at my beautiful friend.

We all have our gifts, and if mine includes making others smile, I can't complain.

Her grin widens as she takes the road that leads to Your Mother's Coconuts, better known to the locals as "Your Mother's". Once off the resort we're no longer lifeguards expected to abide by the rules. We're just fresh college grads ready to run amuck, do some skinny-dipping, and partake in all the fun our young selves demand.

In less than a minute, Becca is screeching to a halt at the far end of the half-filled lot. It is a quarter to eight on a Friday and our work week is done. With a hoot and a few hollers, our buddies jump out the back, rousing the other lifeguards who beat us here to do the same.

"Where the hell have y'all been?" the new girl calls out. "I'm thirsty."

Sean holds his hands out. "Then what're you newbies waiting for? Order up the first round."

"Us?" she asks, looking at her friend. "*We* have to pay?"

"Damn straight, yeah," Sean says like it's obvious. "Everyone knows virgins always buy the first round. Ain't that right, boys?"

The rest of my team, even those loitering on the outside deck, start chanting "virgins, virgins, virgins," pumping their fists in the air.

"Aw, hell," her friend says. "Come on. Let's go get our cherries popped."

They walk in, but we don't follow. Becca's made no move to slip out so I know she means to talk. I smile softly. "What's up?"

She looks to the ocean, where the waves sweep in to bathe the sand with all its salty heaven. But I doubt she really sees it, even though like me, Kiawah is a part of her. She crinkles her nose and then takes my hand. "Last summer," she says.

"Yeah, last one," I answer quietly, knowing how she feels because I'm feeling it, too. I squeeze her hand, my tone mirroring all the emotions fluttering inside me. "Time to grow up, right?"

"I wish we didn't have to," she mumbles, keeping her stare on the sea as if trying to gather some strength from it. "You still serious about applying to the Peace Corps?"

I was hoping we didn't have to have this conversation any time soon, but I've kept things from her long enough. "I applied over winter break, Becks."

Her mouth slowly falls open. "I told you to wait—to not do something drastic just because of what those doucheheads did to you."

The "doucheheads" she's referring to are Hunter, my ex-boyfriend, and Blakeney, my ex-friend. They once held my heart, until I caught them in bed and they ripped it from my chest.

Her words chip away at me. Not because I'm not over Hunter, or Blakeney. I am. I'm just not over their betrayal. I could never hurt anyone I claimed to love or called a friend. But they didn't feel the same.

I try to smile, knowing Becca needs my reassurance. But I can't quite manage this time. "You know I've always talked about going and serving. Ever since I was little."

"So you're telling me, if he'd stayed faithful and been a real man instead of a little bitch—if you'd agreed to marry him like he kept talking about—that you still would have signed up to join the Corps? Come on, Trin. Finding him fucking Blakeney was like a pen being slapped in your hand, forcing you to sign on that dotted line."

"No, it wasn't," I insist.

I don't want tonight to be about the bad things of the past. Not with the five of us together after too many months apart. But here we are, focusing on things I've tried hard to forget. "Becks, as much as I thought I loved Hunter, and as much as I believed that he wanted to marry me, I realize now we never would have worked out. I'm going into the Peace Corps, exactly like I've always planned. But knowing who he is—who he *really* is—he wouldn't have waited for me, and he sure as anything wouldn't have joined up just to be with me."

Even through her sunglasses, I can tell Becca's eyes are narrowing. "He's still a douche head, and so is she."

"I won't argue with you about that," I tell her. My head falls against the seat rest. Do you want to know something about Becca? She's sweeter than maple syrup and about as kind as people get. Until you hurt someone she loves. I'm among the lucky few she loves. But it's because she loves me, that she reacts the way she does.

She pushes her sunglasses up to her head, pegging me with enough disappointment to make me ache. "When do you leave?" she asks.

"September. But I won't know my placement for another few weeks." I answer so softly, I'm not sure if she hears, but her tensing posture assures me she does. "Daddy used his connections at the UN and arranged it so I'd have time to take my boards and have one last summer here with all of you."

"So from Princeton to the Peace Corps. From rich kid, to just another volunteer. "She sighs in that way she does when she's trying not to cry. "Nice," she says, not that she means it.

My attention falls to our hands and to how hard she's holding me. "It's the right thing to do, Becks," I tell her.

"Helping people *is* the right thing to do. Signing up for twenty-five months with no way out, that's above and beyond." She shakes her head. "Hunter and Blakeney are assholes for what they did to you."

They are. But she needs to know that's not why I applied. "Becks, it's time to grow up and move forward, and to do the things we've always planned."

"What if I don't want to?" Her voice splinters and tears glisten her eyes. "What if none of us do? I don't want life to go on without the five of us together—you, me, Sean, Mason, and Hale—especially you, Trin."

Like me, she wishes she could stop time, and that somehow things could be different. But somethings can't be helped, and this is one of them.

Her parents and mine had offered to send us backpacking across Europe, but we chose to come back here. Back home to spend one last summer doing what we loved, and to pretend to be forever young, forever free of life's demands, forever friends. As I look to my pseudo sister, I swallow hard and hope that the latter stays true.

Tears trickle down her cheeks, causing my eyes to sting. But Becks doesn't need me crying with her. Right now, she needs my strength, and maybe a little of my humor.

"*Trin, Becks*!" Sean hollers from the deck. "What the hell? We've got shots waiting and horny women who can't wait to have a piece of me."

"Sorry!" I yell, hopping out of the jeep. "Becca dared me to spell my name across her belly with my tongue and I couldn't refuse."

Instead of taking it for the joke it is, Sean freezes. "No, shit," he says.

Becca doubles over, practically falling out of the driver's side seat. I hurry around to steady her and lead her forward. Sean continues to stare at us, his eyes clouded with whatever dirty thoughts are swimming through his mind as we stumble into Your Mother's.

My laughter fades as I look to where the rustic blue double doors open up to the rear deck. But I'm not staring at Hale as he points to his raised shot glass filled to the rim, or at Mason who's smiling politely at the women admiring his muscles. And my, I barely notice Sean shooting past us.

I'm too busy gaping at the smoking hot bartender with the Army Ranger tat inked to an arm as thick as my thigh.

Holy Baby Jesus in a manger sleeping on a bed of hay.

"Hmm," Becca says in a purr. She leans in close to whisper in my ear. "Who do we have here?"

Brown strands of wavy hair spill around his strong features and startling light eyes, and a thin beard lines a jaw I could probably pound horseshoes on. If I knew anything about horseshoes. Or horses. Or, pardon me, what was my name again?

Not to be rude, or inappropriate—I do have morals, after all—but that tight blue shirt stretching across his broad chest is one pec flex shy of ripping in half. Or me ripping it in half when I straddle him.

"You want to straddle him?" Becca asks, a delighted gleam fixing on her face.

I look at her, realizing I spoke out loud. "No?"

She busts out laughing. This time, she's the one dragging me forward. "Come on, Trin. Time to have fun."

We stroll toward the hot guy. Or as I call him, 'my future baby daddy' because for the first time in too long I'm looking—we're talking full-out gawking—at a man. He has my attention and whether he means to or not he's not letting go.

I smile his way, not because of what he looks like, but because I can't seem to help myself. I think maybe Becca smiles at him, too. But "sex in a tight T-shirt" isn't impressed by her charm, and he sure isn't captivated by mine. He scowls—as in *scowls*—which of course earns him a wink from me.

Hey, sticks and stones, or whatever, I'm going to get this guy to smile. Even if it's clear he doesn't want to smile at me.

Eternal

A Carolina Beach

Novel

by Cecy Robson

Chapter One

Landon

The wind picks up, brushing the gritty sand along the shore in that graceful way it only seems to do during winter. Kiawah is always bustin' at the seams in the summer, drawing tourists from as close as North Carolina to as far as Sweden.

I take a long pull of my beer and dig my feet further into the sand. This time of year there are two a kinds of people: the locals and lonely. I was always the former and only mildly entertained the latter. That changed when I caught my wife blowing her manager with the same wild enthusiasm she blew me.

"God damn it," I mutter.

I'm not sure which part was more disturbing. Her blowing him in the kitchen, the same place we'd fucked earlier that morning, or her finishing him off while I stood there like an idiot.

I'm going to go with her finishing him off.

I can still picture her rising from her kneeling position, the front of the four hundred dollar blouse she insisted on buying flapping open and exposing her bare breasts with each step she took.

"It didn't mean anything, Landon," she told me, wiping her mouth with the back of her hand.

Maybe. But his teeth meant something to him. I could tell by the way he kept batting at his face, looking for them when the police finally pulled me off him.

The pathetic way he looked bordered on comical. Shit, the whole damn thing was comical. I might have even laughed if my heart wasn't busy joining his teeth on the floor.

Bernadette wasn't a perfect person. I knew that long before I put a ring on her finger. But I'm not either so I thought we'd be perfect together. She needed someone to help her, to take of her, and I was willing to do it. Hell, I was willing to do anything for her.

Up until that moment when I found her on her knees.

Call me a fool in love.

But don't make me look like one.

I push my half-drunk bottle into the sand, reminding myself it's been a year, and it's time to move on. Sounds great in theory, but pride to a man is as important as working hard, decency, and family. That's how I was raised. That's how it should be. Bernadette, however brief, was family. She kicked at my pride almost as hard as I nailed Blaze (nice fucking name by the way) in the nuts. All that left me to do was work hard, and damn, didn't I give that shit my all?

The wind picks up, stirring swirls of yellow and sending them to ghost over the water. Mother Nature is doing her best to soothe me, reminding me of the peace and quiet I need and pulling my focus to the vast ocean and the cresting the waves that build and crash along the shore.

Peace, I repeat in my head.

"Quiet," I say out loud.

"Trin," I mumble when my phone vibrates in my back pocket.

I pull it out, sure enough it's my baby sister Trinity. The peace and quiet on Kiawah is no match for her. "Yeah?"

"Now, Landon," she says, her South Carolina accent as thick as mine. "Is that anyway to say hello?"

She doesn't wait for me to answer. "What if I was Miss Universe, calling to tell you I had the cure for diabetes, and whether or not I shared it with the world depended on how you answered the phone? Wouldn't you feel bad that all those people out there with diabetes wouldn't have a cure because you answered the phone with 'Yeah?' sounding broodier than shit, crankier than a leprechaun shoved up some poor unsuspecting bull's ass, and about as pleasant as the matador trying to coax him out—"

"What hell does that even mean, Trin?"

"It means you should go to Becca's New Year's Eve party tomorrow night," she explains like it's obvious.

"I'm busy," I tell her.

"Doing what? Besides drinking a beer and looking at an ocean that's not going anywhere?"

I pinch the bridge of my nose, muttering a curse when she plops down beside me.

Like me, she's barefoot. Most people wouldn't dare walk on the beach in the middle of winter. But ever since we were little, Trin and I have always loved the feel of sand sliding beneath our feet, even in the cold.

Her jeans are rolled up like mine and she's wearing a heavy coat like me. Hers is burgundy, mine is navy. I didn't bother with a hat. She did, a gray beanie tight enough to keep her long black hair away from her pixie face. Even after having my nephew, she's still thin, lacking the muscle that's keeping me warm.

She motions to my beer. "Landon, where are your manners? Aren't you going to offer me a drink? I am a lady after all." She huffs. "Your momma raised you better than that."

I pass her the bottle. She takes a sip and makes a face. "It's warm."

"I kept rolling it in my hands," I admit. "I suppose it's hard to keep it cold that way, even in forty-degree weather."

She nods like she understands. "How long have you been out here?"

I lie. "Not long."

"How long have you been out here?"

I smirk. "A while."

"How *long*, have you been out here?"

"I guess long enough."

I start to stand when her thin arms wrap around me, keeping me in place. "Landon, as your favorite and only sister on God's green earth, I owe it to tell you that dark, hairy, and cranky doesn't fit you." She rubs the scruff on my jaw like she's trying to swipe it off. "Lord, it's like an opossum crawled up your chest and spit out a litter of babies across your jaw."

I edge away. "Your husband has the same damn beard," I remind her.

"Oh, that's not true." She smiles and turns her attention toward the ocean, her stare getting that dream-like look it always gets when she thinks of Callahan. "My man's beard is all alpha and sexy." She makes a face. "Yours is, well, possumy." She holds out her hand. "And if that's not a word, it should be. At least when it comes to whatever the hell is on your face."

"Trin, if you're trying to use your charm to talk me into going to Becca's party, it's not working."

"Why? She was nice enough to invite you." She shrugs. "Besides, it's almost New Year's Eve. Time for a fresh start and a new beginning."

Her voice quiets at her last few words. She doesn't mention Bernadette. But after this year, I suppose I've mentioned her enough, and so has Trin.

If hate were a super-power, Trin's hate for Bernadette would have crushed the Fortress of Solitude and slapped Superman upside the head for being a little bitch. And Trin, she likes everyone.

My family is from money. It's not something I really think about, or obsess over it, it's just always been there. We were taught to take care of it, add to it, but most of all be generous with it, since we had so much. Maybe that's why it was easy for me to give as much as I did to Bernadette. I wanted to see her happy and maybe give her the life she always dreamed of. But where Trin and our Momma would drop a few grand setting up and auction to help raise money for the children's hospital, Bernadette would drop a few grand on herself.

My parents insisted on an air-tight pre-nup. It pissed me off at the time, especially since they didn't insist the same thing when Trin was marrying Callahan. But they saw Bernadette for who she was, not like me. Love makes you blind, but it doesn't make you deaf when the woman you thought you knew calls you a wife-beater to your face.

It should have been an easy divorce. Sign here, initial there, and then walk away. Instead I dropped close to a hundred grand defending the abuse charges she filed against me.

"He's always been violent," she cried to the judge. "Look at what he did to my manager."

Her attorney was more than happy to present the pictures of her manager's busted up face and put the police officers who responded on the stand. Those fine members of law enforcement admitted they pulled me off Blaze (again, nice fucking name), but they were more than happy to mention Blaze's pants and drawers were down to his ankles when they found him.

"Landon," Trin says, her voice sad.

It's never a good sign when my sister grows quiet, and the way she wraps her arms around mine and leans her head against my shoulder. The last time she did that, our granddaddy Palmer had passed.

She knows I'm remembering, and she doesn't like it one bit.

It was bad enough Bernadette had accused me of hitting her, something I'd never do to any woman for any reason. But to try to make me out to look like a monster, and get all the gossip mags talking about Landon Summers, wealthy son of Owen and Silvia Summers, accused of threatening his wife's life, and soiling the Summers' name, it was more than I could take. She wasn't messing with me, she was messing with my folks, two of the best most generous people I know.

"She said I was hitting her," I say aloud, before giving it too much thought.

"I know," Trin says. She adjusts her hold. "But Landon, anyone who knows you didn't believe her."

"But there are a lot of people who don't know me, Trin."

She sighs. "I know that, too."

The waves start drawing closer, but it's not until a large one slaps hard against the shore that she speaks again. "Did she ever hit you?"

I don't bother telling her about all the shit Bernadette threw at me: her hair dryer, the damn crystal jewelry box, or all those dishes she smashed when she wasn't getting her way. But I don't need to. When Trin lifts her head, it's clear she knows enough. "Landon, why didn't you say anything?"

"I couldn't do that to her."

Trin scrambles to her feet, knocking over the beer, her face pink with rage. "But she did it to you—even when it wasn't true!"

"That doesn't make it right," I say. "To be accused of something like that, it's total horseshit."

"Horseshit she was more than happy to fling your way." Her breaths come quick. "She didn't even blink on that stand. You saw that, right? She wanted money and she didn't care what she had to do to get it."

Which was why I spent all that money on lawyer's fees. No way was I giving her more than she was entitled to after she pulled that.

"You should have said something," she says again.

"Anything I said would have made me look weaker than I already was." I shake my head. "Trin, when a man marries a woman who looks like Bernadette, he's supposed to keep her happy at all costs, and in every way possible. If she's fucking around on him, and other men find out, they don't care that you gave her a home, more money than she needed, or that you'd protect and look after her with your life. They assume you weren't man enough where it counted, and where it counts is in the fucking bedroom."

"You're not weak." It's what she tells me, but the way she says it, I think she understands as much as she can.

I tilt the bottle, letting what little beer remains pour into the sand. "It sure didn't feel like that when I found her, and who I found her with."

The foam dissipates, like it never was. It reminds me too much of my marriage, making me mad, bitter, and probably sad too, despite that I'm tired of feeling all three.

I rise and brush the sand off my jeans. "One drink," she says.

I do a double-take. "Now?"

She shakes her head, looking about as happy as I do. "No. Tomorrow night, at Becca's. One drink, a few hellos, and then you can leave." She inches up to me. "Please, Landon. Show me and everyone that's there you're okay." She smiles although the worry behind it dulls her soft brown eyes in the setting sun. "Even though you may not be."

I'm ready to tell her to go home and be with her husband and child, and that she's wasting her time. But Trin, she's trying, and the only person I've allowed in this whole year.

"It's just down the beach," she says like I already don't know. "C'mon, Landon. What could happen?"

What *could* happen? It's what I thought. The thing was, everything did.

Photo by Kate Gledhill of Kate Gledhill Photography

Cecy Robson (also writing as Rosalina San Tiago for the app Hooked) is an author of contemporary romance, young adult adventure, and award-winning urban fantasy. A double RITA® 2016 finalist for Once Pure and Once Kissed, and a published author of more than twenty novels, you can typically find Cecy on her laptop writing her stories or stumbling blindly in search of caffeine.

www.cecyrobson.com

Facebook.com/Cecy.Robson.Author

instagram.com/cecyrobsonauthor

twitter.com/cecyrobson

www.goodreads.com/goodreadscomCecyRobsonAuthor

For exclusive information and more, join my Newsletter!

http://eepurl.com/4ASmj